Sophie Jordan

THE DUKE'S STOLEN BRIDE

The Rogue Files

AVONBOOKS

An Imprint of HarperCollinsPublishers

THE DUKE'S STOLEN BRIDE. Copyright © 2019 by Sharie Kohler. All rights reserved. Printed in the United States of America. No part of this book may be used or reproduced in any manner whatsoever without written permission except in the case of brief quotations embodied in critical articles and reviews. For information, address HarperCollins Publishers, 195 Broadway, New York, NY 10007.

First Avon Books mass market printing: November 2019

Print Edition ISBN: 978-0-06-288543-2
Digital Edition ISBN: 978-0-06-288538-8

Cover design by Patricia Barrow
Cover illustration by Jon Paul Ferrara
Chapter art by Morphart Creation / Shutterstock, Inc.

Avon, Avon & logo, and Avon Books & logo are registered trademarks of HarperCollins Publishers in the United States of America and other countries.

HarperCollins is a registered trademark of HarperCollins Publishers in the United States of America and other countries.

FIRST EDITION

19 20 21 22 23   QGM   10 9 8 7 6 5 4 3 2 1

For Erin, my warrior friend.

The Duke's Stolen Bride

"Kissing?" Her stomach fluttered in anticipation.

"Yes. It's fundamental and typically precedes intercourse. One should always know how to use their mouth."

One should always know how to use their mouth.

Her gaze dropped to his mouth. Kissing him sounded . . . lovely.

She wanted to. Perhaps more than she should.

His gaze, bottomless and deep, gleamed in the flickering shadows of the room. "Go on then," he prompted, his tone rather perfunctory. Cool and unaffected, at complete odds with the dark glitter of his eyes. "Show me what you can do."

By Sophie Jordan

The Rogue Files Series
THE DUKE'S STOLEN BRIDE
THIS SCOT OF MINE
THE DUKE BUYS A BRIDE
THE SCANDAL OF IT ALL
WHILE THE DUKE WAS SLEEPING

The Devil's Rock Series
BEAUTIFUL SINNER
BEAUTIFUL LAWMAN
FURY ON FIRE
HELL BREAKS LOOSE
ALL CHAINED UP

Historical Romances
ALL THE WAYS TO RUIN A ROGUE
A GOOD DEBUTANTE'S GUIDE TO RUIN
HOW TO LOSE A BRIDE IN ONE NIGHT
LESSONS FROM A SCANDALOUS BRIDE
WICKED IN YOUR ARMS
WICKED NIGHTS WITH A LOVER
IN SCANDAL THEY WED
SINS OF A WICKED DUKE
SURRENDER TO ME
ONE NIGHT WITH YOU
TOO WICKED TO TAME
ONCE UPON A WEDDING NIGHT

THE DUKE'S STOLEN BRIDE

Chapter 1

Marian Langley was not given to undignified displays. She'd been employed as a governess for too many years, guiding young ladies into the highest echelons of Society with grace and dignity. She knew dignity. It was her stock-in-trade.

Or rather it had been.

She was no longer employed as a governess. Those days were gone.

So very many things were gone now. Whimsical water-colored wisps of memory. Papa was gone and she had left her comfortable post and returned home to care for her family. She grimaced and assessed her current situation: huddled under a table at Colley's Tavern. Presently, it didn't *feel* as though she were taking care of her family.

It felt ridiculous.

She felt ridiculous and completely lacking in dignity. So far had she fallen.

She was insolvent and, as she was coming to discover, insolvency did not support dignity.

In fact, it did everything to destroy it.

For no other reason did she find herself with her knees tucked close to her chest and her hands gripping fistfuls of her less than pristine skirts in the fervent, desperate hope that this moment pass, and pass quickly.

Her breath fell in hard, rapid little bursts from her lips, partly due to her overwrought nerves and partly from her mad dash through the village and into Colley's Tavern, home of the best shepherd's pie in the shire.

Despite her anxiety, her stomach rumbled at the mere idea of Colley's delicious shepherd's pie. She could even smell it on the air. Directly above her, in fact. The savory, rich aroma drifted from the table above her head.

Her stomach growled, reminding her that she had not eaten in a good while.

She held her breath and adjusted her well-worn boots on the plank flooring. They were her younger brother's boots. She'd claimed them from his room whilst he was away at school. She doubted they would fit him upon his return. Lads his age grew like weeds.

She wrinkled her nose and tried to ignore the dirt and bits of rotted food surrounding her. The proprietor should have a word with his staff regarding their failure to clean beneath the tables.

She might be able to ignore the scraps of food, but the pair of legs crowding her was more difficult to overlook. They were substantial, the Hessians snug on a pair of long calves. She glared at them as though they might somehow disappear.

Yes, the table was presently occupied, but that had not stopped her from taking refuge under it. Marian had glimpsed a person at the table before diving beneath it. She had no choice, however. It was the nearest table and the coal peddler was fast on her heels.

She had a vague recollection of the man's dark shape at the table. Dark eyes, too. Dark boots, of course. Dark like everything else in the shadowy interior of the tavern. Hopefully dark enough to obscure her from the man pursuing her.

The area beneath the table was far from spacious. She feared it barely concealed both her body and the gentleman's considerable legs.

The boots shifted, one solid toe making contact with her hip—purposefully, she suspected.

"Ow." Scowling, she rubbed at the afflicted area.

"What the devil are you doing?"

The voice came, deep and biting, much closer than she expected—a heated huff of breath near her ear.

She turned her face toward the sound of his voice only to find herself pinned by a pair of dark eyes.

For a moment, all speech left her. He was young and handsome. Two things she had not observed in her mad dash beneath the table.

He peered at her, their faces so close their noses almost bumped. "Are you hard of hearing, chit?"

She shook herself and recovered her voice. "Is it not obvious what I'm doing here?"

He did not so much as blink, merely continued to stare at her, waiting, evidently not satisfied with her reply.

She fidgeted anxiously, worried Clite Oliver would enter the room and catch this man looking *under* the table.

"I'm in a bit of a situation," she confessed.

"What manner of situation is that?" he asked in a deep, cultured voice, decidedly *un*amused.

"It's rather a long story. Please. Pretend I'm not here. I promise I will leave you alone soon—"

He nodded as though he understood, but the words that came out of his mouth were far from understanding. "You can leave me alone now."

She glanced over her shoulder and was awarded

with a view of the less than clean floor. No coal-stained boots yet. She had no doubt, however, they would materialize in her line of vision at any moment.

"I implore you. Stop talking to me!" she hissed, looking back at him with a desperate shake of her head. "I will make it up to you."

Not that she had a penny to her name to offer him. That was what landed her into the mess . . . into running from the coal peddler in the first place.

He was unmoved by her plea and her empty promise. His dark eyes stared coldly down at her.

Hopelessness welled up inside her. She'd been battling that demon emotion lately. Often. All the time, really. She refused to give up. If she gave up hope that meant she gave up hope for all of them—Charlotte, Eleanor and Phillip. Giving up meant they were all lost.

Marian could not do that. She could not let that happen. She had to keep their family together.

"Please," she whispered again, reduced to begging. As quietly as she uttered the word, it burned on her lips, stinging her pride.

She couldn't let the peddler find her. He would give no quarter. He was unfeeling. Of all the people they owed money to—and there were several—he was the most persistent. The most ruthless. The one whose eyes promised retribution . . . and pain. He didn't care who their father had been or what Papa had done for the community of Brambledon. They owed the man money. He'd have it or his pound of flesh.

The gentleman peering at her beneath the table said nothing. He blinked those dark eyes. He was impassive. And then he was gone.

There was a rustling of his clothing as he lifted his head back above the table. Footsteps pounded on the old wood planks and she hugged her knees closer to her chest as though she could make herself somehow smaller. The dreaded coal-stained boots appeared.

She sucked in a sharp breath and prayed that the table's occupant wouldn't give her away.

The boots rotated as he scanned the room, searching. She didn't need to see his face to know it was Mr. Oliver and he was hunting for her.

Her eyes widened as those well-worn boots started toward the table—toward her. Heavens save her! Was the man at the table signaling him over?

"Beggin' your pardon, sire. Did you see a lass run in here?"

She pressed shaking fingers to her lips, straining for a sound from the man whose feet nudged her backside.

It was foolishness perhaps. She couldn't hide from Mr. Oliver forever, but when he'd bellowed her name in the village lane, instinct had taken over. She'd taken one look at his merciless eyes, lifted her skirts and ran.

Cutlery scraped against a plate on the table above her, and she looked upward as though she could see through the wood.

Finally, the gentleman spoke, his voice rife with impatience as it floated on the air. "Do you see a lass here?"

Her gaze dropped to his boots again, to those well-formed legs encased in a pair of costly-looking Hessians. Hope fluttered like a bird in her chest. Unbelievably, it seemed he would not reveal her location under the table.

A long stretch of silence met this question, and she could almost imagine the peddler's box-like face scanning the room again. "Nay, I don't see her, but I know she came in here. I saw her, I did!"

He stepped away from the table, his boots stomping in a circle again, apparently searching for her.

"Perhaps you should look elsewhere, and permit me to finish my meal in peace." The words were perfectly polite, but there was an unmistakable edge to them.

Mr. Colley noticed the coal hawker at that moment. His voice rang out as his legs charged toward Mr. Oliver. "What are you doing harassing

His Grace? Take yourself off from here at once, man."

His Grace?

"I'm looking for the Langley chit. I saw her duck in here, I did!"

"As you can see, she is not here. Now leave and don't return unless you're a paying customer."

She could well imagine Mr. Oliver's obstinate face glaring at Mr. Colley. The man couldn't be put off forever. She knew that. She would have to come up with something to appease him. She'd been using what little money came their way for food, but things had reached a desperate level. The coal peddler had to be paid.

"I know she is here somewhere," Mr. Oliver grumbled. His boots moved away from the table, scuffing over the floor.

"She is not in here," Mr. Colley snapped. "Now get out before I have Jasper from the kitchen throw you out on your ear."

Everyone knew Mr. Colley's nephew, Jasper. He was as big as a barge. Not particularly bright, either. He loved to wrestle with the lads, whether they were willing or not. He was often dragging someone into a brawl. He'd been doing this since childhood and seemed unconcerned that he was no longer a child.

She watched Mr. Oliver retreat and exhaled, lowering her forehead to her knees in relief.

"Beggin' your pardon, Your Grace. I apologize for the intrusion. Can I fetch you anything else? More food? Fresh wine?"

"Simple privacy. Please, Colley." The *please* sounded more like an afterthought. A grudging add-on.

"Of course, Your Grace." Mr. Colley shuffled backward.

She lifted her head and stared at the underbelly of the table as though she could see through it to his face.

Your Grace.

He was one of them. *Oh. Dear.* She covered her mouth with her fingers again. A refined snobbish nobleman.

She'd worked for aristocratic families. She'd rubbed elbows with them for years. Granted, that had never been in this village, but confronting one of his class should not intimidate her so much. Even if she was sitting at his feet like a lowly beggar.

His deep voice wrapped around her. "You can come out now, lass."

Chapter 2

*H*is words vibrated through Marian, pulling at her like an invisible thread, urging her limbs to action. She fought the impulse and stayed put, hugging her knees tighter, which was ridiculous. She couldn't hide under this table forever no matter how acute her embarrassment.

"Come now, lass. You're not shy. That much was apparent when you barged in here and commanded me to stop talking to you."

She winced and bit her lip. True. She had been bossy. As comfortable as she had been with her previous employer, she had never spoken in such a way or used such a tone.

"I know you're there. You're sitting on my boots."

When she was a girl—very young, before Charlotte or Nora were even toddling about, before her brother was even born—Papa and Mama had gifted her with a carved wooden marionette for her birthday. This marionette was no doll with an eerie, exaggerated smile. It was a white elephant with a meticulously painted red-and-gold saddle. The gorgeous thing had jointed legs and flapping ears. She'd learned how to manipulate it. She would play with it in her bed at night, making it dance for her, commanding it by pulling its nearly invisible strings.

She felt like that beloved marionette now. Even if she wanted to stay hidden under that table, she was tugged out, pulled, compelled by that voice.

Emerging from beneath the table, she straightened and smoothed a hand down the front of her hopelessly mussed skirts. Once upon a time this dress had been fashionable and as crisp as a fresh morning. She'd been neat as a pin—first as a nanny and then as a companion to the Duke of Autenberry's sister.

Now she was this. A mess.

An unmitigated disaster forced to stand before this man who was handsome and well-appointed in his dark jacket and brocade waistcoat.

He reached for his glass of wine with long tapering fingers. His signet ring glinted in the lantern light. However fashionable his garments and refined his speech and manner, his face had not seen a razor in at least a week. His hair also needed a good trim. Nobleman or not, the ballrooms of London would look askance at him for his rakish mien.

She brushed an errant strand from her face. It rebelled, falling back before her eyes.

In this moment it was difficult to remember that a year ago she had dined with people of his station as a normal course of events. Clara and her family had never treated her like a governess. She'd dressed the part of a lady and was treated with courtesy.

Now she felt like a storybook peasant standing before the lord of the manor. Her gaze flickered to the bountiful fare before him. The crockery holding the shepherd's pie was large enough to feed her entire family. Even if her brother was in residence, it would be enough, and he ate like a ravenous beast.

She looked away from his dinner lest he see the hungry longing in her eyes.

Her gaze dropped to his hand. He loosely gripped his glass, leisurely rotating it on the table. She inhaled thinly through her nostrils and tried not to let his very existence irk her—even if it did.

Why should some people have everything and others so little through mere circumstance of birth? Why should he have such a privileged life whilst she didn't know how she was going to continue caring for her siblings?

She exhaled, forcing the unwelcome emotions out. No sense crying about things beyond her control. This was her lot in life and she had to make the best of it.

He studied her and his expression could only be characterized as bored.

She searched for an explanation for her behavior that would not seem quite so wild and desperate. Even if that accurately described her.

She'd been given a reprieve. She'd avoided the coal peddler for another day. That was all that mattered. Any bit of indignity was worth it. She was simply surviving the best she could these days.

"Er, thank you." She owed him her thanks, of course. He'd permitted her to remain beneath his table undetected.

He merely stared that endlessly dark stare. It unnerved her.

The moments crawled by. She shifted on her feet. Her muddied boots creaked upon the wood floorboards, striking her as incongruously loud in the silence.

She folded her hands neatly in front of her as she waited for him to say something. Anything. His gaze followed the movement of her hands.

She was no longer hunkered beneath a dark table, lost in deep shadow. She was in full view of him now and he scanned her from head to toe, assessing, missing nothing.

He gave his ear a casual rub and looked decidedly . . . uninterested.

It stung. Unreasonably.

Everyone in this village couldn't seem to cease staring at her, gawking and watching her with avidity as though she might suddenly break into song or dance or sprout a second head. She was a veritable Vauxhall performance to everyone. They watched with bated breath to see her next stumble.

He finally answered. "You're thanking me? I did not think you presented me with a choice in the matter."

"Of course, you could have exposed me." She inclined her head. "You did not. Thank you."

He leaned back, stretching a long arm along the back of the seat bench. She was very much aware of the gulf separating them in that moment. He, this powerful man with his demon-dark eyes. He could crush her in every way on a whim and face no consequences for it.

Resentment stirred in her chest.

For a period of time she had supped with men of his ilk only to lose it all. The fine roof over her head. The elegant bedchamber with its private fireplace. The lovely dresses supplied to her. The most current books to be read at leisure. Luscious iced cakes—more than she could ever eat in one sitting. They were there every day at tea. She winced at all the times she didn't clean her plate and sent back half-eaten cakes to the kitchen.

How precarious life was, especially for her gender, to go from *that* to *this* in a heartbeat.

"You're the depraved duke." Mr. Colley had addressed him as His Grace. He could be no one else. There was not an abundance of dukes in these parts, after all, and there could only be one duke in all the realm with such a moniker. "That's what everyone around here calls you." Her voice rang faintly with accusation, and perhaps something else. Perhaps acrimony.

She lifted her chin. If she was to utter such a thing, it seemed like it should be delivered with a fair amount of bravado. That was all she had left, after all. Bravado. And, apparently, the ability to hide beneath tables.

He'd recently moved into Haverston Hall. The late Mr. Haverston had left it to the Duke of Warrington. Apparently there was some loose family connection between them. Not that the duke had ever seen fit to occupy the place before now.

The manor sat high on the hill outside of town. The sprawling country house had been vacant most of her girlhood. She and other children from the village had frolicked and played in the vast overgrown gardens, running through the courtyard and peering into the grimy windows.

She hadn't visited there in years. Idly, she wondered if the duke had restored the place since he took ownership or if the gardens were still overrun with weeds.

Indeed, she had heard tales of this Duke of Warrington. She'd heard about the women who paid call on him. They passed through the village in carriages at all hours of the day and night.

Rumor had it not all of them had left his house. Women went in, but not all came out.

She'd rolled her eyes at such ridiculous stories. Simply because no one witnessed their departure did not mean they had failed to leave.

Mrs. Pratt, her neighbor to the west and the biggest gossip in the shire, had delivered several innuendo-laden morsels on that subject to Marian and her sisters.

Charlotte and Nora had listened in rapt fascination. Mrs. Pratt's farm sat closer to Haverston Hall, so they took her nattering as truth, unfortunately, assuming she was a witness to whatever gossip she recounted.

"I'm sure these women left when you were sound asleep." Marian had tried to interject some sensibleness into the nonsense. She didn't want her sisters to believe everything they heard, especially from a woman with a penchant for gossip.

"As likely not." Mrs. Pratt's face had puffed and reddened in affront over Marian's reluctance to believe her. "Their screams could curdle your blood."

"Screams?" Nora had asked with wide eyes.

"Aye." Mrs. Pratt had leaned forward over their fence. "Mr. Pratt was tending the hogs before supper and he could hear them carrying on up at the manor house, their wails for help echoing on the air like a banshee's shrieks." She nodded fiercely, her cheeks jiggling with the motion.

"I am sure it was just the wind," Marian had attempted to reason. "It howls through the shire. If women were missing, it would be noted and the proper inquiries would be made."

"Who would question a grand man such as he?" Mrs. Pratt had snorted. "What a naïve miss you are for all your worldly travels. Who would dare approach him with such inquiries?"

Marian had designated it as salacious gossip and told her sisters as much.

Except now, staring at him, she thought the moniker appropriate.

"Depraved duke?" he asked. "That's what they call me?" Unlike others who might be concerned or annoyed, he appeared mildly amused. "Alliteration. Clever."

"You mean you're unaware?"

"Now *who* would be so bold as to let me know such a thing?" He looked her over, clearly implying: *aside from you.*

She watched him a moment, waiting to see if he would say more on the matter. When he held silent, she added, "Does that sobriquet offend you?"

"Sobriquet," he mused, sounding almost impressed. "That has a rather gentle connotation. Not what leaps to mind when you hear the word *depraved.*"

"Does it offend you?" she repeated.

After a beat, he answered her, "I'm not a man given to offense, girl."

Girl. The single word had the power to make her feel small and insignificant.

"Are you not?" She frowned. "How singular. Can that even be possible? Everyone is given to offense."

He considered her at length again before answering. "Not me."

"Rubbish," she quickly rejoined.

He angled his head, and she got the sensation that she had caught him off guard. "You refute me, girl?"

Again with the *girl.* As though he sought to remind her of her place.

"I disagree with you, yes," she clarified, not

about to be cowed. He might be a duke, but he wasn't her master—no matter the service he had done her.

"One would have to care to take offense," he said carefully, slowly, as though marveling that he was having this conversation with her. She supposed it was rather personal, rather intimate, for two strangers. Although considering their introduction, not so intimate.

"Oh. And you don't care?" How very fortunate for him. As far as she was concerned, only the very privileged could assert such a claim. She did not possess that luxury.

He reached for his glass on the table. Lifting it, he surveyed the amber liquid. "I care for my lands. A fine whisky. A good meal. A first-rate shag." His gaze dropped back on her, intense and probing. "There is little else."

She sputtered with indignation. The wretch! If he sought to shock her, he had succeeded.

She could not imagine *not* caring. She cared *too* much. About many things. The list was endless, but at the top of it were people. Family.

"That's very sad."

He stiffened, and she knew at once that he did not like that. Contrary to what he'd claimed, she'd struck a nerve—and she was glad of it.

"I'm not the one hiding from lenders beneath tables. *You* strike me as sad."

There was a fair share of disdain in his voice. She flinched, but he'd wanted that. He'd wanted to lash out at her.

"Thank you again for your assistance." She wrapped herself in as much dignity as she could muster, reminding herself that he was no better than she was. A condition of birth placed him at the top of the social hierarchy, but that was all. A vagary of fate could have landed him hiding from peddlers beneath a table. Instead of her.

With her shoulders back, she strolled from the room.

Chapter 3

$\mathcal{N}$ate really needed to stay out of this damnable village.

Up until now he had bypassed Brambledon on his way to Haverston Hall. The last thing he wanted to do was interact with the locals. He wasn't fond of interacting with anyone he didn't have to—not even those of his own rank. *Especially* those of his own rank. Most of them were unbearable. Pompous blowhards, the lot of them.

With the exception of Pearson, his man of affairs, Nate didn't engage with many people at all and he preferred it that way. He wasn't social. He knew that. He wasn't sorry for it, even if Pearson insisted on calling him a misanthrope.

He didn't *hate* people. He simply eschewed their company.

He knew men had friends. Lifelong friends they made at school. Such was the way for many. Only not him. For Nate, school had not been a place to foster friendships.

He'd been small as a boy. His parents had dumped him at school at the tender age of six so they did not have to concern themselves with him as they went about their diversions. They fetched him home occasionally. A few times a year he was briefly spared the abuse of his classmates. As the runt in the pack, his peers enjoyed nothing more than tormenting him . . . beating him. There had been no help, no remedy for him. It was simply his existence. A friendless, lonely existence full of mistreatment.

He'd finally sprouted his eighteenth year—ironically. Once he was free of school, once he had escaped his bullying classmates, he'd shot up. Now he was broad of shoulder and over six feet and could protect himself.

On more than one occasion, he had spotted some of those lads out about Town. They were all smiles and pats on the back, as if they were old friends and not vipers. As if they had not inflicted pain on him.

He had not forgotten those bitter years. Indeed, he had not. All the little lordlings of his childhood were now ready to be his friends, but he had no use for them. He'd rather remain friendless than allow them into his life.

Hunger had compelled him forth to the village tonight. Several of Haverston's staff, including the cook, had quit since he'd arrived. Apparently they found him objectionable. He snorted. And now he knew why. *They call you the depraved duke.*

He had yet to replace the cook with someone who could create an appetizing menu. He'd succumbed to the temptation of a good meal and ventured out from Haverston Hall. Apparently that had been a mistake. Lesson learned.

If he had kept to his usual habits, then a harried village girl with a barbed tongue would not have disturbed his peace while he was trying to enjoy his dinner.

He could still see her in his mind. Fiery eyes. Tendrils of fair hair falling untidily around her face. Her dress was dirt-smudged from her time under the table. She was comely enough, but not to his taste.

He preferred his women more polished. Amenable. Courtesans who knew what they were about and did not possess a saucy tongue. He hired them for their services, and when they were done they left him. It was business. A simple transaction. No harm to anyone. Both were satisfied with the arrangement and compensated in their own fashions.

None of those females were like the little virago who dared to make a place for herself at his boots beneath a table and then flay him with her saucy tongue for his assistance.

He should have exposed her and declared her presence to the tradesman hunting her. It would have been the responsible thing to do. He owed her nothing, after all.

He was not certain why he obliged her. Perhaps it was the plea in her eyes. He could not detect their color beneath the table, but there was no mistaking the glimmer of desperation in her gaze or the ring of it in her voice.

Before he knew what he was about, he was doing exactly as she bade and concealing her. Then, when she'd emerged bold as day, he'd conversed with her. *Talked* to her. He didn't know the last time he had exchanged so many words with a female.

He might eschew Society and friendships, but he had women aplenty in his life. Or rather, in his bed. Tupping did not require conversation. He never talked to any of his paramours at length. It was unnecessary.

Bloody hell. If he had a proper cook at Haverston Hall, he would not have felt so compelled to stray from the comfort of his home.

Home. The word rang hollowly.

All those years spent in hell—at school—he couldn't claim any such place existed for him, but Haverston Hall had been the closest place to a home he ever had. He'd spent one long-ago summer there with Mr. Haverston, a distant cousin of his mother. A summer when he was happy, free of the bullies at school. A summer when he'd met Haverston's goddaughter, Mary Beth.

They'd spent their days fishing at the pond, visiting the fair in town and talking about pirates. Her fascination with pirates had rivaled his own. She had been his first real friend and he wanted to keep her forever. As young as he was, he had known then he would grow up and ask her to marry him.

When he presented himself at the tender age of twenty and asked for her hand in marriage, she had accepted. Even though they had not seen each other in ten years, she had said yes. He'd thought their marriage would be more of the same joy they'd found with each other that summer. He'd thought they would be happy, that they would build a life and family with each other.

Instead he discovered Mary Beth was but a glimmer of her old self and possessed very little memory of their summer together. Just the same, losing her as she attempted to bring their child into this world had been a blow.

When Haverston had expired and left him the manor, Nate could not have been more surprised. The old man had been without heirs and kindly enough, but Nate had no idea he liked him well enough to leave him his estate.

Nate had taken residence at the manor for nostalgia's sake. As though he could recapture his youth here, those days that he had frolicked with Mary Beth.

As though he could go back to being the lad he once was. Unfettered. Carefree.

Free from pain and loss.

Snorting, he reached for his glass and downed the last bit of it. Fanciful bit of rubbish.

The past couldn't be undone. There was no place free from pain and loss. It did not exist for him.

When he walked through the house with its deserted rooms and the grounds wild and overgrown with weeds, he hardly recognized the place from that long-ago summer. He certainly couldn't see Mary Beth in the now musty rooms and shadowed halls. Not as she had been then—a little girl with ribbons in her hair, laughing at all his antics and sharing his childish dreams of the high seas.

He knew he could air the place out and brighten it up—bring it back to its former glory. He could if he had the motivation. Perhaps if Mary Beth and their babe had lived, he would have done it for them.

The place fit him better as it was now. As *he* was now. The *depraved duke*.

That's what everyone around here calls you.

The village girl had not minced words in relating that fact. She let him know what was being said behind his back—and then she had the temerity to call him *sad*. Him! When she was the one so clearly in a sorry, desperate state.

His appetite gone, he dropped a few coins on the table and rose from his seat. He'd been delivered a good many insults in his life. His status and position did not shield him from that. Words far more ugly than *sad* had been heaped on his head. And yet *sad* grated upon his skin.

His stepfather, more than anyone, enjoyed piling invectives upon him. The man never hid his resentment of Nate. He had very few memories of his own father. He'd passed away when Nate was still in swaddling, but his stepfather was scarcely civil to him. It was as though Nate's mere existence served to remind him that his wife had been with someone else before him—someone who happened to be a duke and outranked him. Irrational, but resentment was rarely logical.

Emerging outside, he didn't see the girl anywhere. She'd vanished. A few people strolled on the street, but she was not among them.

A lad fetched his horse and Nate was soon headed home, burrowing into his cloak and pulling his hat low as a fine mist of rain started.

He was chilled by the time he reached Haverston Hall. In the foyer, a servant relieved him of his cloak, hat and gloves. He retired to the library, eager for the warmth of the fire. He held his hands out to the flames.

"Ah, there you are." Pearson entered the room. His father had been the Warrington stable master, but Pearson had expressed no interest in following in his footsteps. When Nate offered him a position as his man of affairs, he'd gladly accepted.

"Here I am," Nate agreed, turning his hands over so the backs could be warmed.

"Why so forlorn? Did you not have a satisfying dinner?"

"Better than anything I would have had here, to be sure."

"Then—"

"They call me the depraved duke. Did you know this?" he asked abruptly. "I suppose that's why the cook quit."

Silence met his declaration and Nate looked over his shoulder. One glance at Pearson's face and he knew she had told him the truth—not that he'd doubted her. She didn't strike him as a liar. If anything, she was too forthcoming.

"Ah. Learned that, did you?" Pearson frowned

and rubbed at the back of his neck. "Who told you?"

Because, clearly, it was not the kind of thing one would share in casual conversation, but then, his conversation with the audacious chit had not been casual. Which only served to annoy him more. Who was she to insert herself with such familiarity into his life?

That's very sad.

It continued to gall him . . . which he knew was in direct opposition to his claim that he didn't care for much of anything.

Apparently he cared enough or she would not have annoyed him so greatly.

"Someone in the village," he replied.

Pearson's eyes widened. "Indeed. Well, he must not have put much weight into the rumors about you to reveal that directly to your face."

"Actually, I think she did believe them."

"She?"

"Yes."

"Intrepid lass." Pearson nodded almost approvingly.

Nate grunted and faced the fire again. "More like foolish," he muttered.

"Hm. Whatever she happens to be, she made an impression on you."

He couldn't disagree with that—even if he would like to.

Chapter 4

$\mathcal{M}$arian pushed thoughts of the depraved duke with his devilish dark eyes and the tenacious coal peddler from her mind as she stepped inside the cozy confines of her kitchen.

She was home. She expelled a happy breath. Even if it was only a fraction warmer inside the house than outside, she was home at last and glad of it.

The kitchen was her favorite room in the house. It was full of fond memories she could wrap around herself. Memories of when Mama was alive. Her mother may have been gently bred, but she had enjoyed spending afternoons in the kitchen, participating in the preparation of their meals.

Marian could envision Mama now, standing at the worktable in her striped pinafore, flour smudged on her nose, wrist-deep in dough as she laughed at one of Cook's anecdotes.

Standing in the threshold, Marian leaned a shoulder against the wall with a quiet sigh and surveyed the current scene. The room seemed a little smaller now, a little darker—certainly not as cozy as in years past.

The years before she became a governess and left home.

The years before Papa died and she returned to take care of the family.

That thought made her wince. *Take care of the family.*

She didn't feel as though she were doing that very well. It was an enormous all-consuming task. The wages she brought in tutoring local children were hardly enough to make ends meet. Coal was the very least of their needs. There was everything else. Food. Maintaining the house. Oh, yes, and *food*.

And Eton, of course. Phillip needed to finish school, and considering he was only ten and three years old, that would be some time yet. He needed to stay there if he was to have any kind of future. If *any* of *them* were to have a future.

Cook was gone, too. Old age had prompted her to move in with her daughter and her family in Dorset. They'd replaced Cook briefly before Papa died, but after his death there had been no possibility of affording such a luxury.

So much change. So much lost. So much gone.

It was up to her to care for everyone. To get them through this. And they would get through it. Somehow. She'd get them over this mountain and onto the other side.

The day her father collapsed, they not only lost him, they lost their livelihood. As the town's only doctor, he'd been a man of modest but adequate means. They'd always had food and clothes and fripperies she would not dream of indulging in now. Now there was only deprivation. So much loss and it was unrelenting.

Nora and Charlotte sat as close to the grate as they dared without catching their skirts afire. Marian watched them undetected from the doorway. They were bent over their sewing. The light in the room was meager, forcing them to peer closely at their stitching.

Marian frowned. They'd be blind before they were old, sewing in such poor lighting, their backs permanently stooped.

Not if she could help it, Marian vowed. They were her sisters and she'd save them from such a fate. She'd save her sisters and keep her brother at school. Somehow.

Chasing away her frown, she cleared her throat

as she stepped forward, letting her presence be known.

"It's almost dark. Put that sewing away," she directed.

Nora looked up and eagerly tossed her sewing aside. Her youngest sister didn't need to be told twice. Nora was an efficient seamstress, but not enamored of the task. She did the minimum required and not a stitch more.

Nora would rather be working in her herb garden or preparing a tonic in what was once their father's laboratory. Nora was more like Papa than any of them—skilled at healing and creating remedies. Marian and Charlotte knew she could mix up a batch of herbs that would shave days off a common catarrh. They did not hesitate to take any elixir Nora concocted for them. Unfortunately, she could not earn money at her vocation, so she was stuck sewing to bring in some much needed coin.

Charlotte, on the other hand, took pleasure in sewing. For her, it was art. She was both gifted and quick. She wanted only one other thing. Someone who was not to be hers. She didn't complain, however. Charlotte accepted that her fate did not hold what she wanted.

And that simply broke Marian's heart.

Charlotte may have accepted that fate, but Marian had not.

"Marian! You're back," Nora proclaimed as though Marian had left for the plains of Gibraltar and been gone decades.

Marian removed her gloves and hung her pelisse on the hook near the door. "Mrs. Walker wanted a word with me after Annabel's lessons."

Not an untruth precisely. Mrs. Walker had wanted a brief word, but it was the dodging of the coal peddler through the village and into the tavern that took so much time and made her later than usual. Of course, she didn't mention that. She hated to see the worry in their eyes. She tried her best to shield them.

"I hope she wasn't trying to dock your wages this week with some excuse or another," Charlotte grumbled, not even looking up. She squinted in the fading light as she worked her needle. "That woman is so stingy with her pennies."

"Awful is what she is," Nora chimed in as she moved to the pot bubbling on the stove.

"Nora," Marian tsked. "Mind your tongue."

Nora pulled a face and continued, "As is that daughter of hers. Annabel is a nasty creature who relishes belittling others." She lifted the lid, and wafts of steam drifted up on the air. Nora stirred the contents.

Marian was well acquainted with Annabel's traits, but she would prefer not to discuss her in her free time. She devoted several hours a week to the difficult girl, and that was more than enough as far as she was concerned.

"Oh, good. You started dinner." Happy for a change of subject, Marian stepped forward and peered over her little sister's shoulder at the pale broth. "What is it?" She was afraid she knew the answer.

"I made a soup with the last of the potatoes." Nora lifted the ladle and let the thin broth dribble back into the pot. Clearly there was more water than potatoes in the soup. It looked nothing like the appetizing fare the Duke of Warrington had been enjoying.

Masking her distaste, Marian turned her attention back to Charlotte still hunkered over her needle and thread. Marian strode over to her and plucked her sewing from her diligent little hands. It was the only way to get her to stop.

"Marian!" Charlotte protested. "I promised the Hansens I'd have that finished by tomorrow."

Marian deftly turned and hung the bodice of the dress on a peg near the door. "You've done enough for the day. The Hansens can wait. You work faster and harder for them than any of their apprentices."

"Yes, about that." Charlotte stood and removed some bowls from a shelf. "Mrs. Hansen offered me that apprenticeship again—"

"Absolutely not."

Dressmaker apprenticeships were generally a miserable existence for the apprentices. Marian would not release her sister to the dubious care of the Hansens. They'd treat her like a slave and never promote her beyond the level of apprenticeship, nor would they ever pay her more than a meager wage, deeming her room and board as sufficient recompense for long grueling hours of sewing by candlelight.

Those were reasons aplenty . . . even if Marian didn't mind the way Mr. Hansen looked at her lovely sister. Mr. Hansen's gaze always followed Charlotte with a keen avarice reminiscent of a wolf eyeing its prey. The very last thing Marian would do would be to send her sister to live under their roof.

Marian knew something about the wickedness of man—especially that of a man in a position of power over a female. She'd witnessed how aristocratic men behaved toward females in their employ.

For a short while her charge, Lady Clara, had been betrothed to one such man. Marian had recognized him for what he was—pure poison. Maliciousness embodied. The Earl of Randall was the manner of man who enjoyed breaking those weaker than himself.

Thankfully Clara had discovered the truth for

herself before it was too late and she bound herself to him in matrimony.

Marian would keep Charlotte safe from men like that. She'd protect her and do everything to see her wed to her young Mr. Pembroke. Her sister deserved a happy and suitable match. She was beautiful inside and out. She was gentle and kind and deserved all good things. A husband. Children.

"One of the Hansens' apprentices left—"

"Ran away 'tis more like it," Nora volunteered.

Nora was likely correct on that score. They treated their apprentices abominably, and Marian would not toss gentle Charlotte into that wolf den.

Indeed not. Her sister wanted to marry young Pembroke. That had *always* been the plan. Unfortunately, it was one of many plans that had changed after Papa died.

Marian knew the Pembroke lad still longed for Charlotte. She saw it in his face every time he stared after Charlotte in town or during church. The lad still wanted her even if his father forbade their union.

Marian had to come up with the dowry. She snorted. Hard to imagine how she could accomplish that when she could not even afford coal.

"It would be very helpful and could alleviate . . .

our situation," Charlotte said delicately, intruding on Marian's desperate musings. Apparently she had not given up on the subject of apprenticing for the Hansens.

Marian stubbornly shook her head. It was unbearable to think how low their circumstances had fallen that this was an offer Charlotte would even consider. She should be planning a wedding, not laboring over needle and thread.

A year ago Charlotte was happily betrothed. Papa had approved the match when he was alive and even agreed to a dowry—a generous dowry and yet one he believed he could scrape together.

If Papa ceased to accept chickens and poorly knitted gloves as payment for services rendered, he could have supported the agreed-upon dowry, and he had started to do that very thing, collecting actual money for his services.

Then he had died.

It was a shame he had not seen to their future before that.

Marian cast out the uncharitable thought. She'd loved her father. She could not fault him for his generosity of spirit . . . even if it left them in dire straits now.

It was a sad turn of events. Especially for Charlotte. Not only had she lost Papa, she also lost her future husband.

"Put the notion from your head," Marian instructed. "I told you not to worry about our situation. I'm working on a solution."

Nora snorted and Marian sent her a swift glare.

Charlotte looked merely unconvinced.

Marian opened her mouth, but was saved from having to prove her claim.

A hard knock sounded on the kitchen door. Before anyone could answer, the door was unceremoniously pushed open.

Mr. Lawrence strode into the room like he owned the place.

She felt the usual tightening of her skin and souring inside her mouth. It happened every time in his presence.

His bright eyes immediately found her. For his great height and girth, the man possessed the smallest eyes. They were dark and small like buttons set deeply in his face. "Miss Langley, there you are."

"Here I am," she agreed dully. In her own kitchen. The most obvious place to find her at this hour. She bit back the sarcastic comment, however. She knew better than to make an enemy of the town's primary blacksmith. He was a man of means in the village.

He dropped a burlap sack on the table with a shuddering bang.

Charlotte jumped slightly whilst Nora, always

fearless, strode forward and opened the bag. "A ham!" she cried in delight.

Almost immediately Marian felt her stomach clench in hunger. She resisted taking a step closer to assess said ham. She hadn't eaten since tea this afternoon with Annabel and her mother. Mrs. Walker insisted they take tea together on the days Marian instructed Annabel. It took everything in Marian not to fall like a ravenous beast on the tray of food.

She had called upon her breeding and years in service to the nobility and gently nibbled at a single sandwich and iced tartlet. To do anything more would earn a frown from Mrs. Walker. The woman was always watching Marian closely, as though she would reveal some grand secret from her time in the Duke of Autenberry's household— some grand secret that would make her daughter more marriageable.

Mr. Lawrence slapped a meaty paw on the hunk of ham. "I saw this today at the butcher's and said to m'self: Hiram, the lovely Langley lasses could do with a bit of ham to thicken their lady frames." He nodded in a self-satisfied manner.

Marian shifted self-consciously on her feet. It was no secret the Langley family had fallen to dire straits. Everyone in the village knew it. Still, it stung to think the townsfolk were remarking how low they had fallen.

"Mr. Lawrence, you are much too kind. We cannot accept such generosity."

"Of course you can." He jerked a thumb toward their dinner simmering on the stove. "Throw a bit of it in the pot. Right tasty. I might even stay to dine with you lasses m'self."

Marian bit back a groan.

Nora gave her a look that conveyed she was glad *she* wasn't the recipient of his attentions. Then, without missing a beat, her sister reached for a large paring knife and went at the ham, the look in her eyes turning decidedly greedy. She was clearly only thinking of her stomach.

Marian reached out and circled her wrist with her fingers, stopping her. "Nora," she admonished.

Her younger sister scowled at her.

Marian frowned back.

"Ladies," Mr. Lawrence's voice boomed over them. "You need the sustenance. Take the ham." He spread his arms wide.

But at what cost?

Marian did not wish to be in this man's debt. He did nothing to hide his interest in her. She would not be beholden to him.

"You need it," Mr. Lawrence added. "Enjoy it."

You need it.

She despised the truth of that statement.

Nora's expression turned beseeching. *Please,* she mouthed.

Marian sighed and looked at Charlotte. Her sister was much too pale and could doubtless use a good meal. Marian felt the defeated slump of her shoulders. "Very well. Thank you, Mr. Lawrence." After all, her sisters had not eaten as she had today. There had been no sandwich and iced tartlet for them. Marian was not even certain what they had eaten. If she had to guess, it was stale bread and jam. Scarcely enough.

Mr. Lawrence beamed in a very self-satisfied manner. "Enjoy, enjoy. It warms my heart to know that I can help you lasses." His eyes rested overly long on Marian. "I enjoy helping. I'd like to help more if you will permit me."

She felt the weight of her sisters' eyes . . . in addition to the weight of Mr. Lawrence's unwavering focus.

The man had not minced words with her a year ago. He had let her know his intentions, and at the time she had let him know that she was in no position to entertain the prospect of matrimony. She was deep in mourning for her father. It was reasonable to reject his suit. Forget the fact that if the Pembroke lad came knocking and wanted to renew his courtship of Charlotte, then they would all happily agree to such a circumstance. That was different, but a moot point as young Pembroke had not come for Charlotte.

Marian had noticed lately that Mr. Lawrence

had renewed his pursuit of her with more obvious intent. Heavy dread settled in the pit of her stomach—alongside all the other burdensome rocks that had already taken residence there.

Clearly her time was up. Reprieve over.

Nora finished unwrapping the ham and started cutting hunks off the pink meat eagerly. The sight pained Marian. Her sister was so hungry she could not stop herself from falling upon the side of ham, no matter who had gifted them the food.

Mr. Lawrence's significant person wasn't budging from where he stood. Indeed not. He looked here to stay, taking up all the space inside their kitchen. She hoped that he didn't really expect them to invite him to dine with them.

Blast. That would be wretched and send entirely the wrong kind of message to the man. She was trying to discourage him, not break bread with him over her kitchen table. No. She would not have that.

She moved toward the door. "Mr. Lawrence, might I walk you out?" There. That seemed clear enough. She was not inviting him to stay.

His eyes lit up. "You may." Taking her elbow he led her to the door.

She stifled a cringe. Apparently the prospect of time alone with her kept him from feeling rejected.

They stepped out into the yard. Dusk had

fallen. Mr. Lawrence maintained hold on her elbow, and she abided his proprietary touch as they moved down the stone path. It was a small thing to suffer in order to remove him from her home . . . in order to set the matter of *them* to rights. She winced. Or rather the *nonexistent* matter of them.

She cleared her throat. "I appreciate all your kindness toward me and my sisters." This, she managed to choke out. She had no wish to offend him.

Mr. Lawrence was an important man in the community. His pockets ran deep. She suspected his interest in her was what had staved off most of their creditors from being too demanding with her this past year. She knew a great many people believed it was only a matter of time before she and Mr. Lawrence married. Even if that misapprehension helped spare Marian and her family, the notion that people thought she might be the future Mrs. Lawrence was intolerable.

He stopped and turned to face her. "I'm here to support you in any way I can. With your father gone, you need someone to look after you." He waved toward her house. "I hate to think of the three of you alone here. Why, anything could happen to you. I would never forgive myself were that the case. You need a good man to stand guard over you."

A good man to stand guard . . .

The words made her want to retch. As far as a good man, he meant himself. There was no question as to that.

"Perhaps," she allowed. "But I'm still deeply in mourning. I cannot, in good faith, take a husband." It was the only thing she could think to cling to.

He clucked his tongue. "Your daughterly devotion is admirable, but well past justification. Why, only this past week, there was a report of highwaymen in these parts. They accosted a carriage that had departed from the Duke of Warrington's. A conveyance full of spoiled womanhood, no doubt." His lips curled. "Nonetheless, I shudder to think what would happen if such rogues befell you and your sisters whilst you live here alone without even a manservant present to defend your honor."

"Mr. Lawrence, there have been no occurrences of homes being set upon."

"Is that supposed to provide comfort? Nonsense, lass." He stepped forward and seized her hand. "These are perilous times. You need a protector, a husband."

"Mr. Lawrence," she reprimanded, attempting to tug her hand free. He only tightened his grip.

"Threats of bandits aside, your finances are dire, Miss Marian. Forgive my bluntness, but you owe money to every tradesman in town."

Mortification stung her cheeks. It was too much to tolerate. She again tried to tug her hand free. "Mr. Lawrence. Your concern is misplaced. I am sure you needn't worry yourself with my affairs—"

"I realize it is the height of gauche to discuss fiscal matters with the fairer sex, but as you've appointed yourself the head of your family, I have no choice." He shook his head, looking at her sternly in the deepening shadows. "You're but a female. You should be sheltered and led through life with a guiding hand. Your father could not have wanted this for you."

That last bit was likely true, but neither would Papa have approved of her marrying Mr. Lawrence. However high-placed in this community Mr. Lawrence happened to be, Papa had never cared for him. He'd found the man uncouth.

She at last managed to free her hand from his meaty paw. "Mr. Lawrence, you go too far. This is beyond improper—"

It was as though he didn't hear her at all. He seized her by her upper arms and stepped so near she was assaulted by the stink of his breath.

"The way I see it, you are out of choices. You're destitute." He nodded again to her house. "You're on the brink of losing your home. Your many creditors are done waiting. Their good will has run out. I know. There is much talk. They care not anymore who your father was. You will be given no further pardon."

His words struck her like the flay of a whip even though he said nothing she had not already told herself. It was still miserable to hear it from him. Miserable and humiliating.

After the day she'd endured, she was in no mood to have these ugly truths thrown in her face from the likes of Mr. Lawrence.

For some reason the image of the Duke of Warrington filled her mind. His handsome face. His haughty bearing. He likely never knew deprivation or struggle. He spent his days in fine privilege. Warm and well-fed, waiting for any numbers of courtesans to visit him. Marian shoved away all thoughts of the dreadful man.

She knew she was out of time, but she could not accept Mr. Lawrence as her savior.

And yet something must be done.

"What of your sisters? Think of them," he pressed. "Have you heard Miss Charlotte's young Mr. Pembroke is paying court to Miss Delia Smith?"

"What?" She shook her head, feeling slightly stunned. "No. It cannot be." It was the first she had heard such a thing. Charlotte would be crushed to learn of this.

Marian had hoped she could get Pembroke to renew his courtship and offer for her sister.

Eventually. Either when he gained the courage to break free of his father's yoke or when her family was restored to its former status and Charlotte once again qualified as eligible.

Marian shook her head. Perhaps it was naïve of her, but the assumption, the conviction, that everything would be well, that a comfortable lifestyle would somehow be returned to her family, burned inside her, clinging to life. Perhaps it was a desperate hope, but what did she have left if not hope?

Now, however, she felt the first wilting of that conviction.

Perhaps it was time she confronted reality.

"It is true," Mr. Lawrence insisted. "He has taken tea with her twice this week."

How could she have not heard such tattle? Pembroke's family was at the helm of local Society— they *were* Society in the shire. It began and ended with them.

At least that had been the case prior to the duke's arrival, but after coming face-to-face with Warrington, she did not think he would be throwing any grand parties or soirees. Pembroke and his wife could continue their reign over Brambledon like a feudal lord and lady without fear of being usurped.

Mr. Lawrence continued, "Considering the history between Miss Charlotte and young Pembroke, no one wished to be the bearer of unfortunate news. I'm sure that's why you were unaware of this development."

"All except you," she said numbly. Indeed, he had no hesitation in telling her. In fact, he seemed to relish it.

His hands flexed on her arms. "That's correct. You may count me as your truest friend for I, dear girl, will tell you the truth."

Her truest friend?

"To what end?" She knew his purpose was not altruistic.

"I have been unfailingly clear about my intentions."

"I cannot marry—"

"You cannot afford to *not* marry me, fool girl." He dropped his hands from her arms, stepped back and looked down at her sternly. "I know you're a sensible lass. If you would just let that good sense of yours lead you to the correct decision, we could cease this tedious dance and you could put all your troubles behind you."

Except she would be married to him.

He continued, "If not for yourself, then think of your sisters. Your brother. How can you afford his schooling?"

Simple. She could not. She could not meet the cost of his next tuition.

He adjusted his hat. "You have my offer.

You'll not get a better one. You might find yourself with admirers, but none whose pockets run deep enough to keep you and your three siblings afloat."

He spoke true. Since her return to Brambledon, she'd been flirted with and propositioned—mostly from tradesmen who thought they could collect payment from her beneath her skirts.

None put forth honorable offers.

None but Mr. Lawrence. His offer was honorable, if not palatable.

"I will leave you to consider all I have said. Good eve." Turning, the man left her standing at the gate to her yard.

Perhaps he was right. Perhaps she really should set aside her aversion to him.

Plenty of girls married for reasons that had nothing to do with love or affection.

Simply because her mother and father had that manner of match did not mean she was due the same. Perhaps she had not been born beneath a lucky star and she must come to terms with that.

She exhaled. Mr. Lawrence rounded the bend in the road and she could no longer see him in the dusk.

He was out of sight if not out of mind.

One thing was certain. There was no happy solution despite her hopes that one would miraculously present itself.

This was no fairy tale, and no knight atop a charger would be arriving to rescue her.

Whatever solution she arrived at, it would not be to her liking. She just needed to decide on the least repellent course of action.

Upon entering the kitchen, she inhaled. Dinner had now taken on a decidedly delicious aroma with the addition of the ham. Even if it came from Mr. Lawrence, she was glad for it—glad that Nora and Charlotte would have a much-needed hearty meal.

"We shall feast tonight," Nora exclaimed in way of greeting as she stirred the contents of the pot.

"Smells delicious." Marian forced a smile. She always donned a smile and feigned as though everything was fine.

"How was Mr. Lawrence?" Charlotte looked at her carefully. She was well aware that he had proposed after Papa's death.

"Yes. Did he propose again?" Nora asked, as straight to the point as ever.

Marian hesitated.

Nora looked up from the pot. "Of course he did. What did you say this time?" For one so young, she was a cheeky lass.

"What do you think she said, Nora?" Charlotte looked askance at her. "She said no, of course. She doesn't love him. She would never marry him."

Now Charlotte turned to look at her, her expression expectant, waiting to hear Marian confirm her belief.

Marian supposed this was all because of their parents. They'd had a love match and Papa had raised them with the full expectation that any marriage of theirs would be founded on love. When so many people around them, if not most, married for reasons other than love, this was a bit more than optimism perhaps. It definitely made them singular among other females.

She shook her head. They were penniless, not a dowry to their names, and yet they still imagined they would marry for love.

"I am not certain I can decline him any longer," she confessed.

"Marian, no!"

"He is a man well-respected and he has been very good to us in our misfortune." The words were meant to make her sisters feel better. Charlotte and Nora did nothing to soothe Marian, but they didn't need to know that.

"And that means you must marry him?" Charlotte shook her head.

"He is twice your age and looks like Mrs. Pratt's dog with his many jowls," Nora said as she served their dinner into bowls. "Too bad you couldn't be a rich man's mistress. Then you wouldn't be bound for life to the likes of Mr. Lawrence."

"Nora!" Charlotte cried. "Where do you get such notions?"

"Oh, you needn't be such a prig, Charlotte. You're only eighteen, but you behave as though you're someone's grandmother."

"You speak of ruin," Charlotte hissed.

Nora sniffed and lifted her nose. "Everyone knows Mrs. Ramsey is no widow, and she leads quite a comfortable life."

"You shouldn't pay mind to rumors," Marian chided even though she suspected those particular rumors about Mrs. Ramsey to be true.

Papa had treated the alleged widow on occasion, and Marian had become friendly with her since her return home. She'd sat in Mrs. Ramsey's parlor a few times, and Nora was right. She possessed a fine house with many fine things. In fact, Marian had often admired a music box on Mrs. Ramsey's mantel.

"Pretty bauble, is it not?" Mrs. Ramsey had remarked.

Marian had nodded, stroking the mother-of-pearl lid. "Yes, ma'am. Lovely."

"He was one of my favorites . . . the man who gave it to me."

"A suitor?" Marian had inquired.

Mrs. Ramsey had smiled somewhat mysteriously. "Yes, you could call him a suitor, I suppose."

"We don't know that it's *not* true," Nora countered, intruding on Marian's reminiscing. "No one knew Mrs. Ramsey before she arrived here, claiming to be a widow." Nora licked a bit of soup off her thumb and fetched three spoons. "No one knows anything of her past and yet she lives in a fine house with two servants and a cook and a carriage and she is always attired in the height of fashion."

"So she must have lived as a courtesan? That's the conclusion we're reaching?" Marian mocked, although she did think Nora's instincts were close to the mark. She simply refused to openly agree on the matter.

"Enough talk of mistresses," Charlotte declared.

Marian nodded in agreement. Nora visibly pouted, but she let the unsuitable subject drop.

They ate their dinner with no further conversation on the matter of marriage or the merits of the demimonde, but it remained at the forefront of Marian's mind long into the evening. As she prepared for bed in her chamber with its cold, empty grate, it weighed heavily in her thoughts.

Nora had a point. There was more freedom in that life. Marriage was forever. A courtesan . . . well, she wasn't bound to any man. She made her own way.

Marian would prefer that to marriage, to spending forever with a man like Mr. Lawrence.

She knew it was scandalous, but taking vows that joined her to Mr. Lawrence felt the far greater sin.

She donned a pair of her brother's woolen socks and wore them under her warmest nightgown. Piling an extra blanket upon her bed, she slipped under the comforting weight. Down the hall her sisters shared a bed piled similarly with heavy blankets.

As little girls, they had all felt so safe under this roof.

She wanted to feel that way again.

She tried to imagine herself as the future Mrs. Lawrence. Such a future did not fill her with feelings of warmth and safety. It filled her with dread.

Her mind strayed to another possibility—a remote and outrageous and wildly improper possibility. She wondered how one even became a courtesan. Was it something one planned? How did one go about orchestrating such a thing?

She wondered all through the night.

Chapter 5

Marian stepped across the threshold into Mrs. Ramsey's drawing room, trying not to feel as though she were taking the proverbial leap into the unknown. She'd called on the lady before. This shouldn't feel so very different from those visits. Except it did. Now there were notions in her head, wild ideas that she couldn't cast out.

She'd deliberately left her sisters at home. She hadn't even mentioned to them that she would be calling on the woman. She didn't permit herself to examine too closely why she had done that.

"Come in. Come in." Mrs. Ramsey waved one pleasantly plump hand toward a sofa. All of her was soft and inviting: from her curvaceous figure to her pleasantly round face with its charming dimples. *Characteristics that must have made her an excellent courtesan.*

Marian couldn't help the inappropriate thought.

Mrs. Ramsey's full lips beamed in greeting at Marian. "You're just in time to join me for tea." She nodded to the tea service in front of the sofa. A book was propped nearby, a ribbon in place, marking her page. Marian knew from their past conversations that Mrs. Ramsey was a voracious reader.

"I'm sorry for intruding." Marian hovered in the threshold.

"Nonsense. I don't get many callers, and I can't recall the last time we had a visit." She waved at her servant. "Diana, please fetch us extra cakes, would you?"

Marian knew Mrs. Ramsey did not entertain many guests. Speculation of her former occupation kept most people at bay. Lack of society did not seem to affect the woman, however. She seemed quite happy with her situation, cheerfully busying herself with her home and garden and other hobbies.

She had one of the loveliest houses in town. It was like a perfect little gingerbread house with its gabled rooflines, scalloped trim and magnificent gardens. Most days, she could be spotted lovingly attending the myriad blooms. It was on one such afternoon that Marian had first made her acquaintance.

Shortly after her return home, Marian had spotted Mrs. Ramsey wrists-deep at work in a bed of roses. She'd never seen such glorious blooms. They'd lifted her spirits and she had stopped to compliment the lady at work.

That conversation led to an invitation to tea, which led to more invitations to tea. Marian had not let the rumors circulating about the woman scare her away. She enjoyed her company.

"Now tell me. What have you been up to? Still tutoring that wretched Walker girl." She tsked her tongue and wrinkled her nose. "That cannot be an easy task."

"Mrs. Walker increased Annabel's lessons. She's determined she be prepared for her come-out."

Mrs. Ramsey snorted indelicately as she poured their tea. "She'd best prepare for a large dowry as that girl has neither the face nor the disposition to land herself a good match. No man of merit will take her to wife."

"Perhaps she will simply settle for a husband and leave out the merit part."

Mrs. Ramsey tsked again. "Poor lamb. 'Tis a shame you cannot imbue her with any of your wit or grace."

Marian winced. "Wit and grace have not gotten me very far in life."

"Not true. You were doing quite well for yourself before you left your employ with the Duke of Autenberry, and you shall do well for yourself again. In time. You will see."

Marian had divulged to Mrs. Ramsey in her previous visits. It felt good to have someone to talk to, and a worldly woman like Mrs. Ramsey was the perfect confidante.

"I appreciate your faith in me, even if you are entirely too optimistic."

"It's not optimism, dear. I just know you're a smart lass." She tapped her temple. "You will see your way out of this. For you and your family."

Marian blew out a breath, feeling that invisible noose around her neck tightening as she acknowledged that Mr. Lawrence might be her only way out.

"Oh, lovely." Mrs. Ramsey clapped her hands delightedly as her housemaid returned to the room, bringing forth a plate of iced biscuits. "Here we are. Have a biscuit. Please be a dear, Diana, and box up some of these lovely confections for Miss Langley's sisters." She lifted one iced biscuit and bit into it with a moan of relish.

"That's very kind of you," Marian said as Diana left them alone again.

"Oh, I recall that Nora has quite the sweet tooth."

"Yes, she does," Marian agreed.

"Any time you girls crave biscuits . . . or a hearty meal, you come here. I have an excellent cook who keeps me well satisfied." She patted the slight curve of her stomach.

Marian smiled tightly. She knew Mrs. Ramsey was being kind, but it was a difficult thing knowing that the woman was aware that food was not something they had in abundance. Goodness, the entire village knew that—or could rightly assume so. Still, Mrs. Ramsey's gracious offer stung her pride nonetheless.

Marian cleared her throat. "I met the Duke of Warrington." It seemed as good a time as any to announce that. She did not often have gossip to share—not when she was so busy concentrating on the struggles of her own life.

"Ohhh, did you?" Mrs. Ramsey sat a little straighter. "Do tell. Is he handsome? His stepfather was a handsome man. I remember him well. He enjoyed some of the salons I frequented in Town. I hear the duke is quite the rogue and young. Well, younger than me." She wrinkled her nose in that charming fashion of hers. "Occasionally I forget I am no longer in the first blush of youth."

Marian shook her head. "Rubbish. You're as fresh as a spring rain, Mrs. Ramsey." The woman had to be approaching her fortieth year, but was as lively and pretty as any debutante. She reminded Marian of Clara's mother. Both were of similar years, but they turned the heads of gentlemen wherever they went. It was not so long ago that the dowager duchess had scandalized everyone by marrying the younger Lord Strickland and giving birth to a set of twins soon after.

Mrs. Ramsey waved her off with a flip of her wrist. "Flatterer. You should have seen me in my glory . . . when I was your age."

"I should have liked that," Marian hedged warily, uncertain how to proceed, but very much determined to continue in this vein of conversation. It was the impetus for her visit, after all. She need only envision Mr. Lawrence's face to bolster her decision.

In the light of day, the idea that had taken form in her mind last night felt bold. *Too* bold perhaps, but she could not stray from her course now. She was at a point where only bold action would save her. This she knew.

"You were in London, yes?" she added. "Before Brambledon?"

"Mostly, yes. Although I spent a few years in Bath, then Sheffield. Wherever my vocation took me."

"Your vocation, yes." She cleared her throat again.

"Are you coming down with an ague?" Mrs. Ramsey looked her over in concern. "I'm sure your clever young Nora could come up with a remedy for that, but let's get you some honey and lemon for your tea. That will be just the thing." She moved to ring for a servant, but Marian stalled her.

"No, no, I'm fine," she reassured and took the plunge. "I've never heard you speak so frankly of your vocation before."

There. No more skirting the topic. It was time she got to the heart of it. Something had to change, and only Marian could make that change.

Mrs. Ramsey stared at her, all frivolity gone from her expression. "Does that make you uncomfortable, my dear?"

"No, no. Not at all. I'm interested. Quite so. In fact, I wanted to ask you about it." Mrs. Ramsey was the only person who would understand what Marian was considering and not deem her mad.

"Did you, now?" the woman asked mildly.

Marian nodded. "I know it's untoward to speak of such matters—"

"No more untoward than *being* the woman who once engaged in the scandalous profession you find of such interest. And yet here you sit in my parlor. So let's talk about what has you so interested, Marian."

So no more assumptions. It was fact. She had been a courtesan.

Mrs. Ramsey swirled some icing off a biscuit as though she were not discussing a taboo subject. She inspected the icing on her finger before licking it clean in the most delicate fashion—like a little kitten.

"Er, yes. Let's do." Marian took a breath, reprimanding herself for stammering. She was not one to stammer. Reticence was not in her nature.

"I did not have many prospects growing up," Mrs. Ramsey explained. "It seemed clear that I was destined to earn a wage on my back."

A soft gasp escaped Marian.

"Oh, I'm sorry. Have I shocked you? You're the only soul in this village who has seen fit to befriend me. We can be honest with each other."

"I appreciate your candor." Marian shook her head and schooled her features to reveal no further surprise. "I should like to know more about the nature of your work . . . or rather, your former work. How did you come to establish yourself in the . . . um, trade?" Marian glanced around them. "You've obviously done well for yourself."

"I see." Mrs. Ramsey leaned back in her chair, her gaze sharp as knives as it settled on Marian. "Well, it's not a vocation for everyone, my dear, but I found it very satisfactory for me."

"You were able to retire in some comfort." Marian again motioned to the well-appointed room around them.

"I made myself essential to a few very wealthy gentlemen."

Made myself essential.

It sounded simple enough, and yet Marian could not imagine ever being essential to any man.

Instantly she thought of Clara and her mother, Lady Strickland. Without a doubt, both were essential to the men in their lives. Marian would characterize them in no other way. They were essential.

But they were wives.

Marian had no wish to be a wife.

Mrs. Ramsey continued, "Indeed, I am comfortable. That is all I ever wanted to be. That was my goal. Comfort. Independence. I wanted a home of my own with a handful of servants to attend to me. I do not require wealth. Merely security and sustainability."

Marian nodded. She well understood that. She wanted the same things in life.

"As to the work . . . the tasks that were required of you . . ." Marian's voice faded. She did not know the precise language to use, which presented some difficulty. She wanted an honest discussion. If she was to go down this path, she wanted no confusion at the onset.

"The shagging? Is that what you mean, dear?"

"Yes," Marian said, grateful for the help. Her

shoulders sagged with an expelled breath. "Is the . . . shagging . . . difficult? To endure?"

Mrs. Ramsey stared at her, her expression turning thoughtful. It was some time before she answered.

"Your father was always very kind to me, Marian. Never once did he turn up his nose at me, and I have no doubt he knew what I was. An honorable man and doctor, he was. He cured me of my megrims when I was most miserable. Well, he and Nora. They gave me the perfect tonic to relieve my aches. I am not certain your dear papa would appreciate me giving his beloved daughter advice on how to become a whore."

It took everything inside her not to flinch. Mrs. Ramsey was watching her, gauging her reaction, judging to see if her constitution could hold up to the ugly word.

It could.

"However honorable my father, he had his flaws. He did not provide for his children. He has left such matters to me. I'm sure you understand that one must do what they can to survive."

"Hm. Indeed, I do." Mrs. Ramsey stirred some sugar into her tea. "Gentlemen oft forget that they are vulnerable. They do not plan for a future where they are not in it, no matter how that might adversely affect their loved ones."

Marian nodded in agreement. She loved Papa, but she did battle some resentment toward him. Some nights, awake in bed, worrying over how she would manage matters, she would curse her father. Then she would quickly repent, beg him to forgive her as though he were standing before her again.

Mrs. Ramsey nodded as though reaching some decision. "I was very good at shagging, Marian. Often, I even enjoyed it. It's always better when you enjoy it. Naturally." A faraway look entered her eyes. "I've had a few paramours who were quite pleasing. They could make me forget that shagging was something I did out of necessity."

"Indeed?" That didn't sound so bad.

Mrs. Ramsey went on, "And then there were times it felt a chore. Make no mistake, you must act the part even when you're not feeling it. A few times even . . ." She shrugged. "Well, it was only unpleasant when I was young. Before I knew any better. Before I realized how to take control."

Control. What a tempting word. It was the very thing Marian so desperately wanted in her life.

Mrs. Ramsey motioned around her. "I have all this because I was very good. I knew how to make men want me and keep wanting me once they had me."

"I'd like to know how to do that," Marian asserted, nodding eagerly.

"Of course you would." Mrs. Ramsey smiled widely. "That kind of skill is power."

"Power," Marian echoed, her heart beating harder in her chest for some reason. *That word was even more tempting than control.*

For so long, she had felt without power . . . but to have control *and* power? It was a heady thought.

"If you make a man want you above all others . . ." Mrs. Ramsey cupped her hand as though she held something in the center of her palm. "You shall possess him."

Marian laughed nervously. "You sound like a witch."

"Indeed, it is a bit like weaving a spell." Mrs. Ramsey looked Marian up and down. "You have it in you to be a great courtesan. I knew it the moment I met you. Some women have it. Others do not. It's not about the body or one's face, not that you don't have a very fine face, but some of the greatest courtesans are not beautiful women. Beauty has naught to do with it." She tapped her head. "It takes your mind. Intellect. That is your greatest weapon. You're clever. Observant. Resourceful. That is essential. Along with a healthy appetite for adventure. You cannot be a prude."

Marian flinched. She was a virgin. How could she *not* be a prude?

"Come now. Don't look so worried."

"I've never . . ."

"Of course you haven't."

"So how can I not present as a prude?"

"A woman who enjoys sex, who wants it, who likes it, is an aphrodisiac to any man."

An aphrodisiac? It was certainly difficult to imagine herself as that.

Mrs. Ramsey smiled. "Don't look so daunted. It's quite simple really. Find a man to play with."

"Play?" How did one *play* with a man? They weren't puppies.

"Indeed. Keep your maidenhead intact, of course." She pointed a finger at Marian. "That will fetch you a high price the first time. But for now find an attractive man, preferably someone who knows what he's about. Practice on him. Learn. Hone your kissing, bring yourself to climax with him."

Her burning face must have revealed some of her shock. "Yes," Mrs. Ramsey went on to reassure. "You can do that and remain a maid. There is much to learn and I could talk myself blue trying to explain it all to you. Simply put, you need a man with whom to experiment."

Marian shook her head. It was too much to digest. "I-I don't know anyone—"

Mrs. Ramsey snapped her fingers. "That duke of yours."

"Warrington?" Marian's stomach dropped to the vicinity of her feet.

"Yes." Mrs. Ramsey nodded and popped a grape into her mouth.

"He's not *my* duke. He's not *my* anything." Except an arrogant man who talked down to her.

"Well, you met him already. That's more than most of the population in this town can claim. What's the problem? He's young and virile, is he not?"

"Y-yes." She really wished she would cease with this stammer. Where was her composure?

"And by all accounts he is not averse to having a woman in his bed."

"So that makes him a-a . . . candidate for me?" There was nothing about him that struck her as willing to . . . *play*. At least not with her. He had looked down his nose at her and called her *girl*. She could not take herself to him and beg him to *play* with her.

Mrs. Ramsey ignored the question. "He would be discreet, I'm sure. He would not wish to compromise you publicly. That would not go well for him, either."

"No. I cannot consider it. Not with him." Marian shook her head doggedly. "I could not."

"Did you find him repulsive?"

"He was boorish and pretentious—"

"Of course he is. He's a duke. But by all accounts he's quite active in the bedroom, and that is excellent for our purposes."

They called him the depraved duke. Naturally, he knew all about fornicating, but that was of no matter to Marian.

She shook her head. "I want no part of him."

Mrs. Ramsey sighed. "If you wish to consider entering into the world's oldest and most venerable profession, you need to stop being so picky. *Liking* the men you're with is not a luxury you can afford."

Marian bristled, trying not to take offense at being called picky. "You said I would have power—"

"Yes. Once you are good. You are not good. You are not anything. Yet."

She flinched at the blunt words.

Mrs. Ramsey continued in a more placating tone, "You cannot have power if you are not good. And you are not good, Marian. You're a novice. You need a tutor to show you the ropes. You were a governess. You, better than anyone, should understand the need for one to properly educate herself."

Marian nodded miserably. She did understand that.

It made sense.

Practice made perfect, and clearly Mrs. Ramsey

had been a perfect courtesan to retire so comfortably. Marian wanted that. Only she could not take herself to a man who had made her feel so foolish and small. She could not approach him and ask him to exercise his wiles on her.

The notion made her ill.

Perhaps there was someone else. Brambledon had a healthy population of men.

She envisioned that, envisioned taking herself to any one of the men she was long acquainted with in town. It made her cringe. She'd known many of them since she was a girl in plaits. All those proper gentlemen would be scandalized at the late Dr. Langley's daughter approaching them requesting lessons in fornication.

She closed her eyes in a slow blink. And who was to say any man she approached would be good enough to teach her? Or maintain discretion? She couldn't bring ruin down upon her family.

No. There was no one in Brambledon she could ask.

Mrs. Ramsey reached over the tea service and patted her hand. "There, there. It's not for everyone, dear. Clearly such a vocation doesn't suit you if you cannot contemplate dallying with one mere man, and a handsome one at that."

"His handsomeness pales once he opens his mouth. He's rude and arrogant and unfeeling—"

"Sounds like a duke—or any man of wealth and importance, which is precisely the clientele you would be targeting." Mrs. Ramsey shook her head and gave Marian a rueful smile. "Clearly this is an impossibility for you. Best put the idea out of your mind."

Marian fought the urge to argue—to insist that the independent and potentially lucrative lifestyle of a courtesan was the right future for her.

It *could* suit her. She wasn't ready to give up on the idea.

The problem was with the duke. Blast the man. She wished she had never mentioned him to Mrs. Ramsey.

Mrs. Ramsey gave her hand a final pat. "You shall come up with something else. Clever girl like you, of course you will. Perhaps you could marry that blacksmith that's always calling on you. He smells of cheese, but he's quite well-heeled."

That decided it.

Marian relented with a pained sigh. "Tell me what I need to say to the duke."

Chapter 6

*M*arian had a great many things to contemplate on her walk home.

She'd agreed to approach the Duke of Warrington, but the idea made her stomach clench. Mrs. Ramsey did not understand. She had not met him herself. If she had, then she would see that he was a completely unsuitable candidate.

The man cared for nothing. By his own admission. *I care for my lands. A fine whisky. A good meal. A first-rate shag.*

The depraved duke, indeed. He was a wretch. How could she bring herself to a man like that?

She muttered beneath her breath and increased her stride.

If he was to tutor Marian in desire . . . should

there not be *desire*? Mutual desire for each other? Per Mrs. Ramsey's instructions, Marian needed to understand the pleasure behind shagging. She snorted. Pleasure was not what came to mind when she recalled the Duke of Warrington.

Mud kicked up at her ankles as she walked briskly across the countryside.

She cut through fields rather than take the main road. The last thing she wanted was to come face-to-face with neighbors. People relished hearing every grim detail of the Langleys' unfortunate circumstances. As though it served as some manner of perverse entertainment for them. Presently, Marian was not in the mood for a battery of prying questions.

She would endure muddy hems and muddier boots to avoid that.

Her basket of goodies from Mrs. Ramsey swung from her hand as she walked briskly.

Her heart pulsed in her ears as she replayed her conversation with Mrs. Ramsey and wondered how she could take all her advice and put it into action. It would take more than bravado to proposition Warrington.

But these were desperate times. Months ago, she would never have imagined herself embracing a future as a fallen woman.

And yet here she was now doing that very thing.

"Who even are you anymore, Marian Langley?" she mumbled to herself, her steps biting angrily into the soft earth.

The air grew steadily darker around her. She eyed the gray skyline and noted a small smudge in the distance, like an ant on the horizon. Stopping, she watched as the ant advanced, eventually turning into a horse and rider.

She inched closer to the hedge on her left that served as a property line between Mrs. Pratt's and the Duke of Warrington's lands.

Squinting, she watched the large and daunting horse advance. A destrier.

No one in these parts owned such a specimen. Such a beast would cost a fortune. It was the kind of animal only the most privileged of men would possess.

With a sickening twist of her stomach, she knew who sat atop that horse. He might be too far away for her to properly discern his features, but she knew.

She knew and she did not want to see him.

She could not see him.

Her heart launched into her throat. With a choked cry, she looked wildly around, desperate to escape. To hide.

Before she could think through the wisdom of her actions, she dropped to the ground and scrambled beneath the hedge, pushing her way through bramble and gorse with foul exclamations no lady should know.

Not until she was tucked beneath tangled branches, poked and prodded on every side, did she fully appreciate the foolishness of her position.

She hugged herself closely, feeling much as she had when she huddled beneath the duke's table.

Except now she was colder. Damp and miserable and doubly shamed.

The sound of hooves grew closer and she waited, eager for them to pass. Eager for the sound of them to fade away.

Her breathing escaped in hard little pants.

The hoofbeats grew louder and louder until they were directly upon her. Until the long, strong legs of a destrier pranced beside her where she hid inside the scratchy hedge.

She pressed her hands over her mouth as though that could muffle her breaths.

"Is someone in there?" a voice called out—a deep voice she remembered all too well.

She flinched and tried to make herself smaller. Through a break in the bramble, she was afforded the barest view of his fine boots nestled in stirrups.

"I saw you dive into the hedge," he said loudly.

She felt her eyes widen.

He saw her?

He continued, "I can also see your dress. The yellow is quite identifiable through the leaves."

She glanced down accusingly at her bright bodice peeking out from her cloak. Marian had chosen it with care this morning, wanting to look nice when she called on Mrs. Ramsey. It was one of the few dresses left to her. She'd brought a vast wardrobe home with her, but that had been a year ago, and she'd divided the dresses among herself and her sisters. Now her best dress had betrayed her.

She closed her eyes and counted to ten, hoping he would just give up and move on his way.

Reopening her eyes, she saw that he was still there. Blast!

"Come out, lass."

He wasn't leaving.

Accepting the inevitable, she squeezed back out of the hedge. She tried to do so as gracefully as possible, but exiting was perhaps *more* difficult than when she had plunged inside the shrubbery.

A thorny branch caught in her hair, nearly pulling several strands out from the roots. Her mouth opened wide on a silent scream as her hand reached up to grab the strands. The move brought a thorn slicing across the back of her hand.

"Ouch!"

"Hold still before your skewer yourself."

Freezing, she watched warily as he dismounted and approached.

He was even more imposing than she remembered. Heavens. He was big. She'd had no proper sense of that before as he had been sitting through their initial exchange.

His gloved hands reached out and began bending and snapping branches free of her.

His expression was intent as he worked. She took advantage of the fact that he never once glanced at her face and studied his features closely.

In the light of day, he was even sterner. And yet that somehow made him more handsome. A bit unfair, that. She had always thought happy people to be the most attractive, but nothing about this man smacked of happiness. He was a bag full of scowls and still heartbreakingly handsome.

Wretch.

Suddenly, his hands were no longer on the shrubbery. They were on her hair—on *her*. She held her breath. It was far more intimacy than she wanted, but she knew better than to protest. Like a hare caught in a trap, she waited, eager for that moment of freedom when she could bolt away.

"Stay still. I don't want to hurt you." His manner might be rough, but his fingers worked gently to untangle the strands of her hair. "You have a lot of hair," he mused.

She grunted noncommittally, unsure what to say to that.

"There," he murmured, his voice a husky puff against her forehead. "All done. Now you're free."

She was free, but unlike a newly freed hare, she just stood there, looking up at him in wonder, pinned to the spot as though she were still imprisoned by bramble and thorns. She might as well have been. His eyes pinned her just as effectively.

For a man who alleged to care for nothing, he was very helpful and considerate of her discomfort. A warm flutter took flight in her stomach. He looked less stern as he stared down at her. His scrutiny was merely . . . intense. Intense in a way that only increased those flutters.

Finally, he stepped away and she breathed a little easier.

"Why is it you are always in places a body should not be?" he asked.

She flushed hotly. It was embarrassing, but true. The first time they met she had been hiding under a table, and now she had taken cover in foliage.

"I thought you were a highwayman," she blurted, stepping farther away from the hedge and yet keeping a respectable distance from him.

"Me?" He looked skeptical. "You thought I was a highwayman?"

"Indeed. They don't always travel in groups. I spotted you from a distance and dove into the bushes to hide."

He looked all around them as though assessing the likelihood of danger.

"If you feared bandits, then why abandon the main road to stroll through the more remote countryside?"

"Everyone knows they always attack the main road. It's more traveled. That's where they go. Of course, I would take an alternate route." That actually made sense. She nodded, pleased with herself for coming up with that.

He looked less convinced. In fact, he looked rather befuddled.

She brought her basket in front of her, clasping the handle in both hands. "In any event, thank you for not being a bandit."

"Er, you're welcome."

"And thank you for helping me emerge from the hedge," she added.

"Of course."

She hesitated. His solicitousness was something to ponder. This—combined with him hiding her from the coal peddler—gave her pause. He could not be entirely wretched and lacking mercy. Perhaps she could approach him about lessons on desire? Her stomach flutters started all over again.

Not right now, though. Not in this moment. She needed more time to think on the matter. As desperate as she was, she didn't want to do anything rash that she would come to regret.

With a final nod, she turned in the direction of home to resume her walk . . . only to stop when she noticed he had fallen in beside her, leading his horse by the reins.

"What are you doing?"

"As you've pointed out, these are dangerous times when bandits could be lurking about. I'm escorting you home."

"Oh, no, no. That's not necessary."

"I think you've perfectly illustrated that it *is* necessary . . . and in the future you should reconsider walking about the countryside unescorted."

As though she had a choice. She bristled. "I assure you, a stroll without a chaperone *with you* presents its own hazards."

His hard expression did not even crack. "I'm certain I do not know your meaning."

"It would not be appropriate."

"Given the manner of our first meeting, I did not think appropriateness would be a concern high on your list."

"You have no idea what concerns me, Your Grace."

He cocked his head. "I have some notion."

She winced. After their first encounter, she supposed that was true. Like everyone else in these parts, he knew she was desperately in need of funds.

"I am certain you can find better things to do." Things like whisky and women and food.

"I might prefer to do better things, but honor demands I escort you the rest of the way home."

Honor? She laughed. She could not help herself.

"I said something amusing?"

"For a man who claims to care for nothing and no one, you seem overly concerned with the notion of honor."

He scowled. "You've a waspish tongue for someone who was just rescued from bramble and thorns."

Rescued? "The only reason I was in there was because you came charging toward me and I did not recognize you. I feared for my safety." He was unendurable and obtuse. "I don't know how much clearer I can be. Being seen with you will be damaging to my reputation."

Perhaps she was exaggerating a smidge, but she did not want to be alone one moment longer with the man. Her face felt hot and flushed and she didn't know how much longer she could stand in proximity to him without doing or saying something that would give away the intimate conversation she'd just had—about him, no less!—with Mrs. Ramsey.

He blinked. "Being seen with *me*? A day ago you were hiding at my feet from creditors and now you're too good for me?"

"My financial status has nothing to do with propriety."

"Bloody, bloody . . ." The rest of his words faded away as he turned from her abruptly.

She watched as he mounted in one fluid motion. The destrier danced in a circle before the duke reined him in. Once he had the beast under control, he looked down, blasting her with a haughty, cold glare. "Enjoy your walk. I'll trouble you no more." With a tense nod of farewell, he whirled his mount around and galloped away.

She stared after him, experiencing mixed emotions but glad that he was departing and glad she had decided *not* to ask him her scandalous request.

At least not yet.

Marian definitely needed more time to consider the matter, and more time to gather her nerve—even if she knew deep down what she had to do.

Chapter 7

*A*fter choking down another barely edible meal, Nate retired to his study to pen the obligatory letter to his mother.

A fire crackled in the great hearth across from him. Nearby, his hound slept on the rug before the fire. The beast was wiry and fit from their many walks through the countryside and swims in the pond, but he was snoring like an old man.

Shaking his head, Nate took a drink from his glass and returned his attention to the matter at hand. The letter was long overdue. His mother had written him again, harping on the fact that he had not replied to her last letter and was he alive still and had he found himself a bride yet because he was not getting any younger.

The usual.

He knew it could be worse. His mother could be in England and within proximity to him and he would have to endure her harping in a face-to-face encounter. Small blessing she was somewhere in Spain.

She had been touring the continent with her husband for well over a year now. His father was long dead. She'd remarried the Earl of Norfolk soon after his father passed. The earl was a few years younger than his mother, a garrulous man with a raucous laugh, given to wild parties and too much drink and flaunting his bastard son all about Society. A perfect match for his mother, who also enjoyed life's excesses.

Nate knew there was a bit of irony in that. His mother liked to surround herself with people. She needed people whilst her son desired only solitude.

A light knock sounded at his door and he bade enter. Pearson stepped inside the room.

His man of affairs was not much older than Nate. Proper. Stoic. Impeccably attired. He only ever wore bland expressions that gave away nothing going on behind his eyes. He was the height of efficiency and his words attested to that. "I've sent inquiries for a proper cook. In the meantime, Dobbs is on his way from Derbyshire."

Dobbs. The Irish cook had been with his family for decades. He would not like being uprooted from the Warrington seat in Derbyshire. Nate had rarely visited his ancestral estate growing up as he had been at school most of the time, but he did recall Dobbs shouting from the kitchen when one of his underlings displeased him.

Nate liked a silent house. Calm. A place where emotions did not rule.

Bringing Dobbs here would add upheaval into his orderly world, but the man knew his way around the kitchen, and it would be worth a palatable meal.

Pearson continued, "I will keep him in check, Your Grace."

Nate nodded once, all brusqueness. "Very good, Pearson. You may go now."

Pearson turned away and departed the room.

Nate returned his attention to his letter. After a moment he wadded it up and tossed it across the room. He pulled out a fresh piece of parchment and started over.

Words never came with ease for him. Even the written word that he could labor over and reflect upon before putting down proved elusive.

He reminded himself that it didn't need to be complicated. His mother only wished to be told everything was right and merry in his life. So that's what he would tell her. He would tell her what she wanted to hear. If he didn't give her such assurances, she might decide to visit him. God forbid that happened.

The last thing he wanted was to endure his stepfather. The man could not hide his contempt for Nate. Norfolk might even bring that wastrel son of his along. For whatever reason, he liked his bastard—perhaps because Kingston was his only offspring or, more likely, because Kingston was cut from the same cloth. A rakehell with no responsibilities who spent all of his time carousing . . . moving from one party to the next drinking, gambling, and seducing anything in skirts.

They were the extent of his family, and he did not want any of them visiting him. His quill scratched over parchment with renewed determination as another knock sounded at his door.

Pearson stuck his head back into the room. "Forgive the intrusion, Your Grace, but there is someone here to see you."

Nate frowned. He knew no one in these parts.

"A woman," Pearson added.

Nate glanced to the calendar on his desk. He kept standing appointments with certain females of the demimonde. He saw to their transport here from London and back. It might be a long carriage ride for just an hour of his time, but he compensated them well.

He never needed more than an hour, two at the most. That was enough. It was a simple transaction. No conversation or flirtation or coddling.

"I don't have an appointment tonight."

"Ah. That is true. I believe she is from the village."

He didn't know anyone in the village. He shrugged. "Then I don't know her." He waved Pearson off. "Send her on her way."

Pearson nodded and turned to leave.

Nate lowered his gaze back to his missive, lifted his quill and froze, the memory of his one foray into the village filling his mind.

"Wait." The word flew from his lips. He looked back up. "This woman. What does she look like?"

Pearson considered the question for a moment. "Young. Fair. A bit shabby in dress, Your Grace. No one would mistake her for one of your lady friends."

Indeed not. All of Nate's lady friends wore the finest silks and brocade and ermine-trimmed cloaks.

He leaned back in his chair. Pearson's description was brief, but it matched with the image in his mind of the chit that preoccupied far too much of his thoughts. He'd encountered her twice, but he could not shake the memory of her words. *You're the depraved duke.*

He knew who was calling on him. He recalled her perfectly. And she was here to see him.

"Show her in."

IT WAS MADNESS coming here, but Marian reminded herself that madness aptly described her life. At least, what it had become. Day after day of drudgery, of grinding penury. That was the definition of tragedy, she supposed.

Somehow, her life had become a Greek play. Who knew what this act would bring? She was at a turning point for certain.

A stiff-lipped fellow led her into the bowels of the house. The place was dark. Under furnished, too, as far as she could see. Not at all like the grand homes of the aristocracy she'd frequented whilst in the Duke of Autenberry's employ. The bones of the house might be grand enough, but it was just that—a skeleton with nothing inside its frame.

Their steps lightly padded over the runner.

They passed windows with heavy damask drapes covering them. Not that it mattered at this hour. There was no sunlight to be had even if they were pulled open.

Haverston Hall was a bit of a trek from her house. She'd left home at dusk with their one horse, Bessie. She was an old mare now. Gone were the days when Marian and her sisters and brother would pile on her back and run across the meadow. Even though Bessie could bring them some coin and it was an added burden to keep and feed her, Marian did not have the heart to sell off the creature. Some things were beyond price.

Besides, Bessie wasn't entirely frail. There was still life in her yet. She had managed to carry Marian to Haverston Hall in the fading twilight, after all.

Sconces lined the walls of the corridors but only a few were lit. Just enough to save them from stumbling about in darkness.

She was led to a pair of slightly ajar double doors. The man pushed a door open and motioned her inside. "Miss . . ."

She nodded and did as he directed, stepping within the well-appointed room. It was dark like the rest of the house, but not quite as bare. All rich woods and leather. No feminine touch whatsoever.

A fire crackled in a great hearth, casting the room in flickering orange light. She clutched the neck of her cloak tightly together in front of her even though she felt quite warm. Warmer than she had felt for quite some time. Since Papa had died.

"Miss . . . you still wish to keep your cloak?"

She nodded and opened her mouth, but stopped at the deep, familiar voice intoning, "Leave us."

The duke's man departed the room, leaving her alarmingly alone with the man she had come to see.

It shouldn't be alarming. She knew that. She'd been alone with him before, out in the countryside, and he had not done anything to make her feel unsafe. On the contrary, he had attempted to escort her home.

Marian took a steadying breath. She had entered into this in full understanding of what she was about. She knew it was an outrageous scheme, but something needed to happen. *Something* needed to change. She had to make something happen or someone else would. Any one of the creditors could bring action against her. She could be sent to Newgate. A frisson of dread danced down her spine. And then it would be too late. It would all be out of her control. Mr. Lawrence's face flashed across her mind, and her dread intensified. Out of her control and not to her liking. *Not her choice.*

Warrington was standing. Or rather leaning against his desk. Even leaning against the edge of his desk he was a head taller than Marian.

"You've tracked me down," he announced.

"It wasn't that difficult. Everyone knows where you live."

He angled his head as though peering to look over her shoulder. "Any other coal purveyors in pursuit of you?" He waved at the desk. "Have you need to crawl beneath this?"

She winced. "No. No one knows I'm here. That is why I came under cover of night."

"Ah." He nodded slowly. "Advisable considering you are an unescorted female. I do believe you are concerned with propriety . . . even if you have a penchant for hiding under tables and inside shrubbery and calling on strange men in their homes."

Of course, he would mention those instances when she had made a complete fool of herself. She glanced away, more nervous than she had ever felt in her life.

"Why are you here, Miss . . ."

She dragged her gaze back to him. "Langley. Marian Langley."

That introduction, she realized, was long overdue.

With an imperious wave of his hand, he prompted her to continue. "Well, Miss Langley. What do you want from me?"

Directly to the point. She supposed she should do the same and get to it.

She squared her shoulders. "I have a proposition for you."

"Indeed." His arms came up to cross over his chest.

She nodded quickly, grasping for her fleeing composure. "I'd like you to teach me . . ." Her voice failed her.

"Teach you?" he prodded.

Find your tongue. Say it. Speak the words, outrageous though they be.

"Yes. I'd like you to teach me to be a good lover." There. She'd said it. She'd done it. Nothing could be as difficult as that. She winced. Except perhaps touching him and letting him touch her, but that was later. She'd fret over that then.

It was some moments before he spoke. "What did you say?"

She swallowed and repeated herself. "I'd like you to show me how to be a good lover." She clarified further. "I want to know everything there is to know about pleasing a man."

His eyes narrowed, but she still felt their dark heat on her in the gloom of the room. "You've never been with a man."

It was more statement than question.

She knew she shouldn't feel offended. A gently bred young lady should be presumed chaste, but a part of her wondered why he was so quick to assume. She was here, after all, for illicit reasons. Did she strike him as a woman no man would want? She was not typically insecure, but around him she felt awkward and uncertain of herself.

"Yes, that is true. I've never been with a man, but I'm not completely ignorant on such matters," she rushed to say. "I understand what goes on between a man and woman . . . the mechanics of it at any rate. I simply lack the experience. That's where you come in."

"No." He shook his head. "I do not."

Her face heated from his rejection. Of course, he needed time to adjust to the idea. She needed to explain herself better. "That is to say, I *hope* this is where you can come into it."

"Even if you were to my taste, I am not in the habit of deflowering virgins. The last virgin in my bed was my late wife. I have no intention of having either a virgin or a wife again."

Even if you were to my taste . . .

Well, that stung, but she pushed her hurt feelings aside. She could almost hear Mrs. Ramsey's voice telling her to be strong. This wasn't personal and she needn't feel so affronted.

"I am not offering you my virginity."

He shook his head once. "My apologies. Did you not just walk into this room and ask me to teach you how to be a proper lover?"

"No. Yes. N-no." She made a strangling sound in her throat. She was bungling this. "Let me explain."

"Please do."

"I'm aware that you're a man of deep appetites."

Laughter burst from him at that statement, and she couldn't help thinking the sound was rough and rusty from lack of use.

Even he looked a fraction surprised that laughter had sprung free from him. He smothered the sound. "*Deep appetites*?" He was silent for a moment as though struggling to grasp her meaning. "I gather there are stories of me being bandied about the village?"

"Yes," she admitted. "Everyone knows of the women coming and going."

He expelled a heavy breath.

She continued, "They are courtesans, I presume? You must know a good deal about the act of congress. After so much experience with . . . er, professionals."

He cocked his head and gazed at her as though she had sprouted a second head. "Why?" he asked. "Why do you want to be a proper lover?"

"Because I want to be a professional. I want to be a courtesan. I want to be good . . . so good that I can name my price and have my pick of clients." *And walk away when I choose, when I'm able . . . with my freedom intact.*

"And yet you don't want me to take your virginity?"

"That's correct. I'm told it can fetch a fine price.

It's my understanding there's a premium on such things." Vile but true. Even before her conversation with Mrs. Ramsey, she knew the way the world worked. For once, she would take advantage of its ugly side and get as much as she could for herself. For herself and her family.

A rush of breath escaped him. "You intend to sell your virginity?"

She flinched, but nodded. "Indeed. It is mine to do with as I please."

Hers. Her body. Her life. No one else's.

"Should you not want a husband to—"

"Just as you want no wife, I want no husband." Her voice lifted an octave. Mrs. Ramsey's words echoed in her mind. "As a courtesan, I choose. I decide." She took a breath and evened her voice. "At least, if I'm skilled enough. And you can teach me. You can help make me skilled."

"Without deflowering you?" he said again slowly, as though trying to keep that detail clear in his mind. Before she could answer, he pushed off his desk, and turned his tall frame, presenting her with his back. "This is madness." He ran a hand through his hair, sending the dark locks into disarray. Lifting the glass up off his desk, he tossed back the amber contents in one fluid move.

She dared to step closer, following him, hoping to still persuade him. "My father left us without funds. I have a family to care for . . . sisters and a brother away at school."

"Then marry. That's what other gently bred girls do."

Why must it always come back to *that*?

"No, thank you. I want to maintain control over my body *and* my fate. If I marry I give that up forever. I'll keep my freedom."

He turned and looked down at her as though she were mad. "You've thought about this." Wonder tinged his voice.

"I won't have to do it forever. Not if I'm . . . good enough. You can recommend me out to your friends. You obviously have ties. Connections."

Something passed over his features. Astonishment, perhaps? "So you not only want me to school you, you want me to give you letters of reference?" He stared at her with incredulity.

She nodded. "In a manner. Please," she whispered, feeling much as she had upon their first meeting when she hid beneath his table. Desperate. Pleading . . . and not a little ridiculous.

She was bumbling this, she was certain of that, but she was also certain that a man such as he possessed the power to help her in this.

"I am no pimp."

She flinched. "I know what I'm asking is a bit unorthodox. I d-did not mean to imply . . . that is, I did not . . ."

Brilliant. She had lost the ability for coherent speech. As a former governess who prided herself on her composure *and* the ability to converse intelligently, it smarted.

Before all was lost, she blurted out, "I was a governess. I am one, rather. I can speak Latin, French . . . I've a head for numbers. I can help you with any bookkeeping you may have. I'm an excellent seamstress, too." Her mind worked feverishly for more to offer him. "My youngest sister is an herbalist. Do you have any aches or ailments? I'm sure some arrangement could be reached in exchange for your—"

"So now *I* am the whore whose services you're offering to buy?"

"No!" she cried in horror. "I'm merely trying to strike a fair bargain."

"I think this concludes our conversation." He dragged a hand over his head, smoothing his unruly hair back into place. "Did you need anything else?" he asked coolly.

He was dismissing her. No doubt of that.

"You won't help me," she said hollowly.

Of course he would not help her. Had she thought he would? He did not know her and, evidently, he did not find her an attractive enough temptation. Had she thought he might help her since he had earlier? Had she thought his streak of altruism ran so deep . . . or that she could barter with him using her math skills? Ridiculous.

"No." The word fell hard. Final.

The senseless burn of tears stung her eyes. She had struggled to simply work up the nerve to come here. Mrs. Ramsey had never discussed the possibility that the duke would say no. Marian hadn't prepared for that. She should have braced for it. It was no small thing she was asking. Especially since she was not to his self-proclaimed tastes.

With her pride in tatters, she turned and fled the room, colliding into a young man in the corridor.

He gripped her elbows to steady her. "Pardon me," he murmured.

She shook him off, continuing on, pushing hard down the stairs until she was out of the house and on her way home.

Chapter 8

$\mathcal{N}$ate watched the female flee the room and resisted the unprecedented compulsion to go after her.

He did not pursue females. Especially not ones who showed up uninvited in his home—not that any had done so before, but it was the principle of the matter. This was what came from fooling about with respectable females. Because contrary to her outrageous proposition, Marian Langley was a respectable young woman. It radiated from her like a fever, and he would do best to avoid her. He did not wish to become afflicted, after all.

"And who was that country miss?" Pearson asked mildly as he entered the room. "She left in quite the hurry. Nearly knocked me over."

"You outweigh her by at least four stones. I doubt you were in danger," Nate returned.

Pearson assessed him critically. "Country misses don't pay calls on you," he accused.

Nate nodded in agreement. "You speak true."

"Then what brought this one to your door?"

"She is no ordinary country miss." That much was evident. He could still hear her outrageous declaration. *I'd like you to teach me how to be a good lover.* Her words, her voice, played over and over in his mind more than they should. More than he wanted them to. Innocent country misses weren't to his taste. He'd said as much. He meant it.

"Indeed? Well, she's certainly established herself as bold. Foolish, even, coming here at this late hour. Unless she had no notion of who you are?" Pearson helped himself to the whisky while sending Nate a questioning look.

Miss Langley was no unwitting female to stumble into his lair. Her entire reason for calling on him was because of his reputation. She knew precisely who—*what*—he was. "Well. This one is looking to be ruined."

A corner of Pearson's mouth kicked up. "Then she came to the right place."

"I don't know what you mean. I am not in the habit of ruining innocent girls. That's more your forte."

Pearson shook his head. "You refer to my stepping out with the poulter's daughter? I'm hardly ruining her. It's called courting. I've her father's blessing. My intentions are purely honorable."

A strange turn, that.

Nate and Pearson had frequented their share of bawdy houses together. Nate never suspected his friend had a penchant for the domesticity of marriage, but he seemed headed in that direction.

Nate wasn't a man given to many leisurely pursuits. He didn't belong to a gentlemen's club. He didn't play cards or bet the horses. He took his seat in the House of Lords when required and performed his duty. The rest of the time he managed his estates. He didn't leave everything to Pearson. He involved himself with the welfare of his tenants. He researched the latest advancements in farming, enjoying digging his hands in soil. In another life, he might have been a simple farmer. A yeoman plowing the fields outside the manor.

Staying busy kept deep thoughts at bay.

A person could do that. Work and stay so occupied he was too busy to think, too busy to feel, too busy to remember. He'd learned how it could be done.

In the lapses, in the pauses when one too many thoughts intruded, he'd take himself to a member of the demimonde. Those excursions helped.

He wasn't a rake, by any means, but if he needed a release, he sought the company of a professional. Better that than a woman who wanted emotion from him. Professionals never disappointed. They gave. He took. He paid. All were satisfied.

Up until recently, Pearson had joined him in his pursuits.

It stopped once they moved to Brambledon and Pearson began his courtship of the poulter's daughter. Now Pearson had no interest in accompanying Nate the two hours into Town to visit their old haunts.

Rather than making the journey himself, Nate sent for his paramours. It was more convenient, less troublesome, and he paid the women handsomely for the trouble.

Pearson could keep his *honorable* courtship.

Nate would stick with what he knew. He would save the innocent for the innocent.

He'd had his chance. His time in the sun. Those days were gone with Mary Beth. A lifetime ago.

There was just this now.

"So, tell me of this girl on the hunt for ruin." Pearson sank down in the chair opposite him and crossed one ankle over his knee, settling in comfortably.

"Miss Langley was . . . interesting," Nate volunteered. *Peculiar* was more accurate a description. Perhaps *insane* was the most accurate word of all.

"How's that?"

He wondered if there was some truth to what she had said. If being mistress to a man was somehow *better* than being a wife. He'd always assumed every girl wished to grow up and marry. He'd assumed matrimony the end goal of every young woman. What sensible lass would wish for the loss of her good name and reputation?

"She had a proposition for me," he finally answered.

"Indeed?"

"Yes. It seems she is interested in learning to become a rich man's mistress. Not mine, mind you. Some other."

Pearson stared. "You jest."

"Not at all. I could not be so creative to conceive such a thing."

"She showed up here and asked you to . . . what? School her? In shagging?"

Nate held up one finger. "In *expert* shagging," he qualified.

Pearson laughed lightly. "Well, you would certainly know. You have plenty of experience."

Nate neither agreed or disagreed to that. "Apparently she has heard of my guests."

"Oh. You mean all the women traipsing in and out of here?"

"You make it sound as though it is every night," he grumbled.

Pearson continued, "It is the talk of the village."

Nate grimaced, annoyed. "Apparently." He had not imagined he would be a subject of such interest to the locals when he moved to Haverston Hall.

"Well?" Pearson looked at him expectantly. "Will you teach her?"

Nate scoffed. "Of course not. I'm not in the habit of dallying with untried girls."

"Yes, I suppose it is your custom to only cavort with experienced females, but she was uncommonly pretty. And she did make it exceptionally easy for you, offering herself up on a platter like that."

Nate paused, digesting that and tracing the rim of his glass with a finger. "To be fair, she didn't exactly offer herself up on a platter." No, she had boundaries. Ridiculous considering her proposition.

"I don't understand."

"It was as I said. She wants instruction on becoming a rich man's leman . . . but she wishes to keep her virtue intact."

Pearson stared at him for a long moment and then laughed. "How very . . . odd."

"Odd is putting it mildly."

"Of course you were right to send her away."

"What is that supposed to mean?"

"You are not a man of restraint." Pearson waved a hand up and down, encompassing Nate's person.

He bristled. "I can restrain myself if need be."

Pearson still struggled to keep his mirth under control. "Indeed?" The single word rang with disbelief.

"You think me some rutting beast?"

"I did not say that. I simply don't see you having the patience to play at intimacy and then restrain yourself. You are no celibate. No wonder you tossed her out of here."

"I did not *toss* her out of here. And I could restrain myself."

Pearson shook his head, his smile a touch condescending. It was insulting to realize his lifelong friend thought him so weak.

"Nonsense. You could not engage in intimacy without sex. You could not make it a fortnight."

"Care to wager on that?"

Pearson's smile widened. "Oh, I'll take that wager. And I'll win. One fortnight with the girl and you'll be beneath her skirts in the truest sense."

"I agree to those terms. A fortnight of instruction and she will still remain a maid in the truest sense . . . *and* I'll have your horse as my winnings."

"Balthazar?" Pearson frowned for the first time. "He's the finest stallion I've ever—"

"Concerned? What are you worried about? I won't last a fortnight, remember?"

"That's true." Pearson nodded, looking smug once again. "Very well. But when I win you have to gift me your new phaeton."

"Agreed." Nate crossed the distance separating them to shake Pearson's hand, convinced winning a wager would never be so easy.

Chapter 9

The sky was dark, storm clouds glowering, threatening rain. Marian was trying to beat the downpour home. In her pockets, coins jingled. Mrs. Walker had finally paid her outstanding wages for Annabel's lessons. Marian knew the woman could afford to pay her. It was merely inconvenience that had delayed her. She didn't keep money on her person. Her husband handled the accounting and Mrs. Walker hated to discuss matters of finance with him. Genteel ladies could not be bothered to fret over such concerns, she had reminded Marian on more than one occasion, forcing Marian into the uncomfortable position of constantly nagging her. Today her nagging had finally met with just rewards—

that or Marian's threat of going to Mr. Walker
had finally worked.

She would have to think carefully about which
debt to pay first. Mr. Lawrence was right. All
their creditors were closing in like vultures. Perhaps she would simply pay the one who knocked
on her door first today, for she knew someone
would.

She had slept very little since her visit with
the Duke of Warrington. Her stomach and mind
churned simultaneously, constantly, searching
for a way out of this mess. There was no choice
without consequence. Without struggle. Without
pain.

In her haste to beat the potential deluge, she
took a shortcut behind Mrs. Pratt's farm and cut
through a thick copse. The alternate route would
allow her to break out onto the main road leading into the village in far better time.

Marian heard the hard beat of hooves before
she spotted the horse and rider.

She emerged from the thicket and was forced
to jump back, clear of the road, to save herself
from being trampled.

Clutching her cloak to her throat, she glared up
at the offender, indignation heating her cheeks as
she clapped eyes on *him*—the object of so much
of her recent anguish.

Of course. It would have to be him. The *wretch*.

She'd hoped to never see him again, but in a community this small she supposed it was inevitable. At least there were no witnesses. They had privacy. She didn't have to feign politeness.

"You should have a care, Your Grace," she called up to him sharply. "You do not *own* the road. Other people traverse here."

He smiled. A fleeting crooked twist of his lips, and then it was gone, as though he regretted the action.

He pulled on the reins of his giant beast. The horse tossed its head and pranced around her, fighting its bit. She turned in a circle, fixing her gaze on the man in the saddle, but also keeping track of his wild-eyed mount.

"Perhaps you should have a care, as well, and not burst out of the trees and into the road," he reprimanded.

She shied back a step from the horse. "He looks as though he's contemplating taking a bite out of my flesh."

The duke dismounted in one smooth movement. "Fear not. He has no appetite for humans. Especially not virginal termagants."

Face-to-face now, she wished he'd never dismounted. She'd much rather contend with a fiery-eyed horse than him. "No need to dismount, Your Grace." She waved a hand down the road. "Feel free to continue on your way."

"I was actually coming to find you."

She blinked. "You know where I live?"

"I made inquiries."

"Oh." She brushed the tendrils back from her face with a gloved hand. "How can I be of service?"

"I changed my mind."

She stared.

He continued, speaking carefully as though he was only just now arriving at a realization. "I've given matters more thought and changed my mind regarding your proposition. I will tutor you."

She worked her lips for a moment before finding the right words. Her pulse thrummed faster at her throat. "You will? You will tutor me in the art of seduction?"

He gave her a bemused look. "Yes. For whatever it's worth."

Oh, it was worth a great deal. A great deal indeed.

He went on, "As discussed, I won't take your maidenhead, so there's no harm in it. As long as we keep our meetings private, no one need ever know."

She nodded. "Of course."

"That way, you're free to change your mind and forget about becoming a courtesan once you've regained your senses."

"I won't," she quickly retorted.

He sighed and gave her an exasperated look.

Marian ignored the look. "And you will help me find clients in the aftermath of these lessons?" That was perhaps the most important piece to all of this. Between him and Mrs. Ramsey, she trusted she would have the necessary connections. Without a client—and without a client soon—she would simply be compromising herself for no reason.

His expression clouded. "I meant what I said. I am no pimp."

"Of course. And how could you be? You gain nothing by doing this. There is no exchange of goods or services. No benefit of money. Isn't that the main criterion of being a . . . pimp? I confess I had to do a little research to make certain my understanding was accurate, but my late father had a very extensive library. I eventually confirmed the definition was as I thought it."

He looked exasperated with her. "Do you always talk this much?"

She sniffed. "I don't think I talk too much. This is a very serious undertaking, Your Grace. I want us to be clear on all the details—"

"I have a friend that could help you." He sighed. "If, at the end of this, it is your wish, I will put you in contact with her."

"Ah." She nodded in understanding. "A former mistress."

"She was no mistress of mine. She has, however, been mistress to a few very prominent men. I'm sure she can give you some direction." He stroked his horse's muzzle as he considered her. "She is precisely the kind of independent woman you wish to be."

"Excellent. When can we begin with the lessons?" Before he could answer, she rushed on to say, "I hope we can begin with all haste. My situation is becoming increasingly urgent," she admitted with a brusque nod even as she loathed giving voice to such a thing.

"Come to me tomorrow night."

The words dropped between them, heavy and resounding.

The late afternoon suddenly felt thicker, warmer, cloying despite the gloom of the day. It took everything in her not to fling her cloak back off her shoulders in an attempt to enjoy a chill breeze.

"Very well." She nodded once. "Thank you."

He turned and swung back atop his saddle.

She retreated a pace and stared up at him, high above her, trying not to feel intimidated with those words ringing in her ears and his dark eyes fixed so intently on her.

Come to me tomorrow night.

It felt intimate . . . lover-like. Except that was far from the case. They weren't friends. They weren't lovers. *They* weren't *that*.

This wasn't that. This was business.

And she would do well never to forget it.

He inclined his head. "Until tomorrow night." Giving a final nod, he turned and rode away, leaving her looking after him with her stomach in a twist of knots.

Chapter 10

*T*he room smelled of leather and books and burning logs. It reminded Marian of her father's small study at home, especially the way it was when he had been alive and they had prospered. She'd spent hours in there, poring over the pages of his books. Once she ran through his collection of novels—he never had enough of those as far as she was concerned—she moved on to his anatomy and surgical texts.

And yet she experienced none of the ease and comfort she had felt in her father's study. Indeed not.

"Have a seat, Miss Langley."

The depraved duke (she really needed to stop thinking of him in such a fashion) gestured to a well-padded sofa in the center of the dimly lit room with an elegant wave of his hand.

She happily sank down on the thick cushion. It was away from him at least. Blessed distance. Immediately, she knew that was the wrong thought. She had come here for schooling on matters of intimacy. Obviously there would be touching and she'd best brace for it.

Moments passed. The clock on the mantel ticked in the silence. He still hadn't budged from where he was ensconced in the wingback chair near the fire, presiding over the room like some king over his domain.

The warmth was luxurious. She winced at the thought of her sisters alone at home, cuddled up in layers of garments to stay warm. Nora had been draped in blankets and wearing a hat and muffler when Marian last saw her.

Marian had feigned an aching head and retired to her room early.

She'd felt guilty deceiving the girls, but she couldn't tell them what she was really doing. They would be scandalized and disillusioned. They still possessed hope. They had not fully absorbed how dire their circumstances were. They still looked to Marian as though she could save them in a manner that would not involve some level of ruin or sacrifice.

She didn't want to shatter that reality, however false it might be.

Lying to them was a small price to pay in order to drag them from the brink of penury. They need never know how she performed that miracle. Those sordid details she would keep to herself.

When the house had quieted, and she heard only the occasional whispering coming from the chamber her younger sisters shared, she'd slipped from her room and crept out of the house, riding Bessie across the countryside to the Duke of Warrington's mausoleum. She knew the area well. Moonlight was enough to reveal her way.

Being at Haverston Hall, late at night, unchaperoned, would have felt wrong if not for the fact that being here was the very thing that was going to save them.

Remember that. Cling to that.

The duke remained seated where he was, a dark shadow with glittering, predatory eyes—watching her.

She swallowed against the perpetual lump in her throat. "Are we to . . . are we to begin?"

"We have."

"Have we? We've begun?"

"Indeed, we have."

They weren't touching. They were hardly even

speaking. She didn't know much about seduction, but she didn't think this was how it was done.

How was this teaching her anything?

He didn't even appear to blink as he watched her beneath his heavy-lidded eyes.

She let out an impatient breath. "I don't see how."

His features were relaxed, his arms resting on the chair arms, fingers hanging loosely. "If you want to rouse a man's desires, anticipation must be built."

"And what we're doing now is building anticipation?"

"Don't you feel it?"

She considered that. All day she'd felt anxious for what was to come. She'd scarcely eaten their meager dinner of cabbage and ham, much to her shame. Food was not to be wasted. Now that she was here, she felt a sparking energy on the air. Her pulse thrummed madly against her neck and her chest ached as though a great weight pressed upon it. She chalked it up to nerves . . . to her continued anxiety of being here alone with this man and their forthcoming intimacy. It could hardly be called . . . anticipation. Could it?

"You mean *you* do?" She cleared her throat. "You feel something?" She motioned to where he sat. "Simply sitting there? You feel anticipation?"

"You're a lovely woman. I'm certain you know that. Undoubtedly you've had admirers." This he uttered so matter-of-factly, with no inflection. As though it mattered not at all to him. "Even if you aren't to my personal taste, you're fresh-faced and young. Any man would feel something."

It would seem he grudgingly counted himself among those men.

"Well, that's . . . heartening." Certainly it should make her feel safe with him. He wasn't likely to become overcome with animal passion for her and disregard her wish to keep her virtue.

He ignored the edge of derision to her voice. "You want to be the best, yes? Isn't that what you said?"

She nodded, feeling a little foolish to have her words tossed back at her. She *needed* to be the best.

She was not oblivious. Gentlemen had responded to her before in a way that suggested she was attractive. And yet it felt arrogant to believe herself so beautiful, so enticing, she could *enthrall* men. She was handsome enough, but there was nothing extraordinary about her. Not like the Lady Graciela or her daughter, Clara, with their sultry, exotic beauty.

Hopefully her evenings with this man would change that. She could learn to be extraordinary. He would show her how to be so extraordinary she could name her price.

"Have you kissed a man before?"

She blinked, startled from her thoughts at this bold question.

She'd have to get accustomed to his bold questions—and the even bolder actions that would inevitably come.

She shifted on the sofa, focusing on his question again. She'd certainly flirted with her share of handsome footmen, but she'd dodged most of their lips.

"Come now," he pressed. "For this undertaking, we must be honest and forthcoming. No prevaricating and no avoidance. That shall be our first rule."

"Rules?" she cut in, disliking that word. It must be her temperament. Papa always claimed she had a fair amount of hoyden to her.

"Oh, yes." His dark eyes glinted. "We need rules, Miss Langley, if this is to go smoothly."

She nodded. That was fair. They should have a mutual understanding of how this was going to work, and rules would achieve that.

"I'll ask again," he said. "Have you kissed a man before?"

She let out a breath. "I can't say that I have been properly kissed, no, Your Grace. A few kisses on the cheek only."

"Kissing is the most natural place to begin. A well-executed kiss can rouse passions."

She nodded. Sound advice.

He patted his knee. "Have a seat."

On his lap?

Her face caught fire all the way to the tips of her ears. She couldn't! She had never imagined such a thing, but she had come here for this. For lessons in seduction.

Her pulse was galloping now. Nerves, for certain. She was about to settle her body upon this very haughty and handsome nobleman's knee and share a kiss with him.

She rose to her feet.

"Slowly. Remember . . . anticipation is everything."

No worries there. She couldn't move with haste even if a pistol was held to her head. Her feet felt leaden as she lifted them, one after the other, toward him.

She stopped in front of him, unsure how to proceed. Her fingers fiddled with the edges of her cloak. She hadn't bothered to remove it, clinging to the layer of protection it offered.

"Remove your cloak," his deep voice intoned.

It was only a cloak. She was still perfectly attired beneath it. The room was warm, too. Almost stifling. And yet she hesitated.

She thought she read amusement in his gaze. He was enjoying her discomfort. "Scared?" he asked.

His words lit a spark within her. Dares had always been her weakness. Her siblings could always taunt her into reacting by calling out her fear, real or imagined. She should be above such behavior by the very adult age of four and twenty. She didn't know how or where this tendency originated. Perhaps it came from being the eldest child and her years as a governess. She was accustomed to giving orders, not taking them. After Mama died, she'd had to compose herself, step into her role as lady of the house, and never reveal weakness or vulnerability.

He tsked and continued, "You're going to have to overcome that if we're to get anywhere."

She defiantly yanked off her cloak and tossed it aside. "I'm *not* scared." She sank down on his lap, settling her skirted legs between his splayed thighs.

Some of his amusement faded then and that filled her with satisfaction—until it penetrated that she was *sitting* on *his* lap.

She'd never been in so intimate a position before, but she fought for her poise. He was correct. She needed to overcome her fear if this was to work.

"Like this?" she whispered, hands clasped in her skirts, her body straight and stiff as a board. She wasn't certain what to do with her hands—

where to put them. She didn't feel comfortable placing them on his body.

"You can come in closer," he directed.

She leaned in until his chest aligned with her arm. His thigh wasn't exactly the best cushion. It felt too firm beneath her. "Am I too heavy?" she asked, her breath a shaky tremor as she fidgeted.

He shook his head once, watching her with deep intensity. No amusement.

"What now?" she asked, wondering why it was suddenly so hard to breathe.

"Tell me what you're feeling."

Her face burned. Reveal her thoughts?

"Is that necessary for seduction? My lovers will need to know what I'm thinking?" She shook her head firmly. No. They would not have that of her. It didn't seem wise for her self-preservation. Wasn't that giving too much of herself? It was enough that they would have her body. Must they have her mind and soul, too?

"No, they don't need your thoughts. But *I* do."

"Is that another one of your rules?"

"Yes. Honesty in thoughts and feelings. I'm instructing you in this matter. I need to know what you're thinking, experiencing."

She moistened her lips, and his gaze tracked the movement of her tongue, his eyes darkening.

Her belly dipped.

"Well. Um." She glanced away and back again. "To be truthful, I feel . . . sick."

His impassive expression cracked. "Sick?" Clearly it was not the answer he was expecting.

She nodded and pressed a hand against her rolling stomach.

"I might lose my accounts," she confessed.

He let loose a bark of laughter and it transformed his face, made him appear younger, less severe. Still handsome, but perhaps more approachable . . . were he not laughing at her as though she were the most ridiculous creature to draw breath.

Her face burned even hotter. "Please don't laugh at me. I'm certain the most artful courtesans don't have men laughing at them."

"True. They likely do not. But you are not yet artful or experienced, are you?" His gaze pinned her.

"No," she mumbled. That's why she was here.

"No female has ever admitted to sickening from my nearness."

"Indeed, no one has *admitted* it before now," she retorted.

"You are a saucy chit." He angled his head and adjusted slightly in his chair. The motion prompted her to move. She started to rise, but his hand shot out to grip her hip and hold her in place.

She hissed out a breath. His hand singed her

right through the fabric of her dress. She could feel each imprint of his fingers.

"For someone who came to me for help, you're proving a difficult pupil."

She was reminded again that there was nothing in this for him. He wasn't getting anything from helping her. They would not even consummate this relationship, and she rather suspected that physical gratification appealed to most men. He could call a halt to this at any time, and then she would be right back where she started.

Marian sighed. "I'm very bad at this."

"You're not a complete lost cause."

"No?"

"It seems not." He cleared his throat. Something flickered across his face then that she couldn't decipher. "You know how I mentioned you weren't to my tastes?"

Yes, that was etched on the fabric of her memory.

"I remember." Perhaps this was it, then. When he would call off this entire business? What did he have to gain, after all, from spending his evenings training a woman he wasn't even attracted to?

"Your hand, please."

"I beg your pardon?"

He held out his hand between them, palm up. "Your hand?"

"Oh." She placed her hand into his.

He took it and turned it over, palm down.

His touch was light. She could have pulled away, but she was here for this. Here to touch him and vice versa. That was the whole point.

Don't flinch. Don't pull away.

He lowered her hand, between his thighs, directly over the bulge of his manhood.

The large, hard bulge.

"Oh, my," she breathed, her fingers resting on the shape of it. "Is that . . ."

"My cock," he supplied, the brackets on either side of his mouth drawing tight.

She gasped at the unexpectedness of his coarse language . . . and the hot thrill it gave her. Certainly that made her wicked. His foul language shouldn't excite her. And yet . . .

He continued, "It's reacting to you."

Reacting to her? So she wasn't unattractive to him, after all.

"Have you never heard that word?" he asked. "Cock?"

"Y-yes. I have." She might be a proper lady, but she wasn't lacking worldliness. Her father had been a doctor, after all. Before she left home, she had often assisted Papa in his work. She knew what the male body looked like beneath garments. She also knew how to clean, stitch and bandage a wound. She could cool a fever and set a bone and prepare a tincture. Not as well as Nora, but she knew the fundamentals.

Marian had also heard men speak words in the throes of pain no gently bred lady should hear. She was no shrinking violet, but sitting here on Warrington's lap with her hand on his manhood, she was on uncharted ground.

"Then say it. No man wants a reticent or miss-ish mistress. Not even sure such a thing exists." He looked faintly repulsed by the notion. "Men can have that in a wife. In their paramour they want more. Much more. They want bold. They want different."

Different. She gave a single nod. Of course, these men would want something different, and she needed them to want her.

"I'm different," she said confidently. She had always been told this. When she'd wanted to leave home and become a governess at eighteen, she'd heard that aplenty. She could have stayed home and married. Instead, she left to make her own way. Papa had supported her ambitions, even when everyone offered their disapproving opinions about his very *different* daughter—how odd she was, how objectionable, how no man would ever want to take her to wife.

Now, for once, being different would serve her well.

"Then say it," he repeated.

Shoving down her inhibition, she held his gaze and exerted the slightest pressure over his manhood, proving that she was able—that she was up for this, that she could be the opposite of reticent.

She could be bold.

"Cock," she echoed, the word dropping between them.

Impossibly, his manhood—*cock*—grew. Swelled against her hand. Her gaze flew down. "Oh . . ."

"It's hard. For you."

Her gaze shot back up to his mouth. That lovely mouth with its well-carved shape, the bottom lip enticingly full as he added, "You must be doing something right."

She must be doing something right.

A sense of liberation washed through her. She could do this. He might be her tutor, but she was free to learn, to explore . . . to do anything she wanted here.

Anything she wanted with him.

Except for one thing, of course. There would be no full act of congress.

She lowered her head and murmured a scant inch from his lips as her fingers increased pressure on his manhood, "Perhaps you've been fooling yourself and you don't know your own tastes."

His eyes flared slightly, proving, to her great

satisfaction, that she had managed to affect him even further.

"Who *are* you?" he whispered.

She arched one eyebrow. "Someone you've underestimated."

"Clearly."

Still watching him, she massaged him and learned the shape of him through his breeches. His breathing grew a little ragged. She eyed him closely, fascinated at the way his eyes went even darker, at the tiny tic of muscle working in his jaw.

She explored freely, tracing the outline of him, feeling no small sense of awe at the way his member swelled even more. It was fascinating and thrilling.

Her blood pumped a little quicker as her palm rubbed him up and down.

He snatched hold of her wrist. "We better stop that."

"Oh." Frowning, she studied him. This close, even in near darkness, she detected a ruddy flush to his cheeks.

He lowered her hand firmly back to her own lap—off him.

"Did I do something wrong?" she asked.

"No. Just the opposite. You're very . . ." His voice faded on a ragged breath. "We have other things to accomplish."

"But—"

"Kissing," he reminded, and she bit back her protest at that.

"Kissing?" Her stomach fluttered in anticipation.

"Yes. It's fundamental and typically precedes intercourse. One should always know how to use their mouth."

One should always know how to use their mouth.

Her gaze dropped to his mouth. Kissing him sounded . . . lovely.

She wanted to. Perhaps more than she should.

His gaze, bottomless and deep, gleamed in the flickering shadows of the room. "Go on then," he prompted, his tone rather perfunctory. Cool and unaffected, at complete odds with the dark glitter of his eyes. "Show me what you can do."

She was on his lap, in a perfect position to kiss him. He was so close. She breathed him in. He smelled heavenly. Like soap and the faint whiff of sandalwood. No overpowering aromas on him.

She had frequented many a rout as Clara's companion and well knew the penchant of gentlemen to douse themselves in cologne in order to mask their unpleasant body odor—never mind that a simple bath would correct the matter. The duke was no such gentleman. Clearly he bathed. Underneath that cologne, she smelled only clean, tempting man.

She nuzzled the warm skin of his throat, grazing her lips against him on her journey to his mouth. Her hands crept around his neck, fingers walking up his nape, into his hair, diving into the silky strands—softness in a man who was so hard.

A small hiss of breath escaped him.

The sound did not make her hesitate in the least. On the contrary. Right now she was caught up in herself, in what she was doing, *feeling*. Her gaze dropped to that compelling mouth of his.

This was it. She was going to kiss him. She was going to do it. Her pulse fluttered wildly at her throat.

She was going to kiss a man who, she assumed, knew how to kiss properly. That was the reason she was here, after all. Why she chose him. Of course, he didn't repulse her. There was that, too. He had a face that could send hearts pounding.

Get on with it, Marian.

Determined, she dipped her head and pressed her lips to his.

All thoughts fled at this first contact.

There was no thinking. No calculation. Just pure sensation.

She tasted the burn of sweet whisky on his lips. She caressed the slant of his mouth, the width, where it was full, where it tapered. The top lip and its delicious dip. The bottom lip.

Her hands tightened in his hair, rubbing the strands between her fingers. She pressed her breasts into his chest, compelled to get closer, and the simple act made her breath rush out.

She draped both arms around his shoulders, her hands playing in his hair as her mouth explored his, forgetting herself and all the rules drilled into her since her youth, primarily the one about unwed ladies *not* doing what she was doing—giving liberties to a man not her husband.

He exhaled a ragged breath, and his parted lips allowed her to deepen the kiss.

She had no idea what she was doing . . . if what she was doing was right—if *anything* she was doing was right at all. For all she knew, she was making a mess of it and he could be thinking how terrible she was at this and merely suffering her efforts.

"Is this correct?" she rasped, lifting away slightly to ask against his mouth.

"Use your tongue," he directed, his soft, dark voice curling around her. His warm breath trembled slightly against her mouth. Just the word *tongue* made her stomach muscles clench.

She flexed her fingers in his hair. "M-my tongue?"

"Yes. Put it into my mouth." His voice sounded strangled now. "Touch mine with it."

Nodding uncertainly, she complied, curling her hand over the back of his scalp, her fingers spearing through his hair. Her tongue brushed his upper lip. Tentative at first, then more thoroughly. She traced the seam of his lips. She didn't know what compelled her to use her teeth, but she did—lightly worrying the tender skin, intermittently nibbling and licking, licking and nibbling.

He growled softly, his hands tightening on her back, gripping her through her clothes, ratcheting up her excitement and bringing her in to him, hauling her ever closer.

She was well aware that he wasn't fully kissing her back. Not yet. She was the one leading the way here, kissing him, her tongue foraying into his mouth, testing, exploring.

She surmised his lack of participation was deliberate and all part of the lesson, but it was no less frustrating. As enjoyable as this was, she wanted more from the experience. She wanted . . . *more*.

She adjusted to straddle him, her knees slipping down on either side of his hips as much as her skirts and space would allow.

She lifted her hands to his face, fingertips sweeping his bristly jaw. She continued exploring him with her tongue, delving inside his mouth.

It wasn't awful at all. It wasn't disgusting.

It was the opposite of awful and disgusting.

She pulled back for an astonished moment—shocked at the sensation of her tongue against his.

It felt intimate. Something lovers did. *Wicked.*

She knew that's what she wanted—what this was all about, why she was here, after all.

Wickedness was the order of the day. She doubted there was a courtesan who didn't know how to be wicked.

But the *idea* of intimacy was so very different than the reality of it.

She searched his face, still holding it in her hands. His breathing was as labored as hers, and she longed to go back to that mouth and keep kissing.

She liked kissing. She liked kissing *him*. A great deal. Perhaps ladies shouldn't. But then, she wasn't here to be a lady. Quite the opposite.

She was here to learn all his wicked ways . . . to become wicked herself.

"Not bad," he remarked. "Still a little cautious with your tongue, though. You can be more aggressive. Cast out your fear. There's no judgment here. You're free to do whatever you want."

Whatever she wanted. No fear. No judgment.

Suddenly she felt lighter, buoyed by his words.

Freedom. Something she coveted. Something she prized perhaps above all things. If not, she would not even be here. She would have married Mr. Lawrence shortly after her father's death. She would have surrendered herself to him with no hesitation and put an end to her family's woes.

But she couldn't. Perhaps that made her selfish, but she needed her independence like she needed air.

Right now, however, air felt like a commodity. Her chest was tight, her breath coming out thin and hard-fought as her eyes traveled his handsome face.

He wasn't clean-shaven like most men of his station. Just another thing he seemed to eschew. Shaving. Propriety. A properly furnished home. A wife. Family.

They gazed at each other, her face probably closer to this man than it had ever been to any person. So close she could admire the crescent sweep of his lashes over his dark, compelling eyes. The proud line of his nose. The mouth he was waiting for her to taste again. And his hard body under her, so solid and strong.

Her fingers fluttered over his cheeks, reveling in the ungentlemanly scratch of his beard against her palms.

Everything struck a visceral chord in her.

Her muscles loosened, liquefied, and she was aware of her own heartbeat—strong and fast beneath her breast.

The world fell away.

He wasn't a duke.

She wasn't an impoverished, desperate woman. And this wasn't a lesson. It wasn't a game. It was real. As real as anything. The most real thing she had ever experienced.

They were a man and a woman in the throes of the most basic act and there was no going back. Everything would be different after this. Everything.

She would be different.

Chapter 11

*N*ate stared back at her, wondering, *hoping* he did not look as she did—wild-eyed and dazed. Bewildered, even.

He had done this sort of thing plenty of times. He should not feel bewildered. Nothing about any of this should bewilder him. *She* should not. He certainly should not feel so rattled by one country virgin. Except he was.

Her flushed face and kissable lips did things to him. She was lovely. Suddenly he felt a fool for saying she was not to his taste. He could not take his eyes off her. Everything about her mesmerized him.

And she was so bloody responsive. More than he could have imagined. Her handling of his cock had been artless but no less arousing. He throbbed and ached to strip off her gown and ease himself inside her welcoming heat. He could seduce her. He felt certain of that. Her body was eager and willing.

But she expressly did not want that. He wouldn't go against her wishes. He wouldn't be that man.

He had not expected resisting her to pose such difficulty.

She might be a novice, but intimacy was intuitive for her. She was a sexual creature. Not every woman had the appetite for shagging. He knew that. But she was a natural.

"How old are you?" he asked in a rough voice. She still held his face and those caressing palms were damned distracting—provocative.

"Twenty-four."

"I thought you older," he murmured. She was self-assured and mature.

"What?" Outrage sharpened her voice. "What manner of man says such a thing to a woman?"

He chuckled. "Did I offend you?"

"Yes." She nodded. "I *am* angry."

"We deal in honesty, you and I."

Her frown softened, somewhat mollified by his words. She was a direct person. Clearly she appreciated forthrightness.

He shifted slightly, trying to keep his hands from freely roaming her. Exploring her body right now would not aid his weakening self-control.

"How old are you?" she countered in a faintly accusing tone.

"Thirty-two."

"You look older." Amusement tinged her voice.

"You're just saying that because I did."

"No," she denied, and he couldn't help thinking she looked adorable in her indignation. "With your hard mien, I thought you older. Aren't most noblemen your age married and busy filling the nursery with heirs and spares?" She shrugged. "That's my experience with the aristocracy, at any rate."

He considered her words, wondering what her experience with the aristocracy could be, but then he reminded himself that this wasn't a relationship where they delved into each other's histories. This was a diversion. A pleasant diversion, and he'd win a wager while he was at it, too.

"Do I strike you as most noblemen?" he asked.

Her soft fingers continued their movement on his face—as though she could not touch him enough.

"At first, yes, but now . . ." She paused in consideration. "No. No, you do not," she whispered in a beguiling voice he felt as much as he heard—

like her stroking fingers on his skin. Both were damn seductive and he could not resist touching her in turn.

He liked that she didn't see him as a duke. At least not primarily as a duke. That was not the case with most women. Usually it was the only thing people saw when they looked at him.

The fact that this woman saw something else in him had Nate reaching for her.

Even Mary Beth had not been able to look at him without seeing his title. When they were children she had not seen it, but he suspected when he showed up ten years later to propose, she had. She had seen it and perhaps only it as he got down on one knee before her.

It pained him to acknowledge that about his late wife. She'd cared for him. He knew that. But there had not been ease between them. She'd been concerned with propriety, and not comfortable sharing their marital bed. He didn't blame her for that. She didn't know any better. She hadn't known how to enjoy that kind of intimacy. She had been brought up to believe that copulation was a burden a wife must bear—not something to be enjoyed. He blamed himself that he had not been able to please her.

Marian Langley looked at him with fire in her eyes. Arousal hummed from her skin. She might be a gently bred young woman, but she was built for passion.

She wasn't Mary Beth. Nor was she a woman paid to endure his touch.

She wanted him. That was real. Her desire was real.

He had to touch her. Had to feel her.

He started with her hair. He seized onto a loose lock dangling over her cheek. One of many things about her that had been beckoning him. It felt like silk between his fingers.

Her blue eyes watched him, wide and luminescent. The air between them thickened, growing as charged as the sky during a storm.

He had held himself still while she rubbed his cock. While she kissed him.

No more.

He wound a finger around that lock of hair and gently tugged her closer, claiming her mouth, using his tongue this time, showing her all that a kiss could be.

He kissed her harder, deeper.

His cock swelled against her thigh, and he knew that wasn't right. It wasn't where it wanted to be, buried inside her.

Evidently guided by her own needs, Marian wiggled, adjusting as much as space and her hampering garments would allow, until he was directly at the apex of her thighs. Better. But still not enough. Not with her skirts bunched up between them. It was too much barrier.

She whimpered, the sound desperate, tormented, and he understood. He understood because his own body was burning for her.

She worked her hips in a clumsy rhythm, grinding down, seeking . . . attempting to ease her own ache despite limitations of clothing. Inexperienced or not, everything she was doing lit him aflame.

Still kissing her, his hands dropped to her waist, gripping her, holding her for him.

He pushed his hips up, seeking relief for his stiff cock, trying to reach her through all their infernal clothes.

Too. Many. Clothes.

She cried out into his mouth, clinging tightly to his shoulders as he thrust against her. Gasping, her mouth broke from his. She buried her face in his neck. Her sweet lips kissed a fiery path over the side of his throat, nibbling along his skin, and he shivered, closing his eyes on a groan.

She was good. This artless girl. She made him forget himself.

His hands flexed in the fistfuls of her skirts, gathering them, tugging them up so that he could reach her . . . *have* her.

Suddenly he stopped. He let go of her skirts and lifted his head. Pulled away to look down at her—at her heavy-lidded gaze and pink cheeks and swollen lips.

She was too good, and that made her dangerous.

"Y-Your Grace?" she queried.

He gulped down a labored breath, flexing and opening his hands, searching for his usual composure.

He seized her wrists and pushed her away from him.

She blinked, disoriented, as though he had ripped her from the euphoria of a dream. Except it hadn't been a dream. It had been real. He'd been swept up in it, too.

This first lesson had gone better—or worse—than planned, and he needed to call a halt to it.

She shook her head and her gaze sharpened. "What—"

"That's enough." As abruptly as he uttered the words, he set her away from him and stood. A good arm's length apart from him, and he still wished she was farther away. He still needed her to be farther away.

She visibly swallowed. "T-truly? We're done as in *done*? But—" She stopped for a breath. "But I haven't been here that long," she finished weakly.

Her gaze fixed on his lips. She wanted his mouth again. She wanted to continue kissing him.

"You're a fast learner. You should be fine." He nodded brusquely, dismissively, the opposite of how he felt, but she didn't need to know how she had affected him or that he wanted to keep kissing her.

"I should be fine?" She stared. "Meaning no more lessons? *Ever*?"

"You understand me perfectly. We're finished." He nodded toward the door. "Now go. Leave me."

He didn't bark the words at her, but she flinched just the same.

Whatever it took, he needed her gone. Before he broke his promise to her and his promise to himself—before this became more than a game. More than a wager made with Pearson.

"This wasn't the arrangement." She stalked toward the door, and then stopped, catching herself and spinning around, pointing a damning finger at him. He blinked. He couldn't recall a woman ever charging toward him in such a manner, with such a total lack of deference. "You know, you're not so very impressive, *Your Grace*," she snapped.

"I'm not?"

"No. We just barely scratched the surface and you know it, so that is hardly honoring our agreement."

He shrugged. "You'll do well enough." More than well enough.

"And what of the reference you're to give me? You promised me."

He winced. He had forgotten about that part. He had promised to use his connections to help her, but he hardly felt inclined to toss her into another man's bed, even if that had been their agreement. The notion was unpalatable. He would not do it.

At his silence, she exhaled. "Was that a lie, then?" She held her arms out wide. "You're not going to put me in contact with your friend?"

"I don't think becoming a mistress is for you."

"Oh." She pulled back in obvious affront. "You don't?"

"I don't see you suited for such a life."

Her lips worked for a moment before finding her words. "How dare you?" Even in the paltry light, he could detect the hot rise of color to her cheeks. "We had an agreement and now you renege? Was this just a game to you? You have no idea, no notion what I'm up against . . ." She stopped abruptly with a swift intake of breath, shaking her head. "I should not be so surprised. A man of your position thinks nothing of toying with a female so irrelevant, so pitiable."

"You know nothing of me."

She had it wrong. Very wrong. He did not think her irrelevant or pitiable. The more time he spent with her, the more he admired her. She had mettle. Not that he would correct her of that misapprehension.

He wasn't toying with her. Quite the opposite. This wasn't a game. He'd approached it that way at first, but it had turned into something all too real. Real enough that he had to end this before it began.

"I know enough about you," she sneered and continued for the door. "All I ever need to know about you, Your Grace."

He stared after her, flinching as she slammed out of the room.

He sat there for several moments, staring into the fire, the fingers of his hand tapping restlessly on the arm of his chair.

Chapter 12

$\mathcal{M}$arian escaped the church into cheery sunlight. She held a gloved hand up to her eyes to ward off the sudden glare. The inside of the church had been full of gloom, quite possibly a deliberate circumstance to complement the day's sermon.

The vicar wasn't the sort to deliver uplifting sermons. If anything, his words gave way to darker contemplations. Most people left him fully convinced they were destined for the fiery pits of hell if they partook in even the smallest of pleasures.

Papa had always jested that if one needed his spirits lifted he would be better served enduring a tooth extraction than listening to the vicar.

She inwardly cringed. If the vicar knew of her latest activities he'd likely grab a pitchfork to send her on her way to that fiery portal himself.

Her sisters stayed close to her side as they emerged outside, well aware that they could be accosted at any moment. Many of the village merchants were present with their families. Usually Marian and her sisters were spared from their demands at church—it was a day of rest and prayer, after all—but one never knew. As Mr. Lawrence had pointed out, their creditors were becoming more aggressive.

"Look." Nora tugged on Marian's sleeve and nodded toward young Mr. Pembroke strolling across the church grounds toward the carriages.

Young William held out his arm, escorting Miss Smith very properly. He was a handsome man, scarcely out of boyhood, his face still prone to spots, but he and Charlotte had grown up together. William had trailed after Charlotte like a puppy since they emerged from their prospective prams. Charlotte was the only one to ever call him Billy.

The girl's parents followed a step behind, looking as though their favored calf had won grand prize at the local fair. The senior Mr. Pembroke also strolled nearby, attired in a shiny plum-colored jacket with a silver brocade vest, looking very much the preening peacock that he was.

Both sets of parents looked on the young couple proudly, and the sight filled Marian with impotent rage. She remembered when the Pembrokes had looked at her sister with such approval—when Charlotte had been the one on young William's arm. When Papa had lived and Charlotte could still claim a dowry. The Pembrokes had loved to remark on what handsome children William and Charlotte would have.

Apparently that was all forgotten now.

"One big happy family," Nora muttered beside Marian.

Marian glanced quickly to Charlotte, worried at how she was taking the sight of her once suitor with a girl she had called friend.

Her sister's face had turned pale. "Billy," she breathed, the sound practically inaudible, but Marian felt the utterance as much as she heard it. She knew her sister well. She knew the pain she felt at the sight of her former beau with another.

As though he felt her stare, William's gaze lifted and searched until he found Charlotte. He stilled. In his eyes, Marian read the heartache. He still loved Charlotte. He had never stopped. His parents' disapproval did not alter that fact.

Foolish lad. Didn't he know Charlotte would have him even if his parents denounced him? Even if he was penniless? She would live in a pauper's shack. Unlike him, she was loyal. She would never have turned her back on him. She was honorable that way.

Miss Smith spoke to him, but he could not be pulled from his examination of Charlotte. *Of course*. Marian appraised her sister. Even wan and too thin, she was the most glorious creature in all of Brambledon, and certainly this churchyard. He did not deserve her sister, a girl whose inner beauty surpassed that of her exterior.

"Come," Nora said, taking Charlotte's hand. "Let him stare at the back of you, eh?"

Charlotte permitted Nora to guide her away.

Marian stayed put for several moments, rooted to the spot as she glared at young William. As her sisters fled from sight, his gaze turned on Marian. The longing in his eyes faded, replaced by contrition. His ruddy cheeks were chronically splashed with color, but they deepened to almost purple now as Marian sharpened her glare on him, letting him feel the full weight of her disdain, letting him know he was not forgiven for crushing Charlotte.

She glanced at Miss Smith, her sister's replacement, and looked back at him pointedly. The girl had not ceased talking. Even as he ignored her, momentarily frozen and gazing at Marian in mute apology, she talked and talked and tugged persistently on his arm, desperately trying to reclaim his attention.

Shaking her head, Marian turned away. As much as she disdained him, she pitied him. His parents controlled him like a puppet on strings. He was young and destined for a lifetime of regret.

It only solidified her commitment to the path she had chosen. Her disastrous first and only lesson with the duke had not changed her mind. She was still determined to become a mistress.

If she could restore Charlotte's dowry, then Old Pembroke would give his blessing. William and Charlotte could still be together. It wasn't too late. If, of course, Charlotte would still have him. Whatever the case, Marian wanted her sister to have that choice. Freedom was about choices, after all. It wasn't something Marian craved only for herself. She wanted Charlotte to have that, too.

The duke's rejection had not swayed her from her course.

She would appeal to Mrs. Ramsey and see if she would go ahead and help Marian using her connections. She'd had one lesson with the duke. Certainly it counted for something. The skin at the back of her neck prickled.

A quick glance across the yard in the direction of Mr. Lawrence found him staring at her with the usual avarice in his eyes. Indeed, she had *not* changed her mind. She would continue on this quest and save herself—save them all.

She only hoped Mrs. Ramsey would empathize and oblige her. Clearly empathy was not something the Duke of Warrington was capable of feeling. She muttered at herself for her continued thoughts of him. She needed to cast him out from her mind entirely.

As she hastened from the church after her family, she contemplated when would be a good time to call on Mrs. Ramsey.

Chapter 13

*U*nfortunately Mrs. Ramsey decided to take a week to visit her grandmother in Shropshire. Marian learned of this when Diana answered the door to her eager knocking.

She could do nothing but wait and count the days until her return.

Wait and stew and give lessons to the spoiled misses of Brambledon and avoid the creditors hunting her. It was exhausting business.

She actually enjoyed finding herself alone at home one afternoon.

Mrs. Walker had sent a message that Annabel was afflicted with an ague, so Marian occupied herself with some much overdue dusting. Without servants, it was up to Marian and her sisters to see to such matters, and with their busy schedules, it was often overlooked.

Charlotte was gone, working at the Hansens', and Nora had gone into town to visit the butcher to barter some of their eggs for a bit of meat. Beef was costly, but they needed the sustenance. They had not enjoyed anything hearty since the ham Mr. Lawrence had brought them and there was none of that left.

It worried Marian how gaunt Charlotte was looking these days. The Hansens were responsible for feeding a noon meal to the shop girls under their employ, but Marian suspected that whatever fare they supplied was meager. Charlotte didn't complain. It wasn't her way, but Marian saw the evidence on the way her clothes hung on her frame.

Altogether, it just heightened her sense of urgency. Marian needed to make certain her sisters were adequately fed. She knew she could always butcher a chicken and cook it in a pot, but they had lost a few hens recently to foxes and she was not inclined to sacrifice any more when they were consistently providing them with eggs. They wouldn't starve as long as they had eggs.

She was slipping off her pinafore and hanging it on the hook when she heard a rider approaching. At the sound of hooves, Marian moved toward the front parlor window, mindful not to reveal herself should it be another creditor calling.

Peeking out the well-worn damask drapes that had once been the pride of Mama, Marian gasped.

The duke was in her yard.

He tethered his horse at the fence and strode forward, assessing her house with an inscrutable expression on his handsome face. She wondered what he was thinking. Was it how very meager her home was? How the roof clearly needed replacing? How the fence needed mending? Whatever the case, she didn't wonder long before panic sank its teeth into her.

Why was he here? What was he doing here?

It wouldn't do for Mrs. Pratt to pass by and see him in her yard given the woman's proclivity for gossip. Hopefully nobody noticed his mount in front of her house and remarked upon it later. She didn't need to be the subject of yet more rumors.

Before he even reached her door, she yanked it open. "What are you doing here?" She waved him inside fiercely. "Come, come inside at once before someone sees you."

Her words did nothing to hasten him. He was moving far too slowly for her liking. She snatched him by the hand and pulled him inside, quickly closing the door behind him.

She dropped her hand from his as though singed by the touch. Stepping back, she crossed her arms over her chest defensively. "You shouldn't be here."

"Shouldn't I?" He arched a dark eyebrow.

"No. You should not. It's untoward."

He looked at her in bemusement. "Need I remind you that *you* called upon me at night. Alone. Unchaperoned," he stressed.

"You don't need to remind me of that fact." That very *regretful*, embarrassing fact. She was doing her best to cast the memory from her thoughts. "But have you by chance looked outside?" She nodded to the window. With its drawn drapes, midmorning sunlight spilled into the room. "It is broad daylight. Anyone could have seen you . . . Anyone could *still* see you."

He removed his hat from his head and ran a hand through his rich, dark hair, tossing it in appealing disarray. Her palms tingled and itched to feel those strands again. She curled her fingers inward as though stifling the impulse.

"I did not realize you were so concerned with propriety. All our previous meetings have hardly been proper. I was unaware of your level of concern for decorum."

She sniffed at the veracity of that allegation, but denied the charge at any rate. "Those encounters were discreet. Mostly," she qualified, recalling herself crouched under his table at Colley's Tavern. "This is not discreet."

"Do you wish me to leave, then?"

She opened her mouth and then closed it with a snap.

Common sense told her he had the right of it. He should leave. She should insist on that at once.

Curiosity, however, outweighed her common sense. She still wanted to know why he was here. Why, after their last encounter, had he sought her out in her own home?

They stared at each other for a long moment as silence stretched between them, and she had no doubt that his mind was traveling back to that last encounter, that night with all its shocking intimacy. The echo of it swelled between them.

She had sat on his lap. They had kissed. Passionately.

She had touched him. Fondled him. Explored the hard outline of him and longed to free him of his breeches. She had no inkling she had such an inclination for passion, for the type of lust that could seethe and storm between a man and woman.

She had stood witness to such a storm when her charge fell in love with her current husband. From the periphery, she had watched in bemusement, thinking she would never know such a thing, that she would never lose her head the way Clara did over her Scottish laird—or that a man would never lose his head over Marian in the same fashion. The latter, in this instance, had proven true.

The memory of how the Duke of Warrington had cast her out had not ceased to sting.

The recollection of that evening never stopped humiliating her. She specifically could not forget the ugly and dignity-shattering way it had ended. Dignity was an advantage of the affluent and privileged and fleeting for those faced with struggle and hardship . . . for those faced with penury. For *her*.

He had demanded she leave as though she was something repellent. As though she had done something wrong. And what did she know? Perhaps she had. She might know about matters of intimacy, but she did not *know* about matters of intimacy. It was a crucial distinction. She had no experience. That's why she had come to him for guidance. It mortified her to think he had to send her away. Was she that bad at it?

"Would you care for some tea?" The question popped out, alerting her to the fact that she had reached a decision without conscious deliberation. Apparently she would not demand his departure.

"Yes, thank you." He clasped his hands behind his back.

Nodding, she ducked her gaze and strolled past him, wiping suddenly moist palms over her skirts. All at once, she felt unaccountably shy as she led him to the parlor.

The room was dusty. They hardly ever used it anymore. Certainly they were no longer in the habit of entertaining guests. Since Papa had died, they took all their meals in the kitchen, even eschewing the dining room. It was just easier to eat and clean up in one place.

His gaze scanned the room, doubtlessly noticing its shabby state, although he uttered not a word. That would have been too rude. Even for him.

"I'll be back directly with the tea." She executed a rather clumsy curtsy as though this were a proper occasion. She had no idea what compelled her to do so foolish a thing. A freak impulse. Her limbs moved before her brain could function.

She was glad to have an excuse to turn and flee the room.

Once in the kitchen she took several deep breaths and gripped the edge of the worktable until her knuckles ached from the pressure. She stared blindly ahead.

Why was he here? Why? Why? Why?

After the last disaster of their lesson, she had never expected to see him again. At least not in close proximity. She would perhaps have to endure the sight of him from afar, but never face to face. That had been her expectation.

Her hope.

With a sharp exhale, she released the table and then set the kettle to boil. She rummaged to see if she could find any biscuits, even though she knew it was useless. There was no bit of food in this kitchen unaccounted for.

Giving up, she examined the woeful status of their tea collection. They had been reusing their tea leaves to an embarrassing degree, much longer than customary, wringing out every bit of flavor possible. Much like her life of late. Her days had become all about wringing out what she could—squeezing out every bit of sustenance.

She hoped he liked his tea weak. She set sugar and milk on the tray. Standing back, she gazed at the meager little tray and tried not to feel too inadequate over it.

"Need any help?"

She swung around, gasping at the suddenness of his deep voice in her kitchen.

He stood framed in the doorway. She had seen her father countless times in that same spot. Never had he looked so imposing, so very tall and overbearing. Not like this man.

Then it struck her. The Duke of Warrington was standing in her kitchen.

The Duke of Warrington was standing in her kitchen.

She doubted he had ever deigned to enter his own kitchens, but here he was. In her kitchen.

"No. I am quite capable of handling this myself. I will be with you in the parlor in a few minutes."

"No need. It's just the two of us, after all." He sank down on a stool across from her, the worktable between them. "We can take tea and talk in here. We are well past formality, I think."

Her face heated. They were well past formality indeed. Formality had flown out the window the moment she placed her hand upon his manhood. Some might even argue that formality had fled the moment she hid beneath the table where he dined.

Or perhaps it was the moment she asked him to tutor her in the art of seduction.

There were several points where social constraints had dissolved between them. She supposed it had been that way from the start.

"Very well," she agreed.

At least he would be spared her shabby parlor. The kitchen was much more to her liking at any rate. It might be small, but it was tidy, warm, and smelled of home. Dried herbs hung before the window, refreshing the room.

She served them. "Milk?" she asked, sighing a small breath of relief when he indicated yes.

Hopefully, it masked the weakness of the drink. Unfortunately, he declined the sugar.

She watched his face closely as he took his first sip, but he showed no outward reaction. He lifted his gaze from the cup and glanced around her kitchen. She followed his gaze and winced when she saw that she had left the cupboard doors open in her fruitless search for biscuits. He could see just how very bare the shelves were. Before she could think better of it, she rose and hastily shut the doors.

Too late, she realized that revealed her shame, drawing more attention to the emptiness of her cupboards than she wanted. Blast it.

She added a hefty dollop of sugar into her own cup and stirred. She knew it was mostly sweet water with the slightest flavoring of bergamot. Still, she took a sip and feigned a look of complete contentment.

In truth she was quite accustomed to the flavor. Whenever she took tea with Annabel and her mother, there was always a startled moment when she first sipped, no longer familiar with what hearty and strong tea tasted like.

She took a bracing breath. "I confess, you were the last person I expected to see on my doorstep, Your Grace."

Indeed, the list of people she expected to see before him was long.

"I thought we had unfinished business." He eyed her expectantly, as though she should understand that.

She did not.

"I thought our business quite finished, Your Grace."

"We had an arrangement. We *still* have an arrangement," he amended. "That has not changed."

She looked down into her cup of tea, her fingers playing along the edge of the rim. They still had an arrangement? She digested that. In his mind it was not over then. It was not finished yet. Butterflies rioted in her stomach as the full implications of that set in.

She gave her head a slight shake. None of this made sense. He'd sent her away.

"I confess some confusion. I thought we were done with . . ." Her words faded. Heat swamped her face at her unspoken words. Unspoken yet no less heard.

His head angled as he considered her. "You are quite fetching when you blush."

She blinked in astonishment. Was he complimenting her? She thought she was not to his taste.

"Am I?" she asked warily.

"I owe you an apology."

He was apologizing? But that couldn't be right. He was much too haughty, too arrogant, too . . . too much of a duke for that.

"An apology for what?" she asked in a voice full of suspicion.

"I might have been hasty sending you away the other night."

"You *might* have been?" She rolled her eyes. "You were a wretch."

"You were quite the apt pupil." He looked down at the rough surface of the worktable. Almost as though he were nervous, which seemed totally improbable. "It is no excuse, but it caught me off guard." He lifted his gaze back to her and she felt ensnared, trapped from the intensity of his stare. "I behaved badly."

"Yes," she snapped. "You *did* behave badly." He had humiliated her, sending her away as though she had done something wrong. Their lesson had just begun and he'd crushed her ending it so abruptly.

"It won't happen again."

Again? She shook her head. "You wish to resume our lessons?"

"Yes."

"No."

He frowned at her quick retort, and she enjoyed that. Disappointing him felt good after how abysmally he had treated her.

"Please reconsider."

"And why would I let you touch me again?" She arched an eyebrow at him.

His gaze crawled over her, slowly, leisurely, leaving a wake of heat everywhere. "Because you want me to."

She sucked in a sharp breath and wished he was wrong, but he wasn't. Of course he wasn't. She should toss him out on his ear, but he spoke the truth. And she still had things to learn about becoming a skilled mistress. Things he could show her. Things she would enjoy for him to show her.

He spoke again, adding, "Because *I* want to."

Her knees started to tremble where she sat. She moistened her lips. "Well, then . . ."

"Are you amenable to continuing our lessons, Miss Langley?" His gaze pinned her questioningly.

This new, kinder, gracious duke bewildered her. She actually felt herself softening toward him.

"Oh, um." A confusing little thrill fluttered through her. She schooled her features into what she hoped resembled impassivity. She didn't want to appear too excited. Or excited at all. This was supposed to be business. A matter void of emotion. "Well. Um. Yes," she agreed. "I would be amenable . . . I suppose."

Tension swelled on the air. A palpable thing, creeping and expanding into a great balloon between them. His hands flattened on the table as though steadying himself.

What happened now?

He glanced around the kitchen. "You are home alone." He stated more than asked.

"Yes."

His gaze settled back on her rather meaningfully.

"Oh." Full understanding washed over her. "You are suggesting that we resume our lessons. Now? Right now?"

"Is the time not convenient for you?"

"Um. I suppose now would be fine, yes. My sisters should not be home for a good while yet." It was her turn to glance around.

Surely her kitchen was not an ideal location for carnal affairs. She cleared her throat nervously. "Shall we adjourn to my bedchamber?"

He stood readily. "That sounds like a fine idea."

She nodded and copied suit, rising to her feet, grateful her skirts hid her trembling legs. "Well. This way."

This was happening, then.

She preceded him out of the room and up the stairs toward her chamber. Her heart beat like a wild flock of birds in her chest as she moved down the corridor, his footsteps solidly behind her. She was glad to be walking in front of him so that he could not read her expression, which must fully capture her panic.

She was taking a man into her bedchamber. To her bed.

She wanted to retch.

She visualized herself losing the contents of her stomach all over him. That would be calamitous. The kind of thing one never recovered from.

She turned the door latch with a shaking hand and entered her room.

Her chamber was tidy and cozy. The bed loomed comfortable and welcoming with a hand-stitched afghan in soft shades of yellow and blue and green at the foot of the bed. Several hand-stitched pillows decorated the head of the bed.

She motioned him to join her inside and then closed the door behind him.

For however cozy the room, it was still much too chilly. The grate was empty, as was the dormant fireplace. She couldn't remember the last time either had burned. Not since Papa had lived.

He glanced to the fireplace. "It's gone cold." She winced. He made the comment as though that was a recent happenstance and not a constant condition of her life. "Would you like me to attend to it?"

She wished he could. No sense circumventing the truth, though. He already knew of her low circumstances. There was no pretending otherwise. "That fireplace hasn't been lit in months," she admitted.

He frowned, his expression puzzled. "Not even this past winter?"

It had been an intensely cold winter. Spring had arrived gradually and the days were still chilly. "Sometimes we managed a bit of coal for the grate. On the worst of nights." Hence the reason why they were so indebted to the coal purveyor. On the most bitter of winter nights they had all three shared a room.

"You have no coal left?" he demanded.

"We have none to spare for any of the bedchambers." What they had was reserved for kitchen use, in order to cook their meals.

He digested that, looking vastly displeased. She suddenly realized he must be cold. He was not accustomed to such deprivation, of course.

"I'm sorry," she rushed to say. "Are you chilled?" She had grown accustomed to the lack of warmth, coping with it by dressing in layers and piling on the blankets.

"No, no. I'm fine." He waved a hand.

She nodded, still uncertain, suspecting he was being less than honest with her in order to spare her further embarrassment.

She fiddled with the collar of her dress.

His gaze went to her fidgeting fingers. "Second thoughts?" he queried.

She lifted her chin a notch. "Not at all."

He moved toward her escritoire near the window. She had vague memories of her mother sitting there, penning her letters as she stared out at the world.

He pulled out the chair from beneath the desk and lifted it, positioning it in front of the bed. She watched as he sank down upon the well-worn seat cushion as though this was the most casual affair and not a clandestine liaison.

What was he doing?

She swallowed against the lump in her throat. "I thought this was to be a lesson . . ."

"Oh, it is." He sat with a relaxed air, elbows propped on the chair arms. "It has begun. Even now as I sit here, we've begun."

She shifted her weight on her feet. She didn't know whether to stand or sit as he was. The only place left for her to sit was on the bed, and that felt much too awkward. She couldn't bring herself to do it.

"You seem uncomfortable," he remarked.

"I suppose I am." No sense lying to him. He could see how very awkward she was. "Temporary, I am certain. Once we begin I will relax."

"The thing you must remember is that reticence gains you no favors. At least in the profession you seek to undertake."

"Of course."

"You must know about all matters of intimacy and be at ease."

"Of course," she said again and then wanted to kick herself for failing to contribute anything verbally significant.

He continued, "You must be knowledgeable in all ways. You don't want to appear frightened. A skittish female will not heat a man's blood."

"I'm not skittish." With her arms still crossed, she brought a hand up to her collar, again plucking at the fraying edge. Her gaze darted toward her bedroom door as though she might make a dash for it. Just an impulse. Naturally, she would not.

He noticed the direction of her gaze, and lifted an eyebrow that seemed to say: *See? Told you. Skittish as a hare . . .*

She squared her shoulders and reminded herself that she had initiated all of this. He was here at her request.

It was difficult to remember that with her nerves running amok, but this wasn't about her. This wasn't about what she was feeling.

She thought of Charlotte's face, her devastated expression when she saw William with another. That was something Marian could fix. It wasn't too late if she was able to restore her sister's dowry. Then she could also continue to fund Phillip's schooling and give Nora a grand come out, too.

He continued, instructing in a flat voice. "A man wants a mistress to do things a wife will not. She needs to be enthusiastic as well as knowledgeable. Otherwise what would be the reason to keep her? To go to her at all?"

Marian nodded. That made sense. Although with her knocking knees, it was difficult to imagine herself as enthusiastic. "Very well. Teach me those things."

"I do not believe I can while you stand there tense as a slat of wood. I cannot teach one *not* to be reticent. Confidence is something you have or you don't."

"This is simply nervousness. I can overcome it."

For some reason she felt even more anxious than she did the first time she was alone with him.

Probably because now she knew.

Now she *knew* what his kiss tasted like, what his hands felt like on her skin, how hard his body was against her own.

Now she knew this man had the power to make her muscles melt. He knew how to reduce her to hot pudding.

He eyed her skeptically.

"I *will* overcome it," she repeated firmly, insistently.

Still studying her, he looked decidedly unconvinced at her insistence.

"I wasn't the one to call a halt to our last lesson," she reminded hotly.

"No, you weren't," he allowed. "But in this moment you're looking a little ill . . . hardly a bedmate to tempt a man, and that is what you're trying to learn here, yes? How to tempt a man?"

She pressed a hand against her churning stomach. "I am quite well, I assure you."

"Your face is green," he pointed out in that exasperatingly even voice of his.

One of her hands flew to her cheek as though she could verify this with a touch. Blast. Her skin did feel clammy.

"Nerves, as I said. Nothing more. I'm ready. Let's begin our lesson, Your Grace."

He sighed and propped one ankle over his knee in a thoroughly relaxed pose. "You hardly look ready to be touched, or to touch in turn, for that matter."

She stomped her foot on the well-worn rug. "I'm ready."

Their eyes locked in silent challenge. She didn't need to see herself to know that determination was writ all over her face.

In his face was something else.

Something out of her scope of knowledge. She thought she read admiration there. Male appreciation, even though he had stated she was not to his preferred tastes.

She had been on the receiving end of male attention before. Obviously, there was Mr. Lawrence, but there had been others, too. Members of the staff when she was in Lady Autenberry's employ. Grooms, valets. Even Clara's suitors had made overtures, the wretched cads. She never gave them a moment of her time, but this man demanded all of her attention.

He was the sun to her universe, sucking everything toward him—including her.

"Tell me what to do," she whispered.

He eased back in his chair, the wood creaking slightly beneath the adjustment of his weight. Suddenly, he did not look quite so relaxed. His eyes glittered hotly.

"Take off your clothes."

Chapter 14

Take off your clothes.

Nate uttered the words with a great deal more calm and authority than he felt. Desire for her hummed just beneath the surface as it had since the night she'd turned the tables on him and left him aching for her. For *her*.

That had not been in the plan, but he'd come to terms with the unexpectedness of it. Now he was prepared.

He was prepared and would not be losing the wager he'd made with Pearson.

He was not weak. Not ruled by his body or baser impulses.

Certainly, he did not live as a monk. He took

his share of women to bed. Since his wife died, he'd been active in that regard. Marian Langley was simply a female with the same parts as any other female. Nothing extraordinary.

Except she hid under tables and called on him late at night in the hopes that he would train her to be a proper mistress.

Very well. Fairly extraordinary behavior that.

He'd do her a favor, help her out, have a bit of fun in the process and win a wager.

"Undress?" she asked as though there could be any confusion in his words.

He nodded. "You cannot be ashamed of your form. Shame should never enter into any of this. Your lover will want to know your body. He will want to know your body better than his own." He looked at her intently, trying to appear detached and not as though he didn't desperately want to know her body for himself. "Now undress yourself."

With shaking fingers, she obliged, starting at the buttons along the front of her dress.

They were little fabric-covered fastenings, but she didn't have any trouble with them.

Nate held still, willing himself not to move, not to react. He willed himself to make no movements that might startle her.

It was harder, however, to will his cock into

obedience. Hopefully, she did not notice from her position. He didn't want to frighten her with the sight of his raging erection.

She shrugged out of her gown, easing it over her slim shoulders. Too slim. He'd have to rectify that. He'd seen her bare cupboards. Tasted her weak tea. As far as he could discern, her kitchen was poorly stocked.

She had not exaggerated about her desperate circumstances. Still, she was an anomaly. Other gently bred females would be looking for salvation in marriage. Instead, she had come up with this plan. Sacrificing her virtue was her solution.

The dress dropped. Puddled at her feet. She stepped out of the circle of fabric, standing before him in her chemise, drawers, corset and petticoats.

Her breasts lifted on several breaths and then her hands resumed their work, stripping away everything until she wore only her chemise. The fabric was of the finest lawn, but it appeared well-worn. The hem ended just past her knees and looked to be mended in more than one spot.

He shifted where he sat in the chair, girding himself for the rest, for the final act—for the sight of her to come. He reminded himself that he had brought himself here. He wanted this and accepted there would be limitations. He could manage it.

She gathered fistfuls of fabric at her hips and pulled the chemise over her head, exposing herself to his eyes.

She was lovely. Skin like peaches. Breasts perfect for the fit of his palms. Hips that flared out from her waist. He was enthralled. He wanted a taste.

"On the bed," he instructed, swallowing against the sudden tightness in his throat that made his voice gravelly and rough.

She hesitated at the command.

"You don't have to do this." He felt compelled to remind her.

A part of him hoped she'd call a halt. For both of them. Restraint would be a challenge. Looking at her now, he couldn't deny that.

"Yes, I do." Her gaze roamed his face before she turned toward the bed. "I want to."

He sucked in a sharp breath. If he had thought her body lovely before, now he was completely undone at the glorious sight of her backside. It was delicious. Plump and full, and instantly his hands gripped the armrests, his knuckles aching from the fierceness of his grip.

Thoughts of his hands on that ass, cupping both plump cheeks, kneading the tender flesh, nearly broke him.

As though she sensed his stare and the impact she was having on him, she sent him a long glance over her shoulder. It was artless and yet no less provocative. Her eyes widened at whatever she read in his face.

He could well imagine what she saw in his expression. It was hunger. As desperate and raw and visceral as he had ever felt. This girl could be his ruin if he were not careful.

"On the bed," he repeated, careful not to move, not to budge from his seat. If it killed him he would not shift from this chair until he was confident he had his lust under control.

She placed one knee on the bed and sank down. For the briefest moment he was awarded with the sight of her ass stretched and perfectly curved in the air.

He bit back a groan. Then the view was gone, replaced by another one of equal torment.

She was on her back on the bed, knees bent and angled to the side like the perfect offering. He tightened his grip on the armrests, determined to stay put.

You're fine. As long as you remain in this chair. As long as you keep your clothes on. As long as you do not go to her.

"Widen your thighs," he instructed.

Her gaze met his and he wondered again if she would change her mind and refuse.

Was this it? Was this when she came to her senses and sent him on his way?

"Marian, we don't—"

She gave a swift shake of her head, silencing him.

Her knees parted and his gaze fastened on her sweet quim, so warm and inviting.

He expelled a breath from where he sat a safe distance away.

He'd braced himself for this. He couldn't deny he was attracted to her. Not after their last encounter, but seeing her like this . . .

It took everything in him to stay in his chair.

Her pink flesh glistened, and his member rose hard and ready to slide inside her, which wasn't going to happen. That was not part of the agreement. He was not a brute who would ignore her wishes. She wanted knowledge of copulation without actually engaging in sex.

He would give her that.

"What now?" she asked breathlessly.

"I want you to touch yourself."

"Wh-what?" She lifted her head from the bed to stare at him incredulously.

He took a steadying breath. "Trust me, Marian. Touch yourself."

"Down . . . there?"

He fought back a smile of amusement. Modesty prevented her from even talking about her own body. She had a long way to go before she was uninhibited enough to be a courtesan.

"Yes. Touch your quim."

She held his gaze for a moment before giving a single nod and lowering her head back to the bed. Her throat worked as she swallowed and followed his instruction, placing her hand between her thighs.

And yet she hardly looked the image of passionate abandon. She was as stiff as a board on her bed.

"Have you never touched yourself?" he asked. "Brought yourself to pleasure with your own hand?"

"No." She sounded shocked at the idea—as though she did not know such a thing could be done.

"You have to know how to please yourself before you can please another."

"What if I can't do that?" Worry creased her forehead.

"You can. You're not frigid."

He'd had her on his lap. He'd tasted her hunger, her responsiveness.

As though to counter his assertion, her hand rested limply over her sex. He resisted the urge to get up and show her how it was done. She needed to master this herself.

"Do you remember how you touched me?" he inquired. "How you moved your hand and explored my cock?"

Hot color splashed her cheeks. "Yes."

"It's as simple as doing that to yourself."

"Not so simple evidently," she muttered.

"Move your hand. Explore. Fondle. Don't be embarrassed."

She nodded jerkily, her expression that of a soldier marching into battle as her fingers tentatively patted her woman's flesh.

He sighed. This wasn't working.

"I don't know what to do." Frustration trembled in her voice.

It was a definite struggle keeping to his seat. He longed to rise from the chair and take his place beside her. To put his hand where hers was and show her how it was done.

He didn't.

"Relax. Take your time. Stroke yourself," he encouraged.

Her movements subtly changed. She stopped patting herself and began sliding her fingers over her sex. Up and down over her folds, and then dipping into her core.

"That's it." He cleared his throat, fighting against the growling thickness of his voice. Watching her play with herself was a torment. "Now find your pleasure point."

"My . . . pleasure point?"

"That's right. It's a little nub nestled at the top of your sex."

"I never read of that in any of Papa's anatomy texts."

"Is that so surprising?" he asked wryly. "Dry medical texts authored by men would likely not focus on such a thing. Now move your fingers up."

Her hand drifted up, following his direction.

She gasped when she brushed the spot, and he felt that sound vibrate through him. "There you go. You found it," he murmured in approval. "Play with it. Press down on that sweet pearl. Do what you like."

She rotated her wrist and pressed down. Another gasp.

He watched, adjusting where he sat, wishing he could free himself from the constraint of his breeches. There would be none of that, though. He knew better. "Find a rhythm. Move however pleases you."

Her hand increased its action between her splayed thighs, moving quickly, feverishly against the little bud buried above her folds.

Her breasts jiggled from her movements, beckoning his hands, his mouth. He couldn't stop himself anymore. His hand dove for his cock. He squeezed himself hard, savagely, desperate to relieve the ache.

His gaze stroked over her body, over glistening skin flushed pink. Her nipples darkened, the distended tips turning a deep plum. His mouth salivated to taste them, knowing they would be just as sweet.

Her body arched, bowing up off the bed as her hand jerked faster between her thighs. A cry tore from her throat and her legs slammed shut, trapping her hand.

He groaned, hating that he couldn't see between her thighs any longer, but he relished watching her lose control. She moaned and rocked on the bed with her hand buried between her closed legs.

"What's happening to me?" she panted.

"Give yourself to it."

"To what?"

"To pleasure."

"I don't know how!" Her voice choked on a strangled cry. "I can't . . . I must not be doing it right."

"Just find what feels good and keep doing it."

She released a whimper, her body writhing on the bed as she continued to jerk her hand between her clamped thighs.

"Please," she begged. "Help me."

"Marian." Now his voice sounded like a plea.

He couldn't go near her. Not when she looked like that. Not when he felt like this.

"I trust you." She wiggled and writhed on the bed. "Please!"

I trust you.

"Just show me. Touch me," she urged. Her voice

was small, barely audible, compelling him, drawing him forward out of his chair.

Standing, he stopped before the bed, looming over her.

She trusted him.

He would not betray that trust.

He sank one knee down on the bed. The mattress dipped beneath his weight. He brushed a hand over her silken calf. Her skin quivered under his palm. "Can you part your legs for me?"

The blue of her eyes locked on him, darker, deeper. With a nod, she opened herself for him.

He looked his fill. "Beautiful," he rasped, taking hold of her other calf.

He lowered his second knee down on the bed, bringing his body fully between her thighs. "This is how you take a man. He will come between your legs just so." He inched higher between the V of her thighs in demonstration. "He will widen your thighs for him." His hands spread her wider. She gasped, her eyes rounding. "Did I hurt you?"

"No." She shook her head, looking up at him.

He looked down, admiring her, exposed and open for him. "He might even test you for readiness." He followed his words, stroking and tracing her with a fingertip, testing her wetness before easing one finger inside her.

She exhaled sharply at the intrusion.

He stopped half a finger in, teeth clenched as her warmth tightened all around him.

She shifted, pushing her hips up in welcome.

It was all the encouragement he needed.

He thrust his finger in deep, exulting in her loud cry.

With his other hand, he seized her wrist. "Now touch yourself." He guided her fingers back to her sex. He placed her fingertips on the little jewel nestled there and forced them down, pressing. He steered her into a rolling motion.

She arched and shuddered and his finger was awash in the evidence of her desire. "Feel how wet you just became?" She nodded, her shudders ebbing. "You just climaxed."

He pulled his finger free and settled his fully clothed body against her, his engorged cock directly prodding her sex.

"This would be the ideal time for your lover to slide inside you . . . when you're wet and ready."

Her wide eyes fixed on his face.

"He will drive inside you." He thrust against her, grinding into her, loathing the shield of his breeches even as he was grateful for the fabric that kept his cock from penetrating her.

Tossing her head back, she moaned and lifted her hands up to his shoulders, clawing into him through his jacket as he rocked into her in the simulation of shagging.

He rode her with his breeches on.

She grew wetter, her juices soaking him through layers of fabric.

They groaned and strained against each other.

It was agony and he couldn't stop. He slid a hand down her bare thigh, wrapping her leg around his waist, angling her into a better position as he drove and thrust and rubbed and worked them both into a frenzy.

A fresh shudder wracked her and she shrieked, her hands flying to his ass, clutching him to her vibrating quim.

He climaxed hard with a shout, the wetness between them intensifying as he spilled his seed in his pants.

He laughed hoarsely and dropped down over her. He hadn't done that since he was a green lad. He propped his elbows on either side of her head to keep from crushing her.

"Oh. My," she gasped as though she had just run a great distance. Her chest rose and fell rapidly, her luscious breasts brushing his chest. How he longed to feel them against his bare skin. How he longed for her nipples to graze him without the barrier of his clothing.

Her blue eyes were clouded, as though she were foxed. "Goodness. Is that what it's like?"

"Almost. The real thing is better." He brushed

a loose strand of hair off her forehead. "My cock inside you would have felt better."

If possible, her eyes clouded over even more. "I want to—"

Before she could finish the sentence, the thud of footsteps pounded on the stairs.

"Marian!"

Her eyes flared wide with instant lucidity. Gone was the fog. Gone was the dreamy haze of pleasure.

Now there was only panic.

"My sister! Go, go, go! She can't find you here."

He jumped from the bed. Fortunately, he was still dressed.

Marian ripped the afghan from the bed and wrapped herself in it. She pointed a desperate finger to the window. "Out that way!"

"The window?"

"Yes!"

"Are you daft?" He took two strides forward to peer out. It wasn't a straight drop. The gabled roof angled so his fall wouldn't be fatal—only dangerous.

"Marian! Are you home?" one of her sisters called.

"Go! Please," she hissed, the color rising high in her cheeks, as though someone had just slapped her. "She can't find you here."

With a curse, he slid open the window and swung a leg over the sill. He cast her one last look. Wrapped up in her blanket, her bare shoulders peeping out, she looked like a woman who had been thoroughly loved. The fetching and far too tempting sight of her convinced him to move—to jump.

But first he reached out and grabbed the edge of her blanket, tumbling her against him. He kissed her hard, tasting her a final time just in case he broke his neck.

He released her. She stumbled back a step.

"We'll resume later, Miss Langley," he promised.

She nodded and he turned.

With what he hoped wouldn't be his final curse, he jumped from the window, sliding down the roofline. There was a brief moment when the air rushed up to greet him and then he landed. Hard.

But alive.

He held still for a long moment, assessing, measuring himself, making certain nothing was broken. When all appeared well, he glanced around. No one was about to witness his ignominious fall. Marian's reputation was safely intact.

He clambered to his feet and crept off, feeling much too old for such skulking about, but knowing he would do it again.

For Marian, he would do it again.

MARIAN PEERED OUT the window long enough to assure herself that he was still alive and unscathed. She exhaled in relief when she spied him popping back up to his feet, his dark hair flying haphazardly in every direction. Her heart clenched at the sight of him, as well as other parts of her anatomy.

She had clambered out of her window plenty of times as a girl and knew he could do it, but it was still comforting to see he was unharmed.

She tightened the afghan around herself and turned just as a knock sounded on her bedchamber door.

"Marian?" Nora called again. "Are you home?"

"Yes. Just readying to leave for town. I'm scheduled to give a pianoforte lesson to Mrs. Kellwood's children." Not untrue. She was expected in an hour.

Without waiting for a biddance to enter, Nora pushed open the door and strode bold as you please into Marian's room.

"Nora!" She clutched the blanket ever tighter about her and glanced wildly around the room as though there was evidence of her interaction with the duke lying about.

Her sister looked her over mildly. "Are you only just now dressing? I thought you were up hours ago."

"Yes. N-no," Marian stammered. "I was up

hours ago. I merely dirtied my dress and needed to change."

Nora frowned, not looking entirely convinced of this fabrication. "Oh."

Her sister turned to go, but then suddenly stopped, her gaze landing on something on the floor. "What is that there?"

With a sinking sensation, Marian followed her sister's gaze. *Oh. No.* There, on the floor, was the duke's hat.

She scarcely remembered him wearing it into the house and carrying it with him up the stairs—but he had and he had forgotten it here on her floor in his hasty escape.

Blast it! And now her sister was gazing at it in speculation.

"Oh. Um." Marian cleared her throat. "I found it out on the road and picked it up," Marian quickly supplied. "I thought I would keep it and try to find the owner."

Nora walked forward and picked it up. She turned it over in her hands, musing, "Very fine quality. I am certain someone is missing it dearly."

Marian doubted it. Nate did not seem the manner of man to worry about such things as a misplaced hat.

Nate. Suddenly she could not think of him in any other way. Nathaniel. Nate. *Her* Nate.

No. *No.* Not hers. He was not hers. Not in any intimate lover-like way.

He was her tutor. Her instructor. This was a professional arrangement. A professional arrangement she just happened to find immensely pleasurable.

"Indeed. I thought I might ask about in town. Perhaps Mr. Simms at the mercantile would know something of it."

At the mention of Mr. Simms, Nora wrinkled her nose. He was one of their more demanding creditors—to such a degree that they avoided his shop altogether of late.

Nora carefully set the hat down on the escritoire. "If you think it best." With a shrug, she turned and faced Marian, her expression rather thoughtful.

It was that curious, thoughtful look that unnerved her. Marian feared Nora was close to realizing just what she had interrupted, and how could she ever explain that to her sister? True, at age sixteen she was precocious, but Marian would like to shelter her a bit more. Was that not her role as elder sibling?

Marian smiled brightly and then pulled back a fraction, fearing she was flashing too much teeth. She did not wish to appear like a grinning madwoman. "Don't you have some sewing to do?" she asked, hoping to distract her sister.

Nora pulled a face. "As always. Yes. Very well."

"And perhaps you could pick from the garden today. One of the cabbages looked ready."

"Cabbage soup then. Splendid." With a roll of her eyes she turned and exited the room, calling out behind her, "See you this evening, Mari!"

Alone in her room, Marian sank down on the edge of her bed.

That had been close. *Too close.*

She lowered her face into her hands and released a ragged breath.

And also amazing. The things the duke had made her feel . . .

It was simply astounding. Beyond pleasant. Mrs. Ramsey had been right. *It's always better when you enjoy it.*

She knew she should get dressed and moving, but she needed a minute to compose herself. Or five.

Her limbs trembled, unsteady after all that had transpired.

As far as lessons went, she felt particularly shattered.

Even so, she could not wait for their next one.

Chapter 15

"Miss Langley! You-hoooo! Miss Langley!"

Marian cringed, and stopped. She lifted her face skyward, sucking in a breath and hoping she was mistaken, hoping it was not Mrs. Pratt hailing her.

Slowly, Marian turned and feasted her gaze on the woman charging toward her at a brisk pace. Of course, it was her neighbor. So much for enjoying her walk in solitude, lost in her thoughts of Warrington—*Nate*—and his impromptu visit.

The sun was out and the day almost qualified as warm. She'd been contemplating when she and the duke might meet again. Was he waiting for her to reach out to him? Or was he planning to connect with her again? They hadn't had time to discuss the particulars in his hasty departure from her bedchamber. *Blast it.* Mrs. Ramsey really needed to return so that Marian could gain her professional opinion on how an individual conducted lessons in seduction.

Mrs. Pratt arrived at Marian's side.

"Good day to you, Mrs. Pratt." Marian pasted a smile to her face.

Mrs. Pratt pressed a hand to her side, breathing heavily from her efforts to catch up with Marian. "Heading to town? Splendid! We shall walk together."

"Splendid," Marian echoed. Turning, they continued on their course.

Mrs. Pratt eyed the empty basket swinging at Marian's elbow. "Doing some shopping?"

"I'm calling on the baker."

"The baker?" Mrs. Pratt arched one eyebrow. "For a hot loaf?"

"Yes, I'm getting two actually."

"Two?"

Marian nodded, trying not to take offense at the woman's incredulity. "Then I need to visit the subscription library."

"Two loaves of bread *and* you're visiting the subscription library?" Her eyebrows arched even higher, practically disappearing into her hairline. "Have your finances improved then?"

Trust Mrs. Pratt to be ever direct.

"The baker's baby is suffering from gripe. He promised me a couple loaves in exchange for some of my sister's cordial water. As for the library, I'm collecting some books for my charge, Miss Walker."

Indeed, she could not afford the annual fee for the subscription library, but the Walkers could. She often collected books on their behalf.

"Ah. That makes sense." Mrs. Pratt nodded, seemingly appeased. "Clever of you to utilize the assets the good Lord has seen fit to bless you and your sisters with."

Marian suppressed a smile. Indeed. She supposed she was doing that very thing in her arrangement with the duke. Wouldn't Mrs. Pratt be so very scandalized to hear of it?

Mrs. Pratt wrenched Marian from her musings and snatched hold of her arm. "Look, there!"

Marian followed her gaze to the horse and rider approaching.

Mrs. Pratt's vise on her arm tightened. "'Tis the duke! He's coming this way." She bounced in place, her cheeks jiggling with anticipation.

"Yes, I can see that." Marian's heart started to thump faster as he drew close. His hat shadowed his features, but she felt his stare as acutely as a touch on her face.

Mrs. Pratt stopped her bouncing, but her grip still clung to Marian. "Stay close to me. It's doubtful he would harm both of us."

Marian nodded mutely, scarcely listening to the woman as the duke pulled his mount up before them.

He touched his hat and nodded to both of them. "Ladies."

"Your Grace. Lovely day for a ride," Mrs. Pratt greeted.

"Indeed, and for a stroll," he returned.

"We're heading into town," Mrs. Pratt volunteered as though he had inquired. "I'm calling on the vicar's wife and Miss Langley here is going to the baker's and the library."

Mrs. Pratt was the one talking, but the duke's eyes remained fixed on Marian with an intensity she hoped the lady did not notice.

Marian glanced down, suddenly self-conscious of her plain day dress. The faded brown would not flatter anyone. He must think her a frump.

"Don't let me keep you from your errands. Enjoy your day, ladies." With another touch to his hat, he turned about and rode away.

"Well," Mrs. Pratt announced as they resumed their walk. "He was civil enough. One would never guess at his ungodly activities." She tsked.

Marian sent Mrs. Pratt a wry look. "We know nothing of his activities. It is all rumor."

The woman chuckled and patted Marian's arm. "Oh, dear, sweet naïve Miss Langley." She shook her head ruefully. "Did you not see him? He looks as though he hasn't seen a razor in a fortnight. And how very big, is he? He's virile like a . . . a dock worker. Not at all as a duke ought to be. And those devilish eyes?" She tsked again. "The way he sat astride his horse was fairly indecent." Mrs. Pratt's eyes took on a dreamy glint as she finished rattling off the duke's negative attributes, which truthfully didn't sound very negative when aired out loud.

"Mrs. Pratt?" Marian prodded. "You were saying?"

The woman blinked and focused again on Marian. "He is all things wicked, that is to be certain." Mrs. Pratt linked arms with Marian. "Fortunately for you, he only seems to favor females of ill repute. You and your sisters should be quite safe from him. Especially that pretty Charlotte. You're all handsome girls, mind you, but that Charlotte is the beauty of your household, as I'm sure you know."

"Yes, I'm aware," Marian said drolly.

Mrs. Pratt smiled and nodded, giving Marian's arm another reassuring pat. "Such fine girls, you are. You are quite safe from that wicked duke."

Marian couldn't help herself. She snuck a glance over her shoulder, seeking a glimpse of the *wicked* Duke of Warrington—a man from whom she was decidedly not safe, contrary to what Mrs. Pratt said.

Unfortunately, he was already out of sight, and she frowned as she faced forward again. She should not even look back at him. Not in the company of the shire's biggest gossip. What if Mrs. Pratt noted her unseemly interest? Marian needed to get in the habit of practicing discretion in his sphere and that meant disguising her interest.

She endured the rest of the walk into town, contributing very little to the conversation. It wasn't necessary, after all. Mrs. Pratt did most of the talking.

They parted ways at the vicar's house and Marian continued on to the baker's shop, delivering the cordial and tucking the two loaves of bread into her basket. The fresh golden loaves would be delicious with their soup tonight.

The subscription library was one of her favorite places. When Papa was alive and had paid their annual fees, she'd spent many an afternoon walking the narrow aisles and browsing books.

"Mr. Wallace," she greeted to the elderly gentleman sitting at the cluttered desk near the front door.

He jolted awake where he dozed, sitting upright in his chair with a sputter. "Miss Langley," he returned, pushing his spectacles up the bridge of his nose.

"I'm here for some books for the Walkers."

He nodded distractedly, gesturing her inside with one old, gnarled hand before he crossed his arms over his narrow chest and closed his eyes again.

She shook her head. It was no wonder people didn't simply stroll inside the place and take whatever they wanted.

Marian moved deeper into the shop, enjoying the musty smell of parchment and leather.

The bells on the front door jingled and she heard the murmur of voices. She smiled slightly. Apparently someone else had dared to disturb old Mr. Wallace.

Marian strolled to the back of the shop where she knew *The Count of Monte Cristo* was located. Not only was it a splendidly entertaining read, but useful for Annabel who needed to practice her French.

Marian slid the book from the shelf and dropped it in her basket alongside the delicious smelling loaves. She then continued to browse, open to anything that popped out as potentially interesting.

The back of the shop was dim and window-less, the only light that which streamed from the shop's front windows. She had to peer closely to read the spines.

She heard a creaking floorboard and turned, expecting to find another patron.

Her breath caught. Nate was not who she expected to see. The last time she saw him he was riding away from town. *Away* from her.

Now he was here.

He was here and advancing down the aisle, moving unhurriedly, one arm stretched out, his fingers brushing along the spines.

"Your Grace?" Was that squeaking her voice? She tried again. "Your Grace?" Much better.

He didn't respond.

She looked up and down the narrow aisle, confirming they were alone.

She flexed her suddenly sweating palm around the handle of her basket. "Are you here to browse? Brambledon has a fine selection."

He stopped in front of her. She edged away a step, her back colliding with the spines of countless books.

"I am here to browse," he agreed, flipping open her cloak to reveal her dull dress. It was modestly cut, exposing very little. Not that it seemed to matter. He surveyed her, examining Marian in her frumpy brown dress as though she were attired in the most provocative of gowns. Or naked. He knew what she looked like without clothes, after all. Heat fired her face at the memory.

He moved in, encroaching, his body flush with hers. His head dipped, nose and lips grazing her exposed throat. He inhaled as though pulling her scent inside himself and she gulped, swallowing down a whimper.

He nuzzled at her throat, his lips finding her skin, nibbling and kissing. Her knees nearly gave out when she felt the velvet swipe of his tongue.

Her basket dropped with a thunk beside her as she grabbed his shoulders, clinging for support. "Wh-what are you doing, Your Grace?"

"What's it look like, Miss Langley?" The heated puff of his words on her skin only added to the delicious sensations spinning through her.

"We're in public," she protested weakly.

He lightly bit her throat and she gasped.

"That's part of the thrill." He spoke against her throat and the movement of his lips on her tender skin spiked sensation straight to her core. "Count this as one of your lessons. Spontaneity can be intoxicating and isn't that what you want to be?" He lifted his face to gaze at her.

"Oh. I see." She inhaled deeply, overwhelmed. He looked at her as though she were the intoxicating creature he described.

"Intoxicating," he repeated softly. "A mistress no man can refuse. What was it you asked me to do that night you came to me? How did you phrase it? *Show me how to be a good lover.* You said you wanted to know everything there is to know about pleasing a man."

She nodded. He spoke true.

She closed her eyes in a long blink, but that didn't get rid of his voice in her head or the sensation of his body against hers. When she reopened her eyes, he was still there, compelling, beautiful, his eyes mesmerizing her.

The way he made her feel, the ideas he put in her head . . .

He completely unraveled her. *Her.* Was she doing the same to him?

Unraveling was what she needed to learn, but what if she couldn't do it? What if she couldn't unravel a man . . . *this* man?

Marian reached up to take his face between her hands. She studied him in the gloom of the library, peering into his eyes, searching, hoping she found even a fraction of the desire he stirred within her.

He turned his face into her hand, kissing her palm leisurely, deeply, closing his eyes as though savoring her.

Oh. My.

It was only her palm, but she whimpered. His mouth slid down to the inside of her wrist, and she hissed out a breath as though in pain . . .

because it felt that good. Incredible. Every nerve in her body hummed.

His mouth opened as he kissed her there, his teeth lightly scoring the fragile skin and she swallowed a ragged cry as all those humming nerves went wild.

She had no notion the inside of her wrist was such a sensitive area.

He looked up, watching her with eyes hooded and dark.

With a soft cry of surrender, she dove for his lips and kissed him, gripping his face between her hands as though he might suddenly vanish.

He met her lips, returning her ravenous kiss. His arms delved inside her cloak and wrapped around her waist, hauling her in, as close as two people could get.

Well, almost as close. They could never get *that* close. That was not part of the agreement. And the fact that they could not ever fully consummate this relationship—that he could never fill the hollow ache inside her with the hard ridge that rubbed against her belly—was just sheer disappointment.

She slanted her head and deepened the kiss, her tongue dancing and twining with his. He growled in approval, his hands sliding down to grip her bottom and hike her higher against the shelves so that they matched perfectly, so that the hard ridge of him prodded directly where she wanted him most—where she ached and throbbed and could *never* have him.

No, she would save that for the highest bidder. She would maintain control over her body and choose a benefactor who would properly compensate her.

Marian would sell herself to a man who wasn't *him*. To someone for whom she felt nothing. That's the way she wanted it to be—the way it had to be.

A sob swelled in her throat. The reminder hit her like a slap. She broke away. "I-I . . . we need to stop."

He stepped back, dropping his hands at his sides.

His breathing was labored in a way that made her feel better. She wasn't the only one affected. At least there was that.

He dragged a hand through his hair. "A bit much for you? Changed your mind?" He held himself stiffly, as though waiting to hear her pronounce that their lessons were over.

"Oh, no. The arrangement still stands." She simply needed to remember the end goal. Security for herself and her family.

"What's wrong then?"

She ran a shaky hand down her face and looked up and down the aisle. "We can't do this now. Not here."

He looked at her hungrily, stepping forward and placing one hand on each side of her head, caging her in. "Then when can we meet again?" His thick growl turned her skin to gooseflesh.

"I . . ." She stopped and swallowed, moistening her lips.

He angled his head, watching her carefully, his gaze on her mouth, following the swipe of her tongue.

"I will come to you," she finally said.

"You'll come to me?" His voice was amused. He was skeptical. He thought she'd lost her nerve and was being evasive.

She lifted her chin. "I will."

"Very well then." He lowered his hands and stepped back. "I look forward to our next engagement."

After a long moment, he turned and left her alone in the aisle. A few moments later, the bells on the door jingled, announcing his departure.

She waited a few minutes until she regained her composure. Satisfied her hands had stopped shaking, she reclaimed her basket off the floor and departed the library without even a glance from Mr. Wallace where he napped in his chair.

Once outside, she took a quick glance around. No sight of the duke. He was gone.

She turned down the lane and set a brisk pace. Mrs. Walker would be expecting her. If Marian was even one minute late, she would never hear the end of it.

"Miss Langley!"

She spun around at the sound of her name, joy filling her at the sight of Mrs. Ramsey.

The finely dressed lady crossed the street, holding her parasol very correctly to shield her face.

"It's lovely to see you, Mrs. Ramsey," Marian exclaimed. "I called on you while you were away."

"Oh, dear, perhaps I should have sent word to you." Her lips pursed in a frown as she considered this. "Oh, dear, dear. I should have considering our last discussion. Shame on me."

"Fret not. I'm glad you've returned now." She expelled a happy breath.

"Where are you off to?"

"I'm on my way to tutor Annabel Walker."

"Come then. My carriage is just down the lane. I will drop you there." She fell in step beside Marian, looping her arm through hers. "And you can tell me all the recent developments." She winked and glanced around them as though to assure they had no audience—not that they had said anything indiscreet.

Mrs. Ramsey's driver was ready with the door open for them.

"We're letting Miss Langley out at the Walker residence, Giles."

"Yes, ma'am," he replied as he assisted first Mrs. Ramsey and then Marian up inside.

As soon as the door shut behind Marian, Mrs. Ramsey whipped around and seized her by both hands. "What has transpired? One look at your face and I know something has happened. Have you seen the duke?"

"Yes."

"I knew it!" She nodded eagerly. "Do tell. Did you explain your proposition to him?"

"I did," Marian said slowly. "And he turned me down."

"Oh." Mrs. Ramsey's expression fell. She sank back against the cushioned seat. "Well, that's unfortunate. Were you very disappointed?"

"I was, yes. And then he changed his mind."

"Oh my!" She sat up straighter, her expression jubilant once again.

"Yes. He agreed to help tutor me and we've met . . . twice now."

Mrs. Ramsey clapped her hands with delight. "Marvelous. And I trust he's the skilled tutor we expected him to be?"

Heat filled her face as she nodded. "Oh, yes, indeed. He is quite skilled."

"Splendid. Well, you are on your way to gaining the experience you need. This is very good news."

"Wait." Marian wagged a finger. "Actually it

was three times. We've had three assignations. We just had another lesson in the subscription library."

"The subscription library?" Mrs. Ramsey queried, her smile slipping slightly.

"Scandalous, I know." Marian laughed, and the sound struck her as both giddy and uncertain.

"Scandalous, indeed." Disapproval radiated from her. "And perhaps a little risky for one trying to safeguard a reputation in this village, hm?" Mrs. Ramsey arched an eyebrow.

"I know, I know," Marian allowed rather sheepishly. "We were the only ones in the library besides old man Wallace, who was asleep at his desk the entire time, but you're correct. It was not the most discreet behavior." She smiled then, her fingers brushing her lips. They still tingled from Nate.

"Oh, dear."

Marian snapped her gaze back to the woman's face. "What is it?"

Mrs. Ramsey examined her closely. "Have a care you do not grow attached to this man, Marian. He is a resource. Someone to be used to help reach your goals. Someone to school you in seduction . . . do not let yourself fall under his spell. It is well and good to enjoy yourself with your lover . . . only do not form too great an attachment. Ruin and heartache lie in that path."

Marian nodded solemnly. Given the way she was feeling right now, these were words she needed to hear, however cold and calculating they happened to be.

"Three lessons, hm? I can only assume you are well on your way. I imagine you should know enough soon to get your start. Of course, I'm laboring under the assumption that he is truly a skilled—"

"He is skilled," she quickly asserted. *Very* skilled.

Mrs. Ramsey eyed her speculatively. "Too many more lessons and your maidenhead could become a thing of the past. The temptation might be too great. Have you considered that? You might not be able to resist him."

Marian winced. The thought had crossed her mind. How could it not? Ever since he'd pleasured her so thoroughly on her bed she throbbed, ached to be filled by him. Already, in the back of her mind, she'd begun to ask herself just how valuable her virginity was. Could she not save her family without it? Wasn't being an exceptional courtesan enough?

She sucked in a breath and shook her head. It was dangerous thinking. Mrs. Ramsey was right. *Do not let yourself fall under his spell.*

Marian would make sure that did not happen.

Chapter 16

*R*ain.

That's all there was. For hours. For days. For nearly a week.

Water dumped in torrents. It was a deluge. A monsoon. A great darkness filled the sky and hammered over the village of Brambledon and the surrounding countryside with no sign of relenting. No one ventured out. They stayed inside, waiting out the rain, hoping it stopped soon.

It was biblical. The type of storm that made one think of the end of days. Nora made plenty of jests to that effect as she peered out the window on the fourth afternoon, claiming she was looking for an ark.

"We're not flooding," Charlotte chided. "Be thankful for that."

"Not *yet*," Nora opined.

"You're such a dramatic creature. It will not come to that, Eleanor." Charlotte only ever used Nora's full name when she was annoyed with her—and trapped indoors together as they were, Charlotte had definitely reached her limits with Nora. They had *all* reached their limits with each other.

On the fifth day, over Charlotte's protests, Marian decided to venture outdoors and inspect the condition of the roads for herself. She had to investigate. One more moment trapped inside and she would go mad. She felt ready to crawl out of her skin. Her house had never felt particularly small before, but it felt the size of a milliner's box now.

It still rained a steady drizzle. She held her parasol aloft and tromped carefully in her brother's old boots, peering through the silvery sheets of water. She didn't get very far, however, before she was forced to turn around. The roads were muddied streams meandering through the countryside. There was no traversing them.

She returned home. Her sisters were waiting anxiously on the front stoop with a blanket for her. They helped rid her of her cloak and wrapped her in its warmth.

Charlotte tsked. "You'll catch your death."

"Come into the kitchen beside the grate," Nora directed. "I've prepared a hot toddy."

"With honey?" Marian asked through chattering teeth.

"Of course."

Nodding, she allowed them to lead her back inside the house, sending one glance of longing over her shoulder. Charlotte was correct. She had been foolish to attempt to leave while it was still raining. She was impatient. Five days. It had been over five days since she had last seen the duke.

Without this blasted rain they would certainly have liaised again. She sank down in a chair beside the warm grate and gladly accepted the cup from Nora, relishing the heat infusing her palms. She drew a slow sip of the hot drink, savoring the slide of the warm brew down her throat.

Was this infatuation then? Foolishly braving rain and inaccessible roads so that she might have another taste of the man she craved? Mrs. Ramsey's words reverberated through her as she stared into the flickering fire.

It is well and good to enjoy yourself with your lover . . . only do not form too great an attachment. Ruin and heartache lie in that path.

"I do hope you will be patient and not venture out again until the rain subsides." Charlotte frowned. "We don't need anything to befall you, Marian."

Marian nodded and smiled weakly. "Of course, you are right. I will be patient."

She would be patient and wait, bide her time until the weather cleared. Then she and the duke could meet again. There was no attachment.

There would *be* no attachment.

BY THE END of the week the rain finally weakened to an inconsequential mist. Marian bundled up in layers at the kitchen door, ready to greet the world.

"Marian? Whatever are you doing?" Charlotte turned from the pot of soup she was preparing for their supper.

"I'm just going to ride over and check on the Pratts."

Charlotte frowned. "I am sure they are fine. They've been on this earth long enough to have the sense to stay in and wait out the rain."

"They are advanced in years," Marian argued. "I should check on them."

A plausible excuse. And she would check on them. She truly would . . . on her way *back* from the duke's home.

"It's dreadful outside," Nora volunteered. "You will probably catch your death."

"The roads are safe. I saw a rider pass by not an hour ago. There is no danger."

She could not stay away a moment longer. She had to see him. Every fiber of her being demanded it. She had not seen him since he left her standing in the aisle at the library. Over a week ago.

Forever ago.

She'd promised she would come to him. Did he think she had forgotten? Or changed her mind? Surely he knew the weather was to blame.

By now she had thought to have several more lessons—several more opportunities to be with him. This blasted rain had put a damper on their activities and delayed her mission to rescue her family from penury. She told herself it was that reason alone that had her so anxious to see him again.

Lies. She cringed. She was lying to herself.

She woke at night afire, her hands fisting her sheets, her body arched and aching, her core clenching in need. She craved relief.

He'd done this to her. Blast him. It was as though he had contaminated her, infected her with a fever for which he was the only cure.

A little mud on the road shouldn't get in the way.

She would see him today and they would continue their lessons as per their agreement. Nothing would keep her away.

A WEEK HAD passed without a glimpse of her. Nate knew the wretched rain was responsible, but the knowledge did nothing to quell his insatiable longing.

She had not come to him and he didn't care the reason, only that he had not seen her. Not heard her voice. Not touched her. Not tasted her.

It had been risky the day he showed up at her house and even more so when he had followed her to the library, and now with this infernal rain he knew that she, like everyone else, was holed up in her home. She wouldn't be alone. Her sisters would be trapped indoors with her. He could not simply ride through the rain, knock on her front door, and make use of her bedchamber to continue their lessons. Unfortunately.

She had promised to come to him. He would not ignore her wishes. She wanted discretion and he would not go against her. He'd give her what she wanted—for some reason that was important to him. It mattered.

He paced anxiously, imagining this was what a tiger felt like in a cage. Trapped. Restrained.

The rain revived just then, drumming on the roof and dancing down the panes of mullioned glass, seeming to mock him, taunt him. He stopped before the window and looked out, hoping the clouds would appear a little less swollen.

Instead of clouds, however, he saw a lone rider

cutting through the steady fall of rain on a direct path for his house.

He rubbed at the fogging glass as though that would somehow clear it. Peering, he noted the individual was slight. Perhaps a child. No, a woman.

He lurched away from the window and bounded down the stairs, not even bothering to reprimand himself for his eager reaction.

It was Marian. Marian had come to him.

Foolish chit. She had risked rain and indiscretion and came to him.

He didn't pass anyone in his hurried descent to the bottom floor. He knew there were servants about somewhere, but he kept only minimal staff, and the house had been quiet these last few days. It was as though the rain had subdued everyone.

He wasn't concerned, though. His staff knew better than to speak out of turn and gossip about matters that occurred within these walls. He was a private man, and they knew not to risk their positions carrying tales. He paid them generously and allowed them time off. He knew his counterparts were not often so inclined.

Even if one of his servants correctly identified Marian, they would keep it to themselves.

And yet if the threat of being exposed were real, he doubted it would slow him down. He didn't care. He would still continue on his path.

He would still rush into the foyer and yank open the front door and yank *her* into the house.

Threat of discovery or not, he could not suppress the urge.

Her expression only reflected mild surprise at the sudden appearance of him before her.

"Nate," she breathed. Then she was stumbling readily into his arms.

Apparently she wasn't concerned with discovery either and that only inflamed him—made him burn hotter.

He slammed his mouth over hers and she met his kiss, just as eager, just as hungry.

She managed to get out a few broken phrases as he kicked the door shut behind her. "Wanted to see you . . . Tried . . . Wretched rain . . ."

"I know," he growled and deepened the kiss, making further speech impossible.

He held her face, cradled it, clung to it, as though she might disappear. As though she might be a figment of his most ardent imaginings and not this real flesh and blood female. *Not his.*

And she was his.

He felt that in every sweep of her tongue against his own, in the wrap of her arms around his shoulders. The desperate press of her breasts into his chest.

He folded her into his arms and lifted her off her feet, bringing her mouth on level with his.

He took the stairs, carrying her with him, mindless in his hunger for her. Servants could be witnessing their display. He couldn't be sure, but he didn't give a damn.

All his attention was focused on her. Marian in his arms. Getting Marian into his bed.

He was in his chamber in moments, kicking the door shut behind them. Moments too long as far as he was concerned. It felt like a lifetime since he last held her, touched her, kissed her.

He dropped her to her feet and growled against her mouth, "You came. You came."

"I had to." She gasped as his fingers attacked the rows of buttons down the front of her wet gown.

"You're soaked."

"I suppose I should get out of these clothes then." His fingers worked feverishly. The boldness of her words made him groan.

"I suppose you should."

She added her hands, helping him rid her of her dress.

All the while his mouth feasted on her, unable to break away. He didn't need air as long as he had this—her.

Her hands buried in his hair, and she pressed against him, into him, practically climbing him in her eagerness.

He lifted her off her feet again and walked her to the bed, his mouth never severing from hers.

He came down heavily atop her and then attempted to lift up, to ease his weight away, but she grabbed his shoulders and hauled him back down.

"Too heavy," he rasped, his tongue in her mouth.

"No," she denied. "I want you on me. I want to feel your weight. All of you."

He kissed her forever, holding her face with both of his hands like she might vanish from him. Desire pumped thickly through his blood. Her thighs widened for him, welcoming him in. Her skirts and drawers bunched between them. He cursed at the surplus of fabric, grinding through the material as though he might reach her. Impossible while they were dressed, he knew, but instinct demanded he move and thrust into her even if penetration was impossible.

Because he had promised.

Her hips rose, seeking the hard rub of his cock. The heat from her core radiated through all their garments, beckoning him.

"I want to feel you. Skin to skin. Please, Nate," she begged.

"We can't."

Her hands fumbled between them, landing on the fastening of his breeches. "Let me feel *you*, then."

He was helpless to stop her. In fact, he assisted her.

Reaching down, he freed himself and groaned as her soft, cool hands surrounded him. She slid her fingers over him, gliding, stroking, her artless touch too much.

"Marian, stop, please. I'm about to spill." He seized her hands.

She whimpered and wiggled, her eyes bright and wild on him. "I need . . . I ache . . . Please, Nathaniel. I've thought about this. I know what I'm doing. I know what I want."

Her broken plea compelled him. He pulled back and hastily rid her of her petticoats and drawers, shoving her chemise up to bare her from the waist down.

He shuddered at the sight of her pretty quim, pink and weeping for him. "Oh, Marian," he breathed, his mouth falling between her thighs with a hungry groan. The first taste of her was as heady and sweet as he imagined.

He devoured her, licking and nibbling, rolling that swollen pearl between his fingers and then taking it between his lips, sucking deep and rubbing it with his tongue.

She convulsed and cried out, writhing on the bed.

He lifted his head to look up at her, his gaze fastening on her face. Her eyes were the color of a night storm with a dark ring of cobalt, almost black, around them. "You're beautiful."

And mine.

It wasn't what he should be thinking at all, but he allowed himself the mistake. His erection bordered on pain and there was no relief forthcoming. He could be forgiven the possessive thought.

He crawled up her length. A body-deep sigh escaped him as he came over her. Skin-to-skin. No part of them was shielded. His cock nestled against her sex.

"This isn't a good idea," he said tightly.

She leaned forward and rained kisses over his throat and jaw. "It's the best idea." Her mouth found his again, kissing him deeply.

She arched and strained against him as her tongue mated with his.

His hips settled deeper, nudging her thighs wider. "You're so wet." He panted, gritting his teeth.

She maneuvered herself so that his erection was pressed directly along the crease of her lips—and then she rocked.

He threw his head back with a hiss, jamming his eyes tight.

"N-Nate," she choked out, thrusting her hips until the head of his cock nudged her opening.

"Marian, stop . . ."

"Why?" She seized his face and forced him to look back at her. "We can do this." She nodded fiercely. "It was my choice not to . . . now it's my choice to do it."

"But you made me promise," he reminded, desperate for her to remember that, to be strong when he felt so weak right now. He wanted her too much, but this wasn't good for her. He didn't want to take her choices away, her options.

Her hand gripped his hair, tugging, forcing his gaze back on her face. "I release you from your promise. Now take me."

He was snared by the intensity of her blue eyes. "Marian, it's not what you want . . ."

"I want this." She moved her hips, searching, seeking penetration. The head of him dipped inside her, just an inch, but that clinging heat sucking him in was bliss.

"Wait . . . no. We cannot—"

"Please!" she entreated, her fingers digging into his shoulders, her face lifting, her lips reaching up to his neck, kissing, sucking . . .

She wanted it. She wanted this—him.

"Nate! Now!"

He drove deep, lodging himself inside her, breaching her maidenhead.

"Oh!"

He held himself still, trying not to hurt her— or hurt her further—even as everything in him cried out to keep moving, keep driving into her snug channel. He watched her face, gauging her expression, her level of pain.

She wiggled her hips, and the friction made her eyes flare wide. "Oh!"

Her inner muscles clenched around his cock and he groaned, dropping his head in the crook of her neck. She was killing him. He might die if he didn't move in her. He supposed that's what people meant by a good death. Buried deep in the sweetest quim he'd ever known.

"Marian," he said against the soft skin of her throat. "I can't not . . . are you—"

"Please! I throb. Move inside me." She bent her knees and hooked one ankle around his waist.

With an exultant cry, he pulled out and entered her again, burying deep.

"I'll make it better," he promised, increasing the tempo, driving into her faster, harder.

Thank. God. She lifted up to meet his thrusts, crying out at every impact.

He still wore his clothes. She still wore her chemise. They were going at it like two savages without a care for the world around them.

She dragged her hands down his back, over his shirt. She grasped his ass in both hands, urging him faster, harder.

He released a guttural sound that could have been her name—or not. He was out of his head and could just be rambling senselessly. He followed her bidding, moving quicker in stabbing thrusts.

She flung her arms above her head in utter abandon.

His hands found hers there. He laced his fingers with hers, pinning her to the bed. Her hands squeezed and held fast to him as his body moved over hers, pumping into her, pushing them both to the brink.

A shrill cry spilled loose from her throat.

He released her hands and she flung her arms around him. Her legs clamped around him until all of him was wrapped up in her.

He slid his hand along one of the thighs draped over his hip, lifting her leg higher for deeper strokes. She shattered around him as he thrust in and out of her.

He drove into her one more time and spent himself, shuddering his release inside her welcoming heat.

The moment he did it, he knew it was ill-advised. He never lost himself so completely with a woman—*in* a woman. He always took precautions. He had never wanted to impregnate another woman again, but everything was so intense, so wild with Marian. He lost himself with her.

Or perhaps he found himself.

He rolled to his side, facing her. She turned to look at him. Neither spoke or moved. Their breaths crashed between them from the toll of their exertions.

He studied her face, tracing her features, committing them to memory. "Regrets?"

She gave a slight shake of her head. "No." She smiled tremulously. "It just means I'll be more experienced."

She was still planning on a future as a mistress. As a prostitute for other men.

That had been the understanding from the start. He should not feel any amount of surprise . . . or disappointment.

"Generally, mistresses are experienced," he agreed. "This night's activities will do you no harm."

As long as she didn't end up with child.

"I just won't have the benefit of auctioning off my virginity."

No, that was her gift to him. He felt his cock swelling between them, ready for another go.

She must have felt it, too. She looked down. "Again?"

"You should rest. Your first time—"

"Is such a thing possible?"

"Yes. It's possible. It can be done multiple times a day. As often as a couple likes."

Her eyes went adorably wide. In truth there was nothing about her he didn't find attractive. "Multiple times in a night? I had no idea."

"We should wait, though."

"Why?" She frowned.

"You might be sore."

"I'm not. I feel fine. Wonderful." She wiggled against him. "I'm ready if you are."

"I don't think you should—" His words died a swift death as she renewed her squirming, raining sweet little kisses along his jawline.

"Nathaniel," she breathed against his skin. She was a siren. A temptress. A seductress. She had achieved her goal. *I want to be good . . . so good that I can name my price and have my pick of clients.*

He could only imagine she had reached that objective. Men would fall at this woman's feet.

He knew he would.

"You're certain—" He sucked in a breath as her hand drifted between them to stroke his cock.

"I am certain you agreed to educate me," she purred.

"Yes," he groaned as her hand stroked him faster. "I'll do that."

And this time he would not lose his seed inside her.

Even as he agreed and let her have her way,

he knew he was lying. There was nothing about what just happened between them that felt rooted in education.

It had been all about lust and need.

It still was.

He speared his fingers through her loosened hair and kissed her.

Chapter 17

*I*t was dawn when they left.

They rode in silence, and Marian was grateful for that. She was glad to have her thoughts to herself with no intrusion from Nate.

Nate descended from his mount first and then approached Marian where she sat atop Bessie.

Without a word, he reached for her and swung her down.

"Thank you," she murmured, "but you really did not need to escort me."

"Nonsense, and we're well past discussing this now."

She nodded slightly. They were past a great many things now.

They were past any hope of their relationship

remaining unconsummated. That was an impossibility now. There was no undoing what had been done. They were also past any hope that matters between them would remain uncomplicated.

Everything felt hopelessly complicated now.

She stroked Bessie's cheek so she would have something to do with her hands.

He stared through the darkness in the direction of her house. "I would still prefer to walk you to the door."

"Such a gentleman," she teased, desperate for a little levity.

"I'm not jesting."

No. She knew he wasn't. "We can't risk that."

It seemed absurd to say that after everything, but she still had a reputation to protect. A family to save. Public ruin was not an option. That had not changed. She shouldn't even be out alone with him now. She glanced around nervously, surveying the sleeping countryside.

"We can leave our mounts here and I can walk you a little closer." He led his horse beneath a tree, tied it off and returned to her side. He took Bessie's reins from her hand as though it was decided and there would be no argument.

She opened and closed her mouth several times, undecided if she should object. He motioned for her to walk and she decided it would be simpler not to argue the point. She just needed to be rid of him. She wanted to reach her bed-chamber, to be alone, to think.

To remember her purpose.

The moon peeked through the leaves over-head, following them. They walked side by side with several inches between them. Hardly like the lovers they now were. She quickly amended that thought. *They once were.*

There was no need for them to continue their lessons any longer. To do so would just be fri-volity. Not for any real benefit. She had learned all she needed to know. She had learned enough, as Mrs. Ramsey would say. Mrs. Ramsey would also tell her to get out while she still could. To end things before too deep of an attachment formed.

The fading night was turning soft purple. Day-break was close. The air throbbed all around them as they cut through the woods toward home. Frogs croaked, enjoying the aftermath of the recent rain. Her boots squelched on the moist ground as she walked.

"Marian—"

"This changes nothing," she blurted, before he could. She was certain he was going to say some-thing similar to that.

He was quiet for several moments. "You still intend to make your way as a mistress?"

"Yes. Even if I won't be auctioning my maidenhead to the highest bidder." She released a dry little laugh.

"Sorry you no longer have that . . . commodity," he replied evenly.

She wasn't sorry. Indeed not. She was rather glad she would always have this experience. It would forever be something she did for herself. Not because she had to. Not because she needed to for some advantage. She had done it for no other reason than that she wanted to.

Because she had to have him or she would die from the want.

"I imagine this concludes our lessons," she murmured.

"Does it?" His feet crunched over loose leaves and bramble. "There is still much you can learn. Much I can show you."

She stopped and turned to face him, considering his offer.

It would be pleasurable, but she had to take care of her family and dallying with him wasn't putting food on the table or paying their creditors. "I can't continue this indefinitely. I must move ahead. I have my sisters . . ."

He knew this song. She'd sung it to him before.

She exhaled heavily. She needed funds. She needed funds now.

No, not now. She needed them yesterday. Last month. Last year.

No more playing at this.

She knew enough to perform the duties of a mistress without being shocked or squeamish. At least, she thought so.

"Will you help me?" she asked. "I recall you mentioned you would put me into contact with a woman. Someone who could help find clients for me?"

As much as it turned her stomach to think of another man touching her—a stranger who might be as repulsive as Mr. Lawrence—she needed to persist with her plan.

Staring up at Nate's handsome face, she felt an unwelcome pang in the chest.

She needed to sever ties with Nate—no. With the Duke of Warrington.

Things were not supposed to become so very personal between them. She should not look up at his face and feel a pang in her chest. It was to be an arrangement between them. Nothing more. No feelings. No engagement of the heart.

He nodded. "I did say that."

She nodded back, waiting expectantly for him to elaborate about this woman and how he might go about introducing them.

He turned so that only his profile was in view in the murky air.

"Your Grace?" she prompted. "The woman? Can I meet her?"

"You might not need to meet her at all. *I* might have a client for you."

Surprise rippled through her. "*You* do?" He had been quite adamant on the matter that he was no pimp. "I didn't think you . . . did that. Or would do that. You said you wouldn't."

"I didn't think I would."

Except he had changed his mind. Why?

She tried not to feel upset, but her stomach churned. She pressed a hand against her middle, trying to quell the rolling sensation. He'd bedded her and now he meant to pass her on to a friend? She had not thought him that manner of man.

"Who is this client?" she asked warily, telling herself to act the professional. A professional would only care about the work—about gaining a new client. In her case, her first client.

"Me," he answered. "The client is me."

"You?" She stared at him and then a small nervous bubble of laughter escaped her. "You jest."

"I assure you, I do not."

"You don't keep a mistress."

"True."

"You said you have no desire to keep a mistress," she reminded.

"That is true, too. Or rather, *was*. I never have kept a mistress before, but that doesn't mean I can't."

She shook her head and pressed her fingers against her forehead. "This makes no sense."

"A man is entitled to change his mind."

"And why have you changed your mind?"

"Why not? Obviously we are good together. You can't deny that. It's convenient. You live a stone's throw from me."

Ah. Convenience. That was what won him over. Not exactly flattering.

She stifled an outright sneer. "I appreciate the—"

"I'm not ready for things to end between us. Are you?"

She felt undeniable longing pulling at her chest. "I had a plan—"

"Forget about your plan. Can you tell me you never want me to touch you again? I can be your plan. I can be your benefactor. I'm wealthy. I can provide for you."

He was earnest, and blast if she didn't feel tempted. No surprise there. The man tempted her in every way.

"We can be discreet," he offered.

She considered that . . . sneaking off to his house in the middle of the night. How long could they keep that up without discovery? Discretion was crucial, and it was already such a struggle even this soon in the game.

As though he could read her mind, he added,

"There's a hunting cottage not far from here on my grounds."

"I know it." Of course she did. She knew this countryside. The hunting cottage he'd spoken of had been abandoned for as long as she could remember. As a girl, she'd spied through the grimy windows, curious about the interior.

"I could have the place cleaned up. It could be quite comfortable for the two of us."

Quite comfortable.

A little love den.

Only it wouldn't be about love. Her face flushed. She knew that. She'd told herself that from the very start, and yet . . .

She gave herself a firm mental shake. There would be no "yet" in her mind.

This thing between them was more intense than she had expected. Evidently it was *more* than he had expected, too, or he would not have had this change of heart. He felt something for her, but it was not love or affection. She knew enough of men to comprehend that.

It was about convenience. For both of them.

If she was agreeing to be his mistress, it would certainly be simple enough to sneak away to the cottage rather than his house. No doubt it would also be easier than traveling to London and entering into liaisons with other gentlemen.

The cottage was on the far end of his estate.

There was nothing in that direction. No one should be about to catch a glimpse of either one of them coming and going. There would be less risk.

"I will have to consider it."

His head pulled back slightly as though surprised at her response. "What's to consider? You wanted a client . . . a protector. I'm offering you that. Your home shall remain your home. Your sisters shall have food and clothing and want for nothing. *You* shall want for nothing."

He was right. It was everything she had sought. It was everything she had set out to achieve and more. So why did the offer feel so very disappointing?

He continued, "Would selling yourself to a stranger be so much better than what I am offering you? Would you prefer that?"

"Of course not," she snapped, although she wasn't so convinced. At least with strangers, it would never be complicated. She would not feel so very confused.

"Then what is it? What is it you want, Marian?"

She resumed walking and bit her lip to stop herself from saying something she could never take back. Something she could not even dare to formulate in her mind.

"I've only ever wanted to provide for my family and keep my independence." A far-fetched dream perhaps, but that was her goal.

"And you'll have that. You're free to come and go, to end our arrangement whenever you please. I'll have my solicitor draw up some papers. If either one of us chooses to end the merger, you'll be left with a stipend regardless."

Merger.

Her head was spinning. She knew she should feel triumphant—like she had just come into some grand inheritance. Any girl in her position would feel such a way. Mistress to a duke. Few would balk at such an arrangement. She was impoverished without even her virtue any longer and he was offering her a way out—salvation.

"I will think on it. It is a very fine offer for me," she murmured, wondering at how very hollow she felt inside.

He said nothing, but she felt his eyes on her, crawling and roving over the lines of her face.

The croak of frogs swelled around them as they stopped at the edge of the trees bordering the side of her house.

A light glowed from her sisters' upstairs bedchamber. They'd just retired for bed when she left last night.

There were two possibilities for the light on this early. Either Nora had stayed awake all night reading from one of her botany texts, or she woke early to resume reading. Charlotte had long ago learned to sleep in a lit room.

Nora had read all the books in their library multiple times, but she claimed that rereading the old material sometimes helped a new formula take shape in her mind. It pained Marian that she could not afford to buy any new books for Nora. Such a simple pleasure had become a luxury they could not afford.

"Someone is awake?" he remarked.

"My youngest sister. She is quite the academic. She reads a great deal of botany texts in her quest to invent new tonics and medicines."

"Impressive . . . and quite the unique pastime for a young lady."

She nodded. "It comes from working so closely with Papa."

"Ah. I see."

She shivered, suddenly feeling the chill on the air. "She'll likely ruin her eyes reading by candlelight." Hopefully, Nora, so engrossed in her reading, would not hear Marian entering the house. "I should go."

She shifted in her boots where she stood, feeling awkward.

His hand reached for her. She braced herself for the contact. He brushed a thumb down her cheek. She leaned into the touch and then he pulled his hand away. It was gone as soon as it started.

She stepped back, feeling foolish. After their night together one would think she had had her fill.

"Good night, Miss Langley."

Miss Langley. So formal. So proper. So very strange, all things considered.

"I-I will . . ."

"Consider it," he finished for her, his voice faintly mocking.

He thought she was being foolish not to immediately accept. Perhaps she was. Perhaps there really was no choice but this now. Perhaps she was just deluding herself into thinking otherwise.

"Good night," she murmured and turned for her home. She felt his stare on her back as she made her way up to the front gate, and she resisted the urge to look behind her.

She felt his stare until she rounded the house, stopping at the kitchen door. She fetched the key she hid beneath a rock. They never used to lock their doors. Since Papa's death and since they had so many angry creditors, they had begun.

She put the rock back in place and straightened. Key in hand, she fumbled in the dark, trying to insert it in the lock.

Snap.

She spun around, peering into the night, expecting to see the duke behind her. She may have told him not to walk her to her door, but he had never been one to follow her dictates.

She searched for a few moments, scanning her surroundings, attempting to make out any suspicious shapes in the darkness.

He wasn't there. No one was.

It must have been a rabbit scurrying about, deciding to make a foray into their paltry garden. Nora kept most of her herbs inside at night where it was safe, carting them in and out every day.

Marian lingered before the door, hesitating, searching the night.

Another twig cracked and she jerked.

"Hello?" she whispered loudly, hoping Nora couldn't hear her from her room on the other side of the house.

Silence met her anxious query. Even the bullfrogs fell quiet.

"Nathaniel?" Her voice trembled on the air, betraying the fact that she was a little frightened and a little certain that someone was out there. Someone not a rabbit.

Heart hammering, she whirled around and unlocked the door, trying not to panic because her back was turned on whatever—whoever—was out there.

Then she was inside. She locked the door and sagged against it with a ragged breath.

She waited several more beats, marveling that it was just slightly less chilly inside. She rubbed at her arms beneath her cloak. As her goose bumps receded, common sense returned.

No one was out there. It was her fervent imagination, seeing things where they were not. It's what came from sneaking about and conducting life-ruinous liaisons.

Liaisons with the duke might be ruinous, she reminded herself, but they could also be the thing that saved her family.

Sighing, she unwrapped her scarf several times from around her throat and proceeded through the darkened kitchen, mindful to keep her steps soft so she did not alert the girls.

She didn't need a light to reveal her way up the stairs to her chamber. She stealthily let herself in her room and moved to her window. She peered out the curtains, her gaze landing on the tree line where she stood moments before with the duke.

Even in the dark she could see no one stood there now. He was gone.

Turning away from the window, she stripped out of her clothes. She could get a quick nap before facing the world.

Once under the covers, she stared straight ahead into the dark.

And considered his offer as she said she would. She played his words over and over in her mind until the full light of dawn crept in between her curtains. There would be no nap.

With the morning light came an awakening of sorts.

A realization that she didn't have a choice. But then, she'd always known that. From the moment he'd shocked her with his proposition, her heart sang with the knowledge that she could agree.

There didn't have to be others. There could be just him.

Chapter 18

A scream wrenched Marian from sleep.

She blinked and looked around, taking in the bright light streaming through the crack in her curtains.

She last remembered dozing off at dawn, telling herself she would nap for a mere hour or two and then face the day. She'd underestimated how taxing a night of copulation could be. She winced. *Copulation* didn't sound right, but neither could she allow herself to call her activity with the duke *lovemaking*.

It must be well past morning now, and from the sound of it, someone was being murdered in her house.

She jumped from bed, grabbed her robe from

the chair where she'd tossed it at some point, and rushed from her room, her heart a wild drum against her ribs.

In the back of her mind lurked the fear that one of their many creditors had come calling and was taking their due out of one of her sisters. Bitterness coated her mouth as she skidded to a stop in the kitchen, her loosened plait bouncing over her shoulder.

Her gaze shot to her sisters. Neither one appeared injured. They were dressed for the day—naturally, as it was afternoon. Both were fresh in one of Marian's made-over dresses.

"What—"

Nora dug inside a crate atop the worktable and lifted out several leather-bound books. Marian swept her gaze about the kitchen, noticing then that there were other crates—several crates—and sacks and jugs and baskets.

"Look!" Nora cried, her eyes glowing as she examined the books. "Botany and horticulture books! It's better than any birthday I've ever had!"

Marian shook her head in bewilderment. "I don't understand. Where did you get—"

"Apricot jam!" Charlotte brandished several jars from one basket. Still peering inside, she exclaimed further. "Pickles! Biscuits!"

"Fresh bread!" Nora unwound twine from a package to reveal a loaf of gold-crusted bread.

She dove for one of the jars of apricots, clearly intent on devouring the delicious-looking bread with jam right then.

Charlotte continued rummaging inside a basket, digging among more undoubtedly excellent and extravagant supplies. "Figs and cherries!" She brought the precious fruit to her nose and inhaled deeply before moving on to another basket.

Marian shook her head, battling her joy at the sight of such bounty.

She knew. Of course, she knew who had sent all of this, and her heart swelled inside her chest.

He did this. The food. The books for her sister. All the things.

"Who could've sent us all this?" Charlotte asked as though she sensed Marian's thoughts, but of course, she didn't know the answer. She couldn't have any idea. Not the slightest notion.

"And look!" Nora mumbled around a mouthful of food as she pointed toward the door. There sat crates of coal for their empty grates. "And outside the lads stacked firewood *this* high." She motioned to her chin.

"Lads?" Marian looked sharply at Nora.

"Yes." She nodded. "They brought everything."

"Who were these lads?" Marian asked carefully.

Hopefully no one recognizable. No one her sisters might see around Brambledon.

"I didn't know them and they wouldn't say who sent all of this!" Nora swept a hand to encompass all the goods and supplies. "They were annoyingly tight-lipped and ignored all my inquiries."

"Who did this?" Awe hummed in Charlotte's voice. "Such generosity . . . who do we know that is capable . . ." She stopped, eyeing their bounty again before her gaze snapped back to Marian. "Lady Clara!"

"Clara?" Marian echoed.

"Of course!" Nora slapped her side. "Your former employer! She is as rich as Croesus and she favored you greatly, Marian. She would not stand by and leave you to perish in miserable penury." She tore off a hunk of bread and stuffed half of it into her mouth while she wrangled to open the jar of apricots.

True. Clara would want to help. If Marian would beg of it, which she never would do. Clara *would* help if she knew how dire their situation, but Marian had not divulged that.

Marian could not bring herself to apprise Clara of her family's grim situation. She had kept that particular truth to herself in all the letters they had exchanged this past year.

Marian could not lower herself to accept the charity of her well-placed former charge. Not when *she* had the power to control her own fate.

Some might consider selling her body unsavory, but what was a loveless marriage to the likes of Mr. Lawrence if not unsavory?

And at the end of every night, she still possessed her freedom. She could go home to her own bed and not have to share it with any man she did not wish to be bound to.

"Marian? Is that it? Did Clara send all of this?" Charlotte looked at her expectantly, waiting for an answer.

It took Marian a moment to find her voice. Lying had never come easily to her. Especially to her sisters. She donned a wobbly smile. "Yes. Yes," she agreed. "It was Clara."

Best they think *that* than the truth—that Marian's lover had sent them these many gifts as an advance on services yet rendered. Heat fired her cheeks as she thought of those services to come. Those delicious and wicked services.

Her sisters could never fathom how completely and irrevocably Marian had embraced her ruination.

She alone knew.

Only she alone could ever know.

SHE KEPT HER appointment with Annabel. Fortunately it was later in the afternoon as she had slept most of the day away.

Keeping her lessons with the young ladies of Brambledon seemed prudent if not a bit audacious considering her secret occupation.

Even if she was now—or soon would be—a kept woman, it would behoove her to keep up the appearance of a woman in need of employment.

There would certainly be talk once they repaid all their creditors, but Marian did not fool herself. Nora could not keep a secret if her life depended upon it. She would soon have it bandied about the village that Clara, sister to the Duke of Autenberry, had come to their aid.

Nora would relish sharing that information, and Marian couldn't blame her. Certain members of the community, people they had considered friends, had treated them abominably once Papa died and they fell into debt. She supposed it had been a test. Now they knew their true friends.

Upon reaching her house, she assured herself that her sisters were still out and she went directly to the barn, intent on saddling Bessie and calling on Nathaniel whilst her sisters were gone from home and busy about their day.

She would give him her answer as promised . . . and her thanks for his generosity. Then she assumed there would be particulars to be discussed. They were entering into an arrangement. A business arrangement. She needed to approach it that way and not with emotion.

She hefted the saddle from its stand and threw it over Bessie's back with a grunt.

"Need some help with that?"

She spun around with a gasp. "Your Grace? I m-mean, Nathaniel." Her gaze darted around the barn. "What are you doing here?"

"You said you would have an answer for me by today."

"Did I say . . . *today*?"

He shrugged. "I thought you might know your mind by now."

His expression was impassive, hardly the image of an anxious man, and yet he was here, less than twenty-four hours since she had last seen him.

He walked through the open door of the stall at a strolling pace, like a lazy jungle cat in no rush.

"Well, I was, in fact, just coming to see you."

"I've saved you a trip, then, have I not?" He stopped and leaned a shoulder against the wood plank wall of the stall.

She moistened her lips nervously, and wondered how it was that this man could still set her so much on edge. After everything they had done, after the shockingly intimate things that had transpired between them, there was not ease. He could still make her cheeks warm and her stomach quiver and her breath catch.

"I agree to your proposition."

He smiled slowly. "Good."

She swallowed. "Shall we discuss the terms of the relationship?"

"I will have my solicitor draw up the papers."

"Papers?" He had mentioned papers before, but until now she had never given it much thought. She had not been ready to consider it before.

She was ready now.

"Yes. A contract. We need no misunderstandings going into this arrangement. I think you shall find the terms favorable, but of course you may feel free to make any changes. It's doubtful I'll have any objections."

She angled her head. "How do you know? What if I have an unreasonable request? You trust me that much?"

"You're not the greedy sort."

She released a short laugh tinged with nervousness. "You hardly know me well enough to say that."

"I think I have an adequate idea of who you are." He approached and she backed up, moving away from Bessie . . . away from him. And yet he followed.

She thrust out her chin. "And who am I?"

"A woman who isn't afraid to break the rules. Who is practical and yet not ashamed to give in to her most innate needs."

She supposed that was accurate, but it wasn't a full description of her. It wasn't everything.

He could never know everything about her. He could not understand the desperation she lived under—the unrelenting threat, the fear of tomorrow.

But then, none of that mattered. This wasn't about knowing each other. This wasn't about closeness.

It was an arrangement grounded in the physical. Not the emotional.

It was only fortunate that she happened to enjoy being with him physically. He heated her blood and reduced her bones to hot pudding.

She hadn't counted on that.

She'd told herself she would tolerate men using her body. She'd learn to tolerate it. She'd told herself it wasn't necessary to enjoy it, only to stomach it.

But with Warrington she didn't feel used. She didn't have to stomach his touch.

She stopped backing away, colliding gently with the far wall.

He stopped before her. "Shall we make it official and seal our agreement, then?"

A small shiver rolled through her at the intent way he looked at her.

"Seal it, how?"

"The only way one would christen an agreement like ours."

She held perfectly still as his meaning sank in.

"Is this another lesson?" she whispered.

"Lessons," he echoed, clearly amused. "Are you still calling them that?"

Wasn't that what they were? Only now the lessons would only be for this man. She would learn everything that pleased him.

He would show her what pleased him, and that prospect excited her. Desire pooled heavily in her stomach because she knew she'd reap the pleasure, too.

So why was there still a hovering unease? A fluttering in her belly that wasn't solely about desire?

His hand landed on her hip, gathering a fistful of the fabric in his grip. "This isn't so much a lesson . . . as a transactional gesture."

"Like a handshake," she murmured as his body pressed flush to hers.

"Yes. Except not a handshake. Something better than that," he said the moment before his mouth came over hers, stealing her breath.

She melted between his body and the wood slats.

This was definitely better than a handshake.

He was a great wall radiating heat, singeing her all the way through her garments.

He wrapped one arm around her waist, lifting her to her toes, bringing her mouth nearer if not quite level to his. His mouth consumed her, lips, teeth and tongue all working to devour hers.

Distantly, over the roar of blood in her ears, she heard Bessie nicker, but Marian clung to him, her fingers clawing deep into his shoulders.

The yearning was back—it had never gone away—but she'd done an admirable job keeping it in check. That savage need from last night broke free now and she kissed him back with ferocity.

When he suddenly broke away, she whimpered, her lips chasing after his. She opened her eyes dazedly.

He was staring directly at her face, looking much more clear-eyed. "Marian."

She blinked at his very solid pronunciation of her name. "Yes?"

"Someone is coming."

That woke her from her passion-clouded fog. "Wh-what?" She shoved past him and took several stumbling steps toward the stall door.

A quick peek out revealed no one in the center passageway, and she heard what Nate must have heard.

"Marian!" Nora called out.

"My sister," Marian hissed. "She's coming! She can't see you here." Marian rotated in a quick circle, glancing all around the stall as though she might find a hiding spot.

"I'm too old to play hiding games."

Her gaze snapped to his face and she accused, "You also promised me discretion."

He inclined his head in grudging acknowledgment. "That I did. So what do you suggest I do, then? She no doubt saw my horse. How will you explain that?"

"Oh." Her shoulders slumped. She had forgotten.

"Marian!"

The voice was closer now. Nora would be upon her any moment.

Sucking in a breath, Marian emerged from the stall with a cheery expression. "Hello, there, Nora."

"Oh, Marian! There you are. I wanted to ask you if I could have Jillian and Henrietta over for tea tomorrow. One of those packages is fairly swimming with the most splendid Indian tea, and there are biscuits—" She stopped abruptly, her eyes drifting just beyond Marian's shoulder. "Oh, hello, there, sir." She turned a wide questioning stare to Marian.

"Nora, allow me to introduce you to the Duke of Warrington." She waved at him—the man, her lover. Her cheeks burned with the secret knowledge. "Your Grace, this is my sister, Miss Eleanor Langley."

He executed a smart bow. "Miss Langley."

Her sister blushed prettily and dipped into an awkward curtsy. "Your Grace." She looked several times back and forth between them, clearly trying to figure out what was happening.

Of course, everything she knew about the duke, everything she had heard, rumors all, were spinning through her mind. Marian fought down a wince and hoped Nora restrained her typical runaway tongue. "And what brings you to our humble"—she eyed their surroundings—"barn?"

"Ahhh—" Nate glanced around as though the answer would suddenly appear before him.

If it weren't such an awkward and desperate situation, Marian might have laughed. Except it was not good.

None of this was good.

Nora was far too clever. Any moment now it would occur to her why the duke was here . . . and then she would take it even one step further and conclude who, in truth, had sent them all the lovely supplies.

Nate. Nate had sent them everything that made life bearable. Everything they had been missing. He'd given them all those fine things. Her heart squeezed anew. He hadn't needed to do that. When he sent them those supplies, he had not even known whether she would agree to be his mistress, but he had done it because he knew it would help them.

He shifted one step over and gave Bessie a pat. "I heard you might be interested in selling this old nag here."

Marian exhaled at his quick thinking.

"Bessie!" Nora cried out in horror, stepping forward and running a hand through the mare's gray-streaked mane. "Bessie is *not* a nag." She turned a quick glare on the duke, not to be daunted by his title, his wealth or his power. The man had just announced himself an enemy as far as Nora was concerned.

Poor girl. She probably thought Marian had broken down and decided to sell Bessie to help with their debts.

Marian intervened before Nora did something rash, like kick him in the shin. "Yes, indeed. I was just correcting His Grace on that misapprehension and explaining that he was misinformed. We are not interested in selling Bessie."

"Who told you this?" Nora scowled, clearly intent on finding the culprit and wringing their neck. She'd do it, too. Marian had no doubt.

The duke looked unperturbed as he avoided Nora's question. "Yes. Quite so. My mistake. I stand corrected."

Marian pasted a smile on her face and nodded. "See now. Everything is fine, Nora."

Nora gave a single nod, appearing mollified. Even so, she did not move from Bessie's side. She

continued to stroke her nose while glaring re-
proachfully at the duke.

Marian cleared her throat. "Your Grace, thank
you for your inquiry. May I escort you out?" She
gestured to the door of the stall.

He gave a perfunctory nod and followed her
from the stall.

They walked side by side, he with his hands
clasped behind his back.

"That was smart thinking on your part," she
murmured.

"I've been known to be resourceful a time or
two."

"I imagine at times you have." No need to
inflate his ego further by letting him know she
thought him quite intelligent.

They stopped before his horse, a beautiful
creature that would make one wonder why he
was interested in dear old Bessie. Best, then, that
her sister remain in the barn and not think about
that too much.

Nate turned to face her, his expression and
voice neutral as he asked, "When can I see you
again? It might take me a day or two to have the
papers drawn up, but I'd like to see you before
then. Tonight."

His eyes conveyed anything but neutrality.
That dark stare crawled over her face, stealing her
breath and sending flutters rioting through her.

"I think I can manage that."

She fought to remain composed . . . to not let the promise of pleasure with him totally dazzle her.

They were lovers. That did not mean they were *in* love.

This was still business and she didn't need to act giddy over the prospect of being with him.

"I will wait for you at the edge of the wood." He inclined his head in the direction of which he spoke, where they usually dismounted from their horses. "I'll have the cottage ready, too. We will go there."

The cottage. The place that was to be theirs.

Her heart warmed and squeezed a little at that, and she sighed at the foolish reaction. Clearly *not* acting giddy would be a challenge.

"I will meet you half past nine." There. Her voice sounded strong and even.

He smiled slowly, deepening the twin brackets on either side of his face and taking him from handsome to irresistible. "Very good. I will see you then."

For a moment he leaned in as though he would kiss her, but then he stopped, catching himself. His gaze drifted over her shoulder.

She turned and looked. Her sister had emerged from the barn.

Nora studied them, still looking rather distrustfully at Nate.

Marian turned back and watched as Nate swung up into the saddle. She shielded her eyes with a hand, admiring him, so strong and impressive limned in the afternoon light.

"I don't think your sister likes me very much," he murmured for her ears alone.

"That might have something to do with the story you fabricated about buying Bessie."

His eyes glinted with amusement. "Would you rather we tell her the truth?"

She snorted and choked back a laugh. That she had agreed to become the duke's mistress? No. She would keep that to herself for all her days. She would take that to the grave.

"I am happy to keep her in the dark."

She would do everything to keep Nora growing up believing in fairy tales. She was only sixteen. She shouldn't have to give up on dreams with the intrusion of adulthood realities. She was still a child. Children should be children for as long as possible.

Marian wanted Nora to have a normal upbringing—the same cosseted existence Marian had before Papa died. Nora deserved that. She would have it. Marian would see to it.

Inclining his head, the duke said in a voice loud

enough for her sister to hear, "Good day, Miss Langley."

"Good day," Marian echoed as he turned his mount and rode from her home.

"Awful man," Nora remarked as she approached. "Handsome or not, he's a wretched fellow. Dukes," she grumbled. "However did you abide them? Arrogant peacocks. Marching about like they can buy anything they wish."

"He was simply inquiring," Marian chided gently.

"Humph." Nora crossed her arms. "Well, now he is clear on the matter that we are *not* selling Bessie. We should not have to see him again."

Marian remained outside while her sister walked inside the house, no doubt eager to return to their stockpile of goodies. She had a tea to prepare for, after all.

Marian lifted her face to a breeze as her sister's words rolled through her mind. *Buy anything they wish . . .*

Even Marian.

She winced and gave herself a mental slap. Of course it wasn't that way. She had offered herself to him. She had practically begged him to take her and quite enjoyed herself in the process.

His offer of protection had been unexpected but quite the coup. She should not feel guilty or sordid.

This arrangement was better than her plan to sell herself to various men—and it would solve their financial troubles.

It was a transaction *she* had initiated. He was her client, but she was the proprietor.

She was in control. She would remain in control.

Nothing would go wrong.

Chapter 19

Marian and her sisters had just finished washing up the dinner dishes when a knock sounded on the door.

"Who could that be?" Charlotte placed a bowl in the cupboard.

Marian tensed. There were a number of people it could be. Any number of creditors, ever clamoring for payment.

At least this time she would mean it when she promised them she would soon pay them. Marian only hoped they accepted her assurance and extended her a little more time. She was certain the topic of her outstanding debts could be broached this very evening when she met with Nate.

She sighed and dropped a drying linen on the kitchen table. "I'll answer that." She gave each of her sisters a pointed look, conveying they should stay put. "Wait here. This won't take long."

She left them in the kitchen and moved to the front door. She was beset with mixed emotions upon opening the door and seeing the man on the other side.

"Mr. Lawrence," she greeted. At least he wasn't a creditor. There was that. And yet he did happen to be a repugnant man intent on wooing her despite all of her protests and many rejections. She wondered about the entitlement of men who did not believe a woman could hold dominion over her own life. Why must an independent woman offend them? Could such a man ever be reasoned with?

He doffed his hat and beamed at her, his smile doing nothing to help settle the contents of her stomach. They'd had a marvelous dinner tonight—thanks to Nate. It would be a shame to lose it.

"Miss Langley, good evening. Might I have a word with you?"

She did not even bother to suppress her cringe. "It is very late, Mr. Lawrence." She snuck a glance over her shoulder before looking back at him. "We were just readying to retire for the night."

That smile of his stretched, and there was

something in it, something that curdled the blood in her veins. "Oh, but it's important. You will want to hear this."

She clung to the edge of the door for a moment before relenting and stepping away. With a sigh, she motioned him into the parlor. He was doubtlessly here with yet another proposal. Days had passed since the last one. He probably thought her desperation all the more acute. He would have no notion that her circumstances had greatly improved.

She would do as she had always done and decline his offer and send him on his way.

Her sisters stepped into their small foyer, obviously curious as to the identity of their visitor. At the sight of him Nora looked visibly disgusted.

"Mr. Lawrence would like a word with me," Marian said evenly.

Her sisters exchanged knowing glances. She tried to convey that everything was fine with a look to each of them.

Charlotte was the first to find her voice and was ever polite as always. "Good evening, Mr. Lawrence."

"Miss Charlotte. Miss Eleanor." He nodded to each of them before his gaze fastened once again on Marian.

Nora only managed a grunt of acknowledgment. She was never one to disguise her true feelings, a definite challenge when navigating social circles, which was a problem, because at the age of sixteen years she was not even officially out in Society. Her exposure to Society would only increase over the next few years.

Not that Nora cared. Marian cared, though. She worried. She'd seen enough of the world to know that outspoken females were ill abided.

Marian led him into the parlor and shut the double doors only partway, leaving them partially ajar for propriety's sake.

"You may want to close the doors fully." He nodded at the double doors. "You wouldn't want our conversation overheard."

She froze, staring at him for a long moment, everything inside her revolting in alarm.

Just the same, she commanded her limbs to move and oblige him, closing the doors fully with a click. It was not above her sisters, especially Nora, to eavesdrop.

Marian clutched the latch in both hands and fell backward against the door as though she needed the support for whatever was to come.

Now she knew what that *something* was in his smile. It was sinister. Pure devious intent.

She couldn't move. Her fingers went numb where they clutched onto the door latch, but she needed that solidness.

He continued to smile that infernal smile at

her as he moved deeper into the room. He circled an armchair before deciding to sink down into it.

"What can I do for you, Mr. Lawrence?"

"I think we are well past the formalities . . . Marian. Call me Hiram."

Never. His name stuck in her throat. Using it implied a familiarity between them that she refused to accept.

Just the sound of her name on his lips felt wrong . . . as wrong as an epithet muttered from him. It simply wasn't natural or wanted.

He sat in Papa's favorite chair as though he belonged there, and she had to fight down the impulse to ask him to remove himself. He splayed a hand over the generous bulge of his stomach, his beringed fingers winking over the glittering brocade of his vest.

"I've been looking forward to this moment."

She stared at him uncomprehendingly, moistening her lips with a quick dart of her tongue. "Have you?"

She was afraid suddenly—afraid to learn, to know, what he was about. His manner told her he felt he had gained the upper hand, and that worried her a great deal.

"Oh, indeed," he said with avid relish. "To have you at my complete mercy is something I have imagined for quite some time."

His gaze slid thoroughly over her, and to her

horror his hand inched down his stomach, drawing ever nearer to his crotch. He stopped just short of touching himself, but she could see that he was aroused. His manhood strained against the front of his britches.

"You go too far, sir," she declared, battling her outrage.

"Oh, I shall go even further with you, Marian."

She was heartily glad to be so close to the door. She turned quickly, ready to bolt when his voice stopped her.

"How long have you been the Duke of Warrington's whore?"

She turned slowly, feeling trapped in a dream—in a nightmare from which she could not awake. "Pardon me?"

"You heard me, love."

"I am certain I misunderstood."

"Shall I repeat myself? I asked you: How long have you been fucking the Duke of Warrington?"

She flinched. "You have no proof."

"Oh, I think people will believe me. It's human nature. We like to believe the worst of others. In your case, you've already fallen so low. All of Brambledon will relish to know you've become just another one of the duke's whores now."

"I want you to leave."

He arched an eyebrow. "Do you really want me to do that? Because if I leave now, I vow to you it will take no less than an hour for the entire village to know you for a whore."

She couldn't breathe. Her chest felt too tight, as though a giant ball were crushing it. "What do you want?"

"Why, what I've always wanted. You." He considered her for a moment, his top lip curling in a sneer. "I confess it disappoints me you will no longer be a maid. I fantasized about you beneath me, busting you for the first time."

She was going to be ill. Right here all over the parlor rug. She pressed her hand to her chest and tried to draw breath. The air escaped her in wheezing pants.

"Oh, don't be so dramatic. Calm yourself. You've already had a man. What's another? At least I will be your husband. I'll make you my wife, not my whore. Which is more than can be said for that bloody duke up on the hill. You should thank me."

The chair creaked as he lifted his weight up and approached her. She backed as far into the door as she could go. Which was not far enough. Nothing would ever be far enough from him, she realized.

He stopped directly before her, his stomach brushing the front of her gown. It was the only contact, but enough to make her skin crawl.

"It won't be so bad," he murmured in a voice

reeking of onions and stale ale. "Not when you consider the alternative." His eyes glinted with malice. "Deny me, spurn me, and I will ruin you. I will ruin your entire family, your sisters, your brother . . . They will all bear the taint of *you*. No man will ever have you for a wife. The entire realm will know that you are naught but a whore and the only way you and those lovely sisters of yours will be able to put food on the table is working on your backs. Imagine that . . . Nora so young and nubile and Charlotte so delicate and lovely. How well do you think they will fare against the lusts of men? Will they break easily, you think?"

She heard his awful words and fought against a surge of bile.

She saw the truth of what he said in his eyes. He would see every bit of his threat come to reality. He would ruin her. Ruin her innocent sisters.

He would ruin them all.

She could perhaps sacrifice herself, but not her sisters and brother. She could not let that happen. They were her family. All she had left.

Briefly, she considered going to Nate for help. But it wouldn't matter. She and her family would be ruined. Lawrence would make good on his threats and talk. He'd shout it to all and sundry. As a duke, the scandal would not affect Nate, but Marian and her sisters, her brother? Their good name would be lost. Their reputations in the gutter.

Nate's face flashed across her mind—so real, so clear. For a moment it felt as though he were standing before her—a flesh and blood man. As though she could reach out and touch him.

But it wasn't real. He wasn't real. He would never be hers.

She lifted her chin. "Very well. What do I need to do?"

"It's a pleasure to see you so accommodating at last. I have longed for this moment. The moment you finally agree to be my wife."

"You truly *still* want to marry me?" Disbelief vibrated in her voice. He'd said that moments before, but she'd told herself she must have misunderstood. Or perhaps he had been mocking her.

She had hoped she misunderstood.

She had hoped he'd given up on that idea for good, but she should know better than to hope. There was no hope with this man. Even if he didn't want to marry her, his intentions were anything but pure. He was the crusher of dreams, the destroyer of hope.

"Of course I do. For years I watched you stroll down the streets of Brambledon on the arm of your father. So proud and haughty, every member of your family. Everyone in this town reveres you, even now when you are penniless. How do you think you've lasted so long? For over a year you've been up to your neck in debt. Were it I, I'd be in Newgate already. I'm tolerated because of my money. Without it, I'd be nothing," he sputtered in outrage, the seeming injustice angering him. "Now you will be my wife. You will be my prize and bring me that final respect."

He reached out and trailed a finger down her cheek. She held still and managed not to shrink away. Not to retch. She would have to grow accustomed to his touch.

She had no choice.

Chapter 20

I just don't understand. How can you marry him?" Nora paced up and down the parlor. She had been haranguing Marian for the last hour, ever since they returned together from town, where they had met with the vicar to see about the posting of the banns. When she informed them of her decision last night, they had been shocked into silence. Today they found their voices.

Marian sat on the sofa beside Charlotte, hands laced tightly together in her lap.

Marian had told her sisters they didn't need to accompany her and Mr. Lawrence, but they had insisted.

They had accompanied her, sulking silently,

glaring at Marian and Mr. Lawrence as though they couldn't decide who angered them more.

"Marian," Charlotte said in her gentle way. "You said you would never marry Mr. Lawrence. I don't understand what has changed."

Everything. Everything had changed.

Marian had been playing a game—a game for her life, her freedom.

And she had lost it.

Marian had allowed Mr. Lawrence to do all the talking today. She couldn't summon much speech. She felt dazed, ill.

Her future with Mr. Lawrence flashed through her mind and she had to fight down bile. The only thing that sustained her was the knowledge that her sisters would be cared for—her sisters could reclaim their lives at long last.

"Marian! Say something."

She lifted her gaze from her lap to Nora. "I'm saving us."

Emotion rippled across Nora's face. "You're doing this for us?" She pounded her chest.

"We don't want you to do this for us. Phillip would never want that, either," Charlotte whispered beside her, her voice small and choked with tears. "We will never be happy if we cost you this."

Nora nodded, the color bright in her face. "The price is too high!"

"I'm not doing anything so unreasonable. Women marry for gain all the time."

"There has to be another way," Charlotte insisted. "He's . . . he's *Mr. Lawrence*."

She said the name as if it was the most wretched thing, and even though she knew marrying him was horrible, Marian fixed her features into an expression of serenity.

Her sisters were a different breed of female. Papa had raised them to believe they were destined to be more than a man's wife, *more* than chattel. Never were they told they *had* to marry. Marriage was a choice, an option for them should they find a gentleman they desired.

Now Marian realized this kind of idealism was reserved for only a privileged class of female. She did not belong to that class.

"We've tried. For over a year." She reached a hand to cover Charlotte's. "He has agreed to reinstate your dowry. You can marry William now."

"You think the ol' Pembroke will let his son marry Charlotte?" Nora asked. "You're marrying a *tradesman*!"

"A very wealthy tradesman," Marian reminded. "I think Pembroke can be persuaded, especially as his son is still in love with Charlotte."

Charlotte was close to tears now. "You think I will be happy knowing I cost you—"

"You cost me nothing," Marian snapped. "If I

blame you, then I might as well blame Papa for failing to provide for us beyond his death. But I don't. I don't blame him. This is simply our situation and I'm getting us out of it, and I'll not hear another word on the matter." She finished rather breathlessly, slicing a hand through the air.

With a huff of breath, she rose to her feet and marched toward the small decanter of brandy Papa had kept in the parlor.

Her sisters watched agape as she poured herself a glass and downed it.

"I'm doing this and you two"—she wagged a finger at both of them in warning—"are going to be blasted happy. You're not going to object or be rude. You will be supportive. Understood?"

They exchanged uncertain glances.

"Yes, Marian," Charlotte dutifully agreed.

Nora was slower to respond. "Fine." She crossed her arms over her chest resentfully, hardly the image of compliance.

Marian cocked her head in continued warning, sending her the same threatening glance she had used when Nora was a naughty child. "Eleanor." It felt necessary to use her full name in this.

"Oh, very well." She dropped her arms in a motion of defeat. "I'll be supportive."

Marian stared at her a moment longer and then returned to the decanter. Pushing aside her lingering suspicion that Nora was going to be anything but supportive, she poured herself another drink.

Her sisters studied her like she was some manner of spectacle on Drury Lane as she drank from the glass.

Charlotte tsked. "Marian. You don't drink."

"There are a great many things you don't know about me," Marian muttered.

Gathering up the decanter and glass, she marched past them and fled to her own bedchamber.

SHE DIDN'T MEET him that night.

Nate waited for over an hour, pacing anxiously, peering into the night, waiting for her to emerge out of the ever-growing darkness.

When it became clear to him she was not coming, he had to stop himself from riding to her house. He envisioned himself climbing his way up to her bedroom window. It was extreme . . . but then, so was his need for her.

He talked himself out of it, of course. There had been enough rashness on his part when it came to Marian. She had asked for discretion. He'd promised to give her that. If she couldn't meet him, there was a good reason. He'd wait.

Even if he spent most of the night tossing and turning and suffering an aching cock.

He exercised restraint.

Upon waking, he took a morning ride through the brisk country air. Following that, he rang for a bath. He was in no hurry. He suspected he would not see her until tonight. That would be the way of it. They would only meet after dark. The nights would be theirs.

He dressed himself for the day in his usual dark breeches, black vest and jacket.

It was almost noon before he broke his fast. He did so overlooking the gardens, browsing the paper, sipping his coffee and eating with gusto.

The rain had finally stopped and he lifted his head to admire the surfeit of green spread before him. Sometimes he found himself glancing to the empty chair across from him and wondering what it would be like if Marian was here with him. Would she read the paper, too? Was she a follower of the scandal rags? Or would she prefer conversation in the morning?

He thought he would like that. Talking to her was always diverting. Never boring.

He would have to see that they had a comfortable place to dine at the cottage. Their cottage. Of course, they could eat in bed. He imagined they would be doing most things there.

Smiling to himself, he cut into another kipper, humming lightly.

Pearson strode into the room. "Ah. There you

are." His gaze swept the table. "Looks to be a fine repast." He bent and snatched a kipper for himself.

"Help yourself," he said as Pearson lowered himself into the seat across from him. "Any word yet from Holleman?" Nate asked. His solicitor should be here at any time.

"I would expect him to arrive by the end of the day." Pearson looked at him expectantly as though he would elaborate on why he had sent for his solicitor in the first place.

But he didn't. He held silent, biting into his jam-lathered toast. Pearson would likely find out eventually. As his man of affairs, it would come out.

No matter how much he wished to keep this development to himself. Their arrangement was private. It was between him and Marian. He would involve his solicitor only for her protection, and he knew that Holleman was a professional. He would not share confidences. The man had been in his employ for some time. Nate knew he was too ethical to break his trust.

For now he held silent beneath Pearson's inquisitive gaze.

"I should really stop eating these, but they are delicious." Pearson selected another kipper from the platter between them. "I will be stuffed by the time I take tea with Allison."

"Ah, another afternoon in the village with your young lady."

"Actually I already ventured to the village this morning so one of the blacksmith's apprentices could have a look at Balthazar. I might as well have stayed at home, however."

"Why is that?"

"The man was hardly attentive. The entire village, in fact, was abuzz over the announcement of the blacksmith's betrothal."

"Eh. And that is so very newsworthy?"

"I think it is more the matter of *who* he is betrothed to."

"Oh?" Nate selected another piece of toast and began slathering it with jam.

"Yes. It happens to be someone you are acquainted with."

He ceased chewing, freezing, slow dread spreading through his chest.

Pearson continued, "I suppose it fortunate that your, er . . . association with her ended when it did, before anything really began. For the best. It prompted her to pursue a more traditional arrangement. Much better for her to be a wife to one man than a leman to another. Even if that man is you. Certainly you see that."

Nate very carefully leaned back in his chair and set his knife down upon the table. He sat composed even as a loud roar filled his ears.

"Miss Langley? You speak of Miss Langley?" As obvious as it seemed, he needed clarification. He needed there to be no doubt.

Pearson nodded, looking at him curiously.

Nate knew he was behaving oddly. Reacting strangely to news that should not have had any impact on him at all.

He didn't know what he felt precisely, but he felt.

He felt. Damn it.

And that was the crux of the matter. Problematic indeed.

He'd loved once. He had loved Mary Beth as a child and even as an adult. It had not been the grand passionate love he hoped for when he proposed at the tender age of twenty, but they could have lived all their lives together quite satisfactorily.

They could have had she not died just three years into their marriage.

Their relationship had never been very complicated. Mary Beth liked her clothes, her servants, iced biscuits, her cat. She liked Nate most of the time. Usually, she seemed to care for him. They never fought. As long as he did not place excessive demands on her, she was quite happy.

Again, it was not the marriage he had envisioned, but it was fine. Simple. Uncomplicated. And he had resigned himself to it.

This, with Marian, was complicated.

What he felt right now was complicated. The churning in his gut should not be present. He should not care that she had reneged on their arrangement. The arrangement had barely begun. No papers had been signed.

He'd had her. They had both enjoyed themselves. It was for the best.

He would never have to end things with her. She was doing that for him—for them both.

Chapter 21

Marian escaped her sisters and their incessant haranguing into the quiet of her chamber.

Nothing she said would satisfy them.

They couldn't fathom why she would agree to marry Lawrence, and the last thing she could do was admit the truth—to inform them that they were the reason. Her sisters and her brother. She was doing it expressly for them. *Because* of them. If she had only herself to worry about, she could have left Brambledon over a year ago and saw to her own well-being. However, she would not place that burden of responsibility and guilt on them.

She hadn't undressed yet—only taken the pins

from her hair and shaken the long tresses free—when a sudden banging erupted downstairs.

Voices and pounding feet soon added to the fray floating up from downstairs.

She hurried to her door and yanked it open just as those voices drew nearer—on the stairs, advancing.

"Marian!" Charlotte cried out, coming up the stairs. For once, it seemed, Nora, wherever she was, held silent.

Charlotte came into sight, her panicked gaze landing on Marian as she waved wildly behind her. "He forced his way inside, Marian!"

Her stomach sank.

"He who?" Marian demanded, even though she feared she already knew. It was Lawrence returning to assert himself. A shudder racked her because she knew if he chose to, there would be no resisting him—there was nothing she could do except submit to him.

Nate crested the second floor. His head emerged, followed by the rest of him. His dark eyes immediately found hers.

"Nate," she breathed.

He passed up Charlotte in a few strides and came to a stop before Marian.

His very solid chest lifted on an audible breath. From the periphery of her gaze, she spotted

Nora arriving to join them, her hands balled into fists as though preparing for a battle.

"Is it true?" he demanded, eyes still only for Marian.

He did not look pleased. Hot emotion raged in those eyes.

"What?" she asked even as she knew what he was asking.

"You're to marry. You've agreed to marry the blacksmith. Is that so? Is it true?" Something in his face urged her, compelled her, to refute this. He didn't want it to be true.

She didn't want it to be true, either. She wished she could tell him it was all a lie. A horrible rumor.

She longed for this not to be her life. Not her fate.

She stared back at him, ensnared, pinned by those dark eyes.

After some moments, she nodded. Her fate could not be denied. "It is true."

"You renege on our agreement, then?"

She flinched at his hard tone, but nodded anew. "I fear I must."

"What agreement?" Nora demanded, but Marian couldn't even bring herself to look at her. Not in this moment.

Not in the awfulness of this moment.

There would be unavoidable questions later.

She would contend with them then. Later she would tell her sisters what she must. Not the full sordid truth. They didn't need to know everything. She was entitled to some privacy.

"You never even drew up those papers," she reminded him.

"A formality."

"What is happening?" Nora cried.

Charlotte added her own bewildered voice to the uncomfortable situation. "Marian! Please explain."

Marian shifted uncomfortably, wishing this wasn't so hard. Wishing he wasn't here. Wishing she didn't have to see him again. Lawrence was bad enough, but being face-to-face with Nate again made her eyes burn with the threat of tears.

She shrugged and attempted to be dismissive—to get him to spare her and leave. "We scarcely began—"

He moved quickly then, his hands seizing onto her arms, pulling her close, hauling her to him.

"Don't do that. Don't act like we didn't have anything." He kissed her then. Deep and punishing, right in front of her sisters. Even over the sounds of their gasps, she melted into Nate like she did every time he touched her. Even as mortified as she was to have an audience, she was helpless to resist him.

When he came up for air, she shoved him hard

with both hands and fell back against the corridor wall. "We can't do this. Lawrence knows about us. He will see me ruined unless I marry him."

He sprang closer, his face in hers, his hands flattening on the wall on either side of her head. "Why didn't you tell me? Why didn't you come to me?"

"Because you can't fix this. Not even you can make it right."

"Don't do this." His deep voice vibrated through her.

She drank in the beauty of his face and ached for it—for him. For what could never be. "He will destroy us. I have to do this," she whispered.

He bowed his head, his breathing ragged. When he lifted his gaze, his brightly dark eyes settled on her with frightening intensity. "Marry me."

She knew she heard him correctly because her sisters exclaimed excitedly. One of them even clapped.

"You don't mean that," she said evenly. "You said you never wanted to marry again."

"It's not something a man says lightly," he quickly returned.

She stared at him for a long moment, digesting this. It was tempting. Except she knew he didn't mean it. It was momentary—this pity. This wild compulsion that stemmed from who knew what or why.

He would regret it.

Tomorrow he would wake and wonder how to get himself out of a vastly unsuitable marriage to the likes of her. She couldn't bear that.

She couldn't do it.

"No," she said in a small voice, closing her eyes in a pained blink. "That would be a mistake we would both come to regret."

"Marian!" Charlotte's tone rang with reprimand.

"He's better than Mr. Lawrence!" Nora added.

Marian shuddered at the mention of Mr. Lawrence, and a weak part of her wished for Nate to say the right words, to persuade her—to make this something she could agree to. Something she could convince herself was right.

"You'll not do this," he proclaimed, with a swift shake of his head. "I won't let you."

Before she could speak to refute that, he grabbed her and flung her over his shoulder.

"Nate!" Hanging upside down, she rained fists on his back.

His deep voice rumbled through her. "Would one of you pack her some garments? Anything she might need for a few days?"

She spied Nora rush past them into her room eagerly. "Nora!" she cried in reproach. The traitor!

"He's better than Lawrence!" Nora called again, apparently her newfound mantra and what she would cling to.

Marian twisted around to glare at him. "What are you doing? Where are you taking me?"

He ignored her and spoke to a gaping Charlotte. "Spread the word about the village. Let everyone know that your sister has eloped with the Duke of Warrington."

THEY JOURNEYED NORTH in silence. Not a word beyond the perfunctory: *Are you hungry? Watch out for that puddle. This way to the carriage.*

Marian held silent their entire journey. Not a word passed between them in the carriage. Not when they stopped to change horses. Not when they stopped overnight halfway to Gretna Green. They shared a room and a bed but not one word passed between them.

When they arrived in Gretna, Nate found a room and settled her in it whilst he went to make the necessary arrangements.

It was an easy enough matter to find a reverend. They were all about town, happy to perform a hasty wedding for a fee.

The silence gave him more than enough time to think, to ponder what he had done.

She was wrong. The regret didn't come.

He didn't care what brought them together. He didn't care that she had wanted him only as an instructor in the finer points of seduction. He didn't care that he'd ever made that idiotic bet with Pearson. He didn't care that he had vowed to never marry again.

None of that was relevant. He only cared that she would be his.

His one regret would have been if he'd stood by and allowed her to be forced into marriage.

Aren't you forcing her?

He shoved the silent query aside. She'd already agreed to be his mistress. He was offering her marriage now. Lifelong security—not just for herself but for her siblings. He would not be lumped into the same category as the bastard who was threatening to ruin her.

He was a duke, damn it! Mamas had been attempting to manipulate him into marriage ever since Mary Beth died.

Marian should be pleased. Thrilled, even!

Still, he felt guilt over her lack of real choice in the matter. It was Lawrence or ruin or Nate. He was the obvious choice, but he felt regret that she had no real power in her life.

He returned to their rented room to find her staring out the window and down at the bustling street, her fingers tapping against her lips pensively.

"I've found a reverend. He will take care of acquiring the proper witnesses. We've an hour."

She looked over her shoulder. "Why are you doing this?"

"It was this or let you marry Lawrence." He shrugged. "A simple enough decision."

"You didn't even want me to be your mistress. How can—"

"I asked you to be my mistress, did I not?" he countered. "I wouldn't have done that if I didn't want to." He advanced on her near the window.

"But you didn't want a mistress. Not really."

"I asked you—"

"And you don't want a wife." She laughed mirthlessly and flung up her hands. "I know this. You said that. You most assuredly do not want a wife. You claimed that, too."

He frowned as he closed the distance between them. "Listen to me, you vexing woman. I do nothing I don't want to do. I wouldn't be here with you right now if I didn't—"

"What? Pity me? Or is it some other motivation I've missed?" She eyed him up and down. "You have some dark need in you where you can't be denied or rejected. Is that it? You feel like you would be losing if you let me marry Lawrence." She snorted. "You won't feel that way for long. One morning you will wake up and whatever you feel for me will be gone. You will feel trapped. Imprisoned in your marriage to some-one so beneath your station."

"Enough," he growled, reaching for her. "You talk too much."

Her eyes sparked. "Perhaps *you* don't talk enough. The entire way here you didn't say a word. I waited . . . I waited and hoped you were going to give me some explanation as to why you're doing this."

"Isn't it clear why I am doing this?" His hand crept behind her neck to haul her against him. He kissed her to silence her and himself. So neither one of them had to talk.

And then he was kissing her because it was all that mattered. All he wanted to do.

Once his lips met hers everything else faded.

Chapter 22

*M*arian knew kissing him ran counter to everything—primarily the *words* she had hoped they would finally speak. She had hoped to have an actual conversation with him that might reveal what had prompted him to steal her away in the first place.

But that didn't happen.

The kiss became another kiss and another and another.

The partial removal of their clothing followed.

His hands on her breasts. His hands everywhere. He broke away only to yank shut the curtains—they probably should have done that prior to the removal of their clothing.

Then they backed up and fell together on the bed.

He pressed against her, over her, his bigger body fitting against hers so perfectly that she had the sudden thought they were made for each other. It was a ridiculous fancy, but it intruded nonetheless.

The ache was back, slamming into her with rocking intensity. It still felt new even as it was familiar.

His hips pushed into her and she felt him there, between their hampering garments, his hardness nudging where she most needed him.

She shook her head even as a current of heat raced down her spine to pool in her core.

His fingers went to the hems of her dress and petticoat, tugging them up hastily.

"Always too many bloody clothes," he muttered.

She nodded, incoherently . . . impatient.

There was a rip and then she was free of her drawers.

"I'll buy you more," he growled.

A bubble of laughter escaped her.

He looked at her in surprise and then he chuckled, too.

Cool air caressed her exposed flesh, but he warmed her, dragging his fingers in a fiery path that made her squirm and arch under him.

With her skirts bunched and gathered around her waist, his big hands slid down her bare hips and around to her derriere. "Do you know?" he growled. "You have the most delicious bottom?"

She shook her head almost violently, dazed by his touch and his mesmerizing voice.

"I nearly spent myself the first time I saw it, and touching it, having it in my hands." He groaned and gently flexed his hands over her cheeks. The act sent a rush of moisture between her legs and she moaned. She thrust her pelvis and reached behind her to find his hands, to guide them.

"I won't break. You can squeeze me harder."

His eyes glittered and he obliged, squeezing and kneading her bare backside while she simultaneously ground herself into his hardness.

"Oh!" She cried out as something burst inside her. She shuddered.

His eyes widened. "Did you just . . ." His voice sounded hoarse and she choked out a whimper, nodding. She'd just climaxed.

He kissed her. "So sweet, so responsive," he said against her mouth.

Still nodding, she gasped as he brought one hand between them, unerringly finding and landing directly on that little bud between her thighs that throbbed and ached for him.

He rolled expert fingers over her slowly in dragging strokes that reignited the pressure between her thighs until she was crying out and surging against his hand.

"That's it," he spoke against her ear.

He slid a finger inside her and curled it, hitting some invisible place that he seemed to know existed.

Again, she shuddered and came apart, flying into pieces under him.

Her hands grabbed hold of his shoulders, hanging on for dear life.

Waves of sensation eddied through her. He pulled away and she whimpered at the loss. She heard him stripping his clothes, but it didn't matter. She writhed, impatient.

He came back and guided her to roll over, positioning her on all fours, keeping her skirts still shoved to her waist.

"What—"

"Trust me," he said. "Let me pleasure you."

He smoothed his hands over her bottom in worshipful strokes.

She moaned, her core clenching and aching, desperate to be filled with him.

"Marian," he breathed, kissing down her spine as he kneaded and massaged her round cheeks. "This sweet ass . . ." His mouth moved lower, kissing each cheek.

Moaning, shaking, she sank down to her elbows on the bed and looked over her shoulder.

His heavy-lidded eyes, dark as night, met hers over the curve of her hip. He splayed a big hand over the small of her back and she shuddered anew. Never had she felt like this—so deliciously possessed, *claimed*.

He lowered his head and she suddenly felt his teeth. The light scoring edge bit into her, the barest nip of teeth against her tender skin.

"Oh," she gasped and adjusted herself on the bed, instinctively parting her legs wider in invitation. "Take me, please."

He rubbed against her, the swollen crown of him nudging against her womanhood. She pushed back into his hard cock and he tsked at her, keeping himself from fully entering her.

"Nathaniel!" she begged. "Please, now."

His hands seized her hips, fingers digging deep into her skin, positioning her, gripping her, holding her for the perfect thrust.

He drove into her and she tossed back her head with an exultant shout, the force of his body against hers, *in* hers . . . paradise.

He rode her, and she reveled in it.

The force of his thrusts, the sliding friction of his cock, left her breathless and dizzy, her limbs as substantial as pudding.

She felt stretched, full in the best way. He hit that magical spot hidden deep inside her. Over and over, he unraveled her. She wouldn't have been able to stay upright or in place if not for his hands on her hips.

She shot a look over her shoulder at him, feeling brazen and alive. Not herself. Not Marian Langley. Daughter to the honorable Dr. Langley. Former governess to the Duke of Autenberry's daughter. Responsible older sister.

Saliva pooled in her mouth as her gaze locked on his face, so fierce and savage.

He gave a strangled cry as he pounded into her. Groaning her name, he continued pumping his hips. Their bodies came together with loud smacks. All the blood rushed to her head . . . and other parts of her.

She pushed her bottom back up to meet his thrusts . . . seeking, needing . . .

Her mind danced toward the thought that he was to be hers. Her husband.

She could have this . . . him, always.

Then there was no more thinking.

His body bowed over hers, his thrusts slowing, becoming more leisurely, deep and grinding.

He kissed her nape. Her neck. Her shoulder. He dragged his lips over her skin and she shivered uncontrollably. Her hands clenched in the bedding.

She blabbered, unaware of what she was saying.

She fisted the counterpane, pushing back into

him, meeting his every plunge, racing toward the end.

She was close. Her vision went fuzzy as she shook all over.

"That's it." He panted against her ear. "Let go."

She tottered on the edge and finally broke. Shattered. Splintered to tiny pieces, fragments of herself.

With a cry, she slumped beneath him. He pumped once, two more times, and then stilled, his hands tight on her hips, clinging. She felt his cock twitch and give a final jerk inside her.

He sighed her name and slid out from her body. "Are you . . . was that . . ."

"I'm fine. It was . . ." Brilliant. Splendid. She was overcome. All things she would never reveal to him. It gave away too much. She already felt vulnerable. He didn't need to think she was in love with him.

In love with him . . .

Oh. God. Had it come to that?

No. No. No. It hadn't come to that. Please, no. She didn't want or need to love the man she was to marry.

His weight lifted, and he rolled off her and pulled her close. She curled against his side, trying to catch her breath. His hand stroked up and down her spine, and she wished they could stay just this way.

Perhaps he was right and no words were for the best. Unfortunately, she couldn't turn off her brain. Her thoughts continued to spin as she lay there on that bed with a naked man curled around her.

"Tell me about your family." The words dropped into the silence between them. An unsubtle attempt at conversation. His family seemed a good place to begin. She was to be his wife. His family would become hers—or at the very least, they would be people floating about her life.

Wife. They were to be married. It still seemed too incredible.

"This is where we talk, then?" he inquired lightly. Light enough that she did not think he was resistant.

"We're to marry," she reminded. "Should we not talk . . . and know things? About each other?" She should know some things about him. She should know more than the rumors that abounded or tidbits she picked up from Mrs. Pratt. None of that information could be deemed reliable.

He was silent for some moments. She began to suspect he would ignore her attempt at conversation, and then: "Very well. Shall we start with my family then?" He nodded as though turning that over in his mind . . . as though he wasn't even certain he understood the question. As though the word *family* was a foreign word on his tongue.

Of course, that was strange to her. Family was

everything. It motivated so many of her decisions. "Yes, your family. You've met all of mine. Well, except for my brother, but you'll meet Phillip when he comes home for holiday. What of your family?"

"I haven't any. Not really."

She knew his father was gone. Clearly he was in possession of the title. It occurred to her that they had that in common. Fathers lost.

She didn't talk about Papa very much with her sisters. Especially not with Nora. She had been the closest to him, often working side by side with him in his lab and visiting patients.

Glancing at Nate, feeling the stroke of his hand along her spine, she felt a loosening in her chest. She had not realized *all* of his family was gone. How terrible that must be . . . to be alone. *He's not alone anymore. He has you.*

"I'm sorry," she said. "I did not realize you had no other family."

"Oh, I have relations. My mother and a stepfather." He shrugged. "I'm forced into their company now and then. There's even a stepbrother, my stepfather's by-blow. He surfaces occasionally. Thankfully, only that. But they are not family as you think of it. You will rarely ever see them."

Forced? That was not a word she thought of when she thought of her family.

"Why don't you see them more often?"

She had so many questions. It was a bewildering thing . . . to have a family and not have a family.

He released a huff of breath. "My mother and her husband are currently abroad. Not sure where my reprobate of a stepbrother is at the moment. I don't keep track of him. I usually only have to endure him when my mother and her husband drop on my doorstep . . . and that happens once a year or so when they remember my existence."

Marian shook her head. It was unfathomable to her that a family could be like this. She didn't know what to say.

"You're speechless," he correctly surmised.

"A little."

"What you have with your family, it is not in my experience. I was shipped off to school at a very early age, where I was not coddled or shown affection."

Her heart broke a little, imagining him as that little boy, a child without anyone to nurture him. Her hand started a slow circling stroke against his chest.

"I'm not saying this to solicit your pity. It's simply best you know. Don't expect me to be capable of warmth and affection." Her hand stopped its motion on his chest. "You're my wife. I'll give you all the respect due a wife, but . . ."

But he would not give her love. He was saying "but" without saying that.

Hopefully he wouldn't finish his sentence. She did not want to hear it spoken aloud. She did not want to suffer the sound of those words coming from his lips.

"I understand," she supplied, hoping to stop him from elaborating.

He fell silent and she was grateful for that. Grateful for the silence once again between them.

Now she knew there were worse things than silence.

She wished she didn't have to think about what was to come or what she meant to him—if anything.

She wished she didn't have to wonder if she was making the greatest mistake of her life.

In one year, in five, in ten . . . where would they be? She couldn't see it and that terrified her.

She couldn't see it.

But she knew she wanted it to *not* be a mistake.

She wanted it to be *good*.

Living together without conversation, without the warmth and affection he just claimed himself lacking, did not bode well.

Even if he continued to touch her and fulfill all her most ardent physical needs . . . that did not seem enough. She wanted more than that in her future with him.

His voice rumbled beneath her ear. "We should probably dress. The reverend will be waiting."

She hesitated a moment and then stood up from the bed. They dressed in silence. Of course.

He escorted her from the room and from their lodging house.

As they strolled down the sidewalk, she glanced down at herself. It was her wedding day and she wore a faded blue muslin riding habit. Not the elegant piece she had imagined wearing on her wedding day.

Yes, in a less practical era, when she was a girl, she had imagined such things.

In fact, nothing about this fit with what she had imagined.

She had imagined a beautiful gown, fresh flowers, her family and guests surrounding her. And love. There had been love.

Standing before an elderly, doddering reverend with a drunkard and a tavern wench serving as their witnesses did not come close to her imaginings.

But then, this was her reality, where dignity remained as elusive as ever, and Marian had long ago resigned herself to the trappings of reality.

Chapter 23

$\mathcal{T}$he return home was an improvement on the journey north.

They talked, at any rate.

Not that they spoke of anything significant. Not of the future, not *their* futures, which were now indelibly and forever entwined.

The carriage pulled to a stop before the massive double doors of Haverston Hall and woke her from her surprisingly comfortable nap.

Traveling by carriage always tired her. She had traveled great distances before. Distances much farther than Gretna. She had escorted Clara all the way to the Black Isle close to two years ago. Was it *only* two years ago? It felt like a lifetime ago. She had been so much younger then. So hopeful . . . with no idea of all that was to come.

One could not go much more north than the Black Isle. It had been a cold and arduous journey. She and Clara had huddled for warmth, with heated bricks at their feet.

She had rested peaceably every night of that trip. Unlike now.

On the return journey, Nate kept her awake and occupied into the long hours of the night. There was nothing peaceable about that. Not that she was complaining about their carnal activities. And yet as they drew closer to Brambledon, Marian dozed off to sleep.

She supposed she should have expected for Nate to bring her Haverston Hall. It was his home. She was his wife. He wouldn't deposit her at her house—her *former* home, she mentally amended. As his wife, she would live with him.

"Come, Marian." He shook her shoulder lightly.

"I'm awake," she said groggily, rising and permitting him to lift her down onto the ground.

She blinked and noticed several staff members standing very correctly by the front of the door, watching her avidly as though she might break into song or dance or perform a neat trick for them. She swallowed against the sudden lump in her throat, fighting against the irrational urge to cry.

She was no duchess.

They all knew. They saw that at once. They saw through her for what she was—an imposter. A common woman without any rightful claim to this role thrust upon her. What's more . . . she didn't want it. She had never wanted to be a member of the nobility. Not after living in their world as a servant—even if an upstairs servant.

An elegant, well-dressed young man stepped forward. She recognized him from her previous visit. Her face heated, aware that he knew of her late night visits with the duke. Likely all of his staff did.

Misery swallowed her whole.

She forced a smile as Nate introduced her to the waiting staff.

Once they entered the foyer, she gave his sleeve a tug and pulled him aside to whisper, "I need to go home to my sisters."

He frowned at her. "This is your home now."

She opened her mouth to protest, but the words never came. Not when she heard—

"Marian! You're back!"

She turned just as her sisters excitedly rushed down the stairs toward her. She looked from them to Nate in bewilderment. "They are here?" she murmured.

He gave a single stiff nod.

Her heart swelled a little. "Thank you."

He shrugged just as she was surrounded and embraced by her sisters. From over Charlotte's head, she watched him silently slip away as though uncomfortable with the emotional display.

"We're so glad you're back! We can't wait to tell you everything you've missed. The entire village is aflutter over news of your elopement."

She'd been gone only four days, but staring at her sisters' animated faces, it felt so much longer. Likely because her world had changed so dramatically since she'd gone and returned. Life as they knew it had vanished and was replaced with something else, something new and exciting and a little terrifying in its strangeness.

Her sisters started rattling off names of people and their various reactions.

". . . the Pembrokes are in quite the shock. They've called on us here twice since you—"

Her gaze swung to Charlotte. "Is this true?" Hope tightened inside her chest. "The Pembrokes called on you?"

Charlotte smiled rather vaguely. "Yes," she murmured. "Billy and I took a stroll about the gardens."

Marian studied Charlotte's face, trying to gauge how she felt about this, but as usual Charlotte revealed nothing. She was that way—the opposite of Nora. She kept her emotions in check, carefully tucked away and out of sight.

"And this is . . . good, yes?" Marian wanted confirmation that Charlotte was happy. She had her suitor back . . . perhaps even her fiancé again.

"The ol' Pembroke dragon insisted on it." Nora snorted. "She was practically throwing William at Charlotte. Predictable, is it not? We are kin to a duke now and suddenly deemed worthy."

Marian continued to gaze at Charlotte, waiting for her reaction to all of this.

She finally nodded in agreement. "Yes. It's good."

Not exactly an exuberant affirmation of joy, but Marian accepted it. Charlotte had her suitor back. Her sister's life was returning to how it had been before Papa died.

Everything Marian had done would be worth it, after all.

"Come." Charlotte led her from the foyer and up the stairs. "You must be weary from your travels. We'll show you to your room."

They chattered all the way up the stairs, still very excited over their change in circumstances.

Halfway down the corridor, Marian stopped and looked at each of her sisters. "Wait. What of Mr. Lawrence? Have you heard from him?" How could she have forgotten him? When she last left Brambledon she was still betrothed to him. She winced.

Nora and Charlotte exchanged uneasy glances.

"What?" she pressed.

"Well, we weren't there to witness . . ."

"What happened?"

Charlotte moistened her lips. "Billy was at the draper's with his mother when the news came through the village. Mr. Lawrence happened to be there, too."

Marian nodded, dread pooling in her stomach. She wanted to believe he wasn't so terribly offended at being jilted. At least, not so offended that he would make her life difficult. The despicable man had bullied her into a betrothal. A humiliating jilting was the least of what he deserved.

"Billy said Mr. Lawrence did not take it well."

Even though Marian was free of him, safe forever from all his ugly threats, a little tremor ran through her. "What did he do?"

"Oh, there was some jeering and mocking. A crowd gathered. It was not nice. Well, not nice for Mr. Lawrence. People laughed. He smashed a jar and stormed out. No one has seen him since."

"Oh, he deserved it." Nora shrugged. "Now, let's help you get settled in and you can tell us all about your trip. How was your wedding? Was it romantic?"

"We eloped to a border town," Marian said dryly.

"Oh, la!" Nora clasped her hands together. "I

hope someone sweeps me off my feet like that some day."

Shaking her head, Marian followed her sisters down the corridor.

NATE FOUND LAWRENCE at his house.

There had been no question ever in his mind that he would call on the brute and take him to task for all his misdeeds. Marian was his wife now. He could not let insults against her go unpunished.

And yet it was more than that—more than Nate doing what he *ought* to do. There was a whole host of emotions churning and simmering through him. Feelings he'd never experienced before.

Even if Marian had not been his wife, someone should thrash the lout for what he had done to her—what he had *attempted* to do. He deserved no less.

He deserved to bleed.

Never far in the back of Nate's mind was the thought—the fear. What if he had never come to know Marian? If she'd never hid herself beneath his table? If she'd never knocked on his door and offered herself to him in such a bold and tempting manner?

She would have married the blacksmith. She

would belong to him. She would have spent her days trapped, broken, miserable, crushed beneath the boot of a man with no measure of empathy for her.

Nate knew a bit about the hell of living among bullies. Only his hell had come to an end. He'd finished school and escaped them. He'd grown into a man who could defend himself.

There would never have been an end for Marian. Never an escape.

And that fed his rage, carrying him to the blacksmith's door, intent on collecting reprisal, to mete out justice.

When he knocked at the door, a servant answered. "Mr. Lawrence is not at home," she informed him, but her shifting, nervous gaze told Nate a much different story.

Nate stepped back off the stoop to assess the house with a critical eye and noticed a second floor window with parted drapes. He caught a glimpse of a man there before the figure quickly stepped back into the shadows.

"Pardon me." Nate pushed the door open wider and stepped past the woman.

"Wh-what are you . . . you cannot barge in here even if you are a grand lord," she sputtered.

Nate ignored her and took to the stairs, quickly locating the room abovestairs that faced out to the front lawn where he had seen the man in the window.

The door was ajar and he strode inside, stopping to sweep his gaze over the room.

The bastard was waiting for him, his face splotchy red, his hands opening and curling into fists at his sides. He was panting like a bull, a veritable giant, each of his hands reminiscent of anvils.

Lawrence might own a successful smithy with several men working under him doing the day-to-day labor, but the man was a blacksmith by trade, and here was the evidence of that. He was thick, his hands work-scarred and ready to bring abuse, and he was apparently undeterred by Nate's title or position.

The hulk of a man charged him with a roar, which was fine with Nate. He detested bullies. He had that on his side—a lifelong aversion to bullies. And one could not discount his rage. It was powerful fuel.

This man's treatment of Marian filled him with such anger that he was only too ready to unleash it and meet the charge.

Lawrence ducked low and rammed hard into Nate's torso, wrapping his thick arms around his waist and lifting him off his feet with the howl of a wounded bear.

Nate's vision darkened for a moment as he was slammed against the wall. Every dirty trick Nate had ever learned from school rushed to the front of his mind, instinct awakened.

He lifted his arms above his head, locked his hands together and brought them down hard on top of Lawrence's skull.

Immediately Nate was free. The blacksmith fell to the floor with a moan. Nate wasted no time. Hesitation marked the difference between triumph and pain.

Nate kicked him. Once. Twice.

This was brute battle. There was no fairness, no holding back.

Before he could land a third kick, Lawrence twisted surprisingly swiftly for a man of his size and grabbed Nate's foot, yanking up so that Nate landed on the floor on his back. Lawrence delivered a fist to Nate's ribs that had him gasping for breath.

With another roar, Lawrence jumped and came down, on the verge of dropping all his considerable weight on Nate.

Nate rolled at the last moment, saving his body from being crushed by the bigger man.

Lawrence cried out when he crashed down on the floor, clutching his arm, which took the brunt of the force. The rug offered thin cushion, but that gave him little pause. He grunted like an animal as he got up on his knees and kept coming. He was unstoppable.

But so was Nate.

A quick glance around and Nate snatched a vase from a nearby table and brought it crashing down on the man's head.

Lawrence fell, rolling onto his back amid shards of vase. His dark, small eyes glazed over in pain, staring straight up at the ceiling, seeing nothing, Nate suspected. Feeling only pain.

Panting, Nate loomed over him. "Stay clear of my wife. I don't ever want to have to come here again."

Lawrence released a low groan, and those beady eyes rolled back in his head before his lids drifted shut.

With a satisfied grunt, Nate held his sore middle and gingerly walked from the room and out of the house.

Chapter 24

$\mathcal{M}$arian wasn't sure what to expect, but she had thought perhaps she would share a bedchamber with Nate.

Her husband certainly had no hesitation when it came to indulging in the perks of the marriage— at least, he had since the day of their marriage. There might be things lacking in their union, certainly, but physical intimacy was not one of them.

She brushed out her hair at the dressing table. She had just started plaiting the long strands when a knock sounded. Her gaze flew to the door of her bedchamber.

Another knock and this time her gaze moved to another door along the wall of her room. She had not given it much thought when she was first shown to her chamber, but now she called out, "You may enter."

Nate stood on the other side. She looked beyond his shoulder and noted the lavish room with its own bed behind him. "We have adjoining rooms?" she asked. She had assumed a maid was knocking.

"You were not aware?" He lifted an eyebrow.

She shook her head.

She supposed that was how it was done for those of the upper echelons of Society, but she knew that wasn't the case for Clara. She shared a room with her husband. In fact, she believed the Duke of Autenberry shared the same bedchamber with his wife, too. Separate rooms weren't a necessary standard.

She glanced at her reflection in her dressing mirror and tried not to visibly pout.

"It makes matters more convenient," he elaborated.

Rubbish. She'd thought marriage might bring them closer. Despite his warning of no warmth and affection, she had hoped it might feel . . . special. So far it didn't feel very different from when she was his paramour. Not that she had a great deal of experience being his kept woman prior to marrying him. However brief it had been, she understood how it was to have worked.

It was just to have been shagging. A physical exchange.

Intimacy without intimacy.

So far that described her marriage accurately. No wonder he had been so agreeable to marrying her if this was to be the way of it.

He stepped inside, shut the door and strode over to her. He tugged her up from the bench and hauled her into his arms.

All thoughts fled then.

He kissed her.

She wrapped her arms around his neck because that's the kind of weak creature she was. They kissed until they were both panting. She slid her hands down his chest, reveling in his broad chest, in the firmness of his body beneath his robe. Marian dipped her fingers inside his robe, eager for his warm skin. She brushed her hand over his ribs.

He jerked and hissed out a breath.

She pulled back in alarm. "What's wrong?"

"Nothing." He attempted to kiss her again, but she parted his robe, searching, unsure what she was looking for—

She gasped. "Nate! What happened?"

Ugly bruises of varying shades of blue marred the skin of his torso.

"Nothing."

"It does not look like nothing." Her alarm twisted into real fear. He was injured. Hurt. It had never occurred to her that something could happen to him, but now that the realization was there, she could not chase away the fear. "Tell me. I demand to know—"

"I got into a bit of a scuffle."

She stilled. He was a duke. Who engaged in fisticuffs with a duke? "A scuffle? With whom?"

He sighed, avoiding her gaze, clearly resistant.

"Who?" she pressed sharply.

"Lawrence."

"Mr. Lawrence?" she echoed. Then she felt her eyes widen as understanding washed over her. "For me? You went after him?"

Nate gave a single hard nod, his expression resolute.

"Are you mad? He's a giant."

He shrugged. "You know what they say. The bigger the man, the harder the fall."

She looked back to his torso. "Are you hurt badly?"

"It's just a bruise. He got in one good punch. I'll be fine. I've had worse."

She returned her gaze to his face, gaping. "You have? But you're a . . . duke!"

His lips twisted. "Dukes can get in fights."

And get hurt . . . they could get hurt. She did *not* like that.

She brushed her fingers gingerly over his battered flesh. "You should not have done that," she scolded.

"You're my wife," he said gruffly, his breath rustling the tiny hairs at her temple. "He threatened you. That could not go unanswered."

So it was the principle. She was his wife . . . his property, in a sense.

And yet as his gaze traveled hotly over her face, she did not feel like a mere possession. She felt like something more. He brought his hand up to her face and brushed a tendril back off her cheek. She felt like something cherished. He stroked a thumb against her bottom lip. She felt wanted. Needed. She felt as though he would go to battle for her again and again because of this . . . because of what there was between them.

They were so close now their breaths collided and mingled into one fusion of air. "I would gladly take a thousand beatings, if it kept you from harm," he whispered thickly.

She slid her hand down from his battered ribs, parting his robe wider, seeking the hot length of him. When she found him, she wrapped her hand around his already stiff member and squeezed. He pulsed and swelled in her grasp.

With a groan and a curse, he bent and picked her up, starting for her nearby bed.

"You're injured!" she cried out in alarm.

"The only thing hurting right now is my cock. It needs to be inside you."

Instantly, she was breathless, aroused. They came down together on the bed, and her hands shoved his dressing robe fully off him.

Sighing in pleasure at the sight of him, her hands skimmed his male form, so strong and warm. Her belly quivered, knowing the pleasure to come, the pleasure his body could give.

He lifted her nightgown, stroked over her thighs and touched her between the legs.

His fingers slid against her, inside her, filling her. She arched with a moan.

He kissed her. "You're already wet for me."

She moaned into his mouth as he thrust his manhood inside her.

He drove into her and she rose up to meet every thrust, spiraling closer and closer—

Suddenly he was gone.

She whimpered in disappointment.

Groaning, he moved away.

She lifted up on her elbows, watching as he spilled his seed on the bedding.

Her arousal faded away as confusion filled her. *What was he doing?*

His gaze met hers. "Sorry. You didn't finish, did you?" He reached for her. "I can—"

"What did you do that for?" she asked. No, she demanded.

"Do what?"

She paused, thinking how to say it. When it came to matters of intimacy, she still had a lot to learn, it seemed. "At the end . . . you curtailed yourself."

He lifted his head to look at her, his expression befuddled. "Curtailed?" Understanding lit his eyes. "Oh. That. You mean why did I not take my release inside you?"

Her face heated. He had no problem expressing himself when it came to such matters.

She nodded. "Yes. Why did you do that?"

"So I would not get you with child."

Because that would be bad.

Unwanted.

She had rather suspected that, but she had to know for certain. She did understand how anatomy and procreation worked, after all.

She could only stare at him, thinking about that. Thinking that he did not want to get her with child. This was to be her life. Her future. She needed to understand.

"Why?" she whispered.

"I lost my first wife in childbirth. I'll not take such a risk again."

She sucked in a sharp breath. Moistening her lips, she began carefully, "You do not want children?"

"God, no."

She could not stop her flinch.

He noticed it and continued in an almost gentle voice, "I was careless, I admit. With you. In the beginning, that first time. I will not be so careless anymore."

She reeled from what he was saying, her mind working, absorbing the significance.

He did not want children.

He would not have children with her.

She would not have children. Ever. Not as long as she was his wife. Which would essentially be . . . forever.

As far as she was concerned, children were the one benefit to marrying—the one perk that made giving up her freedom tolerable.

When she had decided that she would never marry, never give up that much of herself, never lose her freedom, that had been the one point, the one fly in the ointment.

Marrying him, she had thought she would at least get this out of the union.

But she had been wrong.

She would not have even that.

She would not have love in this union, and she would not have children. She felt these blows keenly.

"Good of you to explain this to me before you stole me away to be married," she accused hotly.

He released a rough bark of laughter. "As though you had a choice?"

Fury seized her. "I have a choice. I will always have a choice in my life!" she argued even as doubt crept through her.

"Do you believe that?" he demanded, the anger in his voice matching hers. "You believe Lawrence to be a choice? Public ruin? Cruel ridicule? Poverty? You believe these choices? Valid choices over me?"

She hated that he was right. She hated that she felt such a fool in this moment. "Oh, you are an arrogant bastard."

"Well, you have the right of it there." He shrugged, reaching for his robe.

"You seem very proud of that."

"I simply know who I am. Tell me, Marian. Do you know who you are?"

"Of course I know myself."

"Because you don't seem to have a very good handle on your situation. You are a woman without family to care for you. Without wealth. Without position. You seem to be missing this self-awareness if you think you have any choice better than me."

She released a stinging breath. "Thank you. Thank you so much for relating to me how utterly powerless I am." Her voice choked a little at the end of her words. "I suppose I should just fall at your feet in gratitude that you should want me as a wife."

"I didn't say—"

"Didn't you?" She hopped up from her bed.

"Where are you going?"

"Away from you," she snapped.

"Save yourself the trouble. This is your room. I'll leave."

"You do that," she agreed, the sting of unshed tears burning her eyes.

She was being foolish. She knew it. This was all about the fact that he didn't want to have children with her. He wouldn't even consider it. Not that he had ever promised to give her children in the first place.

A week ago she had not possessed the comfort and security and luxury of being his wife. Some would call her greedy. She was certain of that. Some would say she should be content. Satisfied.

She was not. She wanted more from him. She wanted more from their life together. Perhaps even everything.

She could not talk herself out of her disappointment. Her anger flared hot in her chest and had her thinking horrible things—had her saying horrible things that she did not mean.

She called out after him before he passed through the adjoining door. "Should I find that I want a child, I am certain I can find someone to give me one . . . if you will not."

He stilled.

She froze as well. The only thing moving was the violent hammering of her heart, threatening to burst free of her chest.

He took two steps toward her and stopped. His dark eyes fastened on her and reminded her of the first time she met him and thought him the very devil—all ruthlessness.

"No man, save me, will ever touch you. As you pointed out, you made your choice and I'm it."

Fury radiated off him. She thought he would say more on the subject.

Some men abused their wives. She knew of this shameful behavior. Her father had tended to more than one such wife on different occasions. Marian braced herself, wondering if this was the moment when she discovered he was such a man. She didn't think it possible. She didn't think he had it in him.

Turning, he stormed from the room, proving her correct. Nate was not such a man.

She had pushed him, angered him, hinted to him that she might cuckold him. He had not lifted a hand to her. Naturally. Because he was a good man.

She fell upon the bed. Dropping her face into a pillow, she let the softness absorb the sound of her sob. She almost wished he wasn't the man she thought him—a man she could esteem. A man she could love.

Then she wouldn't be so disappointed. She wouldn't hurt so much.

THE DAY DAWNED colder than expected, certainly colder than it had been of late. It might be spring, but apparently Mother Nature hadn't been alerted to that fact.

Marian dressed warmly in the bedchamber she had been assigned.

Attired in a wool riding habit, she descended the staircase. Voices carried, and she followed them into the small, dark-paneled dining room to find her sisters eating as though they were preparing for a month-long fast.

"Marian!" Nora cried out around a mouthful of food. "Join us!"

Marian stepped forward and filched a piece of toast. "I shall just take this."

Charlotte eyed her up and down. "Are you going somewhere?"

"I thought I would ride over to the house and get a few of my things."

"Oh, Mr. Pearson promised to send a crew of servants—"

"I just want a few things of my own for now. I'd like my favorite shawl."

She really just wanted some time for herself to walk the floors of her own home. This was the duke's house. She felt like a stranger here. She didn't know if she would always feel that way, but that's how she felt right now . . . and she presently craved a return to what she knew. To what felt safe.

Bessie had already been settled in to the duke's stables. A lad appeared to help her saddle her mount.

"Would you like me to accompany you?" He moved as though to ready himself for the task.

"No, I will do well on my own. Thank you."

He looked at her doubtfully. "Are you certain, Your Grace?"

She stopped, startled at the formal address. He meant her. She was *Your Grace*.

A blasted duchess now.

"Yes. I am quite capable. Thank you."

And then she was off, riding into the bitter cut of wind despite the offer of company. She didn't want company. She wanted solitude.

She felt like a fraud. An imposter. She was no duchess, and she actually knew something on the matter. She had been in the employ of a duchess once upon a time. Clara's mother had been elegance and nobility personified. Marian could never be that.

She pushed Bessie as hard as safely possible. The old girl still had it in her. She broke into a trot, seeming to relish the cold breeze on her face.

The front gate to her house swung open with a neglected air, and she felt a pinch in her heart as she passed through the gate, a longing for all those happy days through the years.

After securing Bessie in the stables, she took herself inside her house.

It already felt empty. Vacated. Even though they had not officially moved out yet, there was a lifelessness to the house that brought tears to her eyes.

She walked through every room, examining it and its items and thinking how she might incorporate some of those things into her new home. The duke's home was so dark. Maybe they could lighten a few rooms with paint or a lovely wallpaper.

"I thought you would turn up here sooner or later. I wasn't certain you would be alone, however, so this is quite the gift."

She spun around with a gasp. Lawrence stood in the parlor's threshold.

She swallowed against the boulder-sized lump that formed in her throat. "What are you doing here? You shouldn't be here."

"I think an explanation was owed me," he replied with a flare of his nostrils.

"You were *threatening* me!" Heat flashed through her.

"You were promised to me—"

"You're a monster! I never wanted to marry you. Never! You knew that! I don't owe you any explanation."

Shaking her head, she stormed past him, ready to flee.

He had intruded upon her quiet time. She no longer wanted to be in this house. She no longer wanted to be anywhere if he was there.

He grabbed her arm, seizing hold of her, stopping her from fleeing.

She looked down at his hand circling her forearm. His fingers were as wide as sausages. "Unhand me."

His lip curled in a sneer. "You made a fool of me, *duchess*." He spit the last word as though it were the foulest thing.

She tried to twist her arm free, but he only tightened those fingers. "You're hurting me."

"Maybe you deserve to be hurt."

She stared into his face, fear washing over her as that penetrated.

She was all alone with him in this house.

He thought she deserved to be hurt. He could hurt her. It was that simple.

She searched deep inside herself for the courage she did not feel right now. Determined to at least feign it, she growled at him through tightly gritted teeth, "Unhand me at once, sir."

He brought his face closer, his rancid breath a hot puff against her skin. "You think yourself so much better than me?"

He was incapable of reason, of compassion. She managed to wrench her arm free of him. She rubbed at the bruised flesh. No doubt there would be marks.

Stepping back as far as she could, she squeezed past him in the threshold. She exhaled, relieved that he had let her go without attempting to stop her.

She had thought that he might—

Pain exploded in the back of her skull. Her knees buckled and she went down, her hands coming up to catch herself, but it did no good.

She hit the ground. Hard.

Spots danced before her vision. She managed to roll to her side. She tried to lift a hand to her head, but her limb felt like lead. She couldn't move. She couldn't move at all.

She blinked tearing eyes. Lawrence's face swam above her.

A scream lodged in her throat as his thick hands came toward her.

Darkness closed in, descended, blotting out everything else.

Chapter 25

*N*ate stayed away all day.

He told himself it wasn't avoidance. He wasn't running away. He wasn't hiding from his wife. One uncomfortable argument wouldn't send him fleeing.

It was all bollocks, of course.

He'd never wanted to marry again. He'd never wanted another wife—and he certainly didn't want to have a child.

He well remembered that night. It was the stuff of nightmares. The screaming agony. The blood. So much blood and loss. All for naught. For death only.

He would not put Marian through the trauma of childbirth. He would not wish it on any woman, much less one he cared about, one he . . .

He stopped himself from taking the thought one dangerous step further.

From the moment Marian entered his life, she had challenged everything he thought he wanted for himself.

No one had forced him to marry her. There had been no family pressure. Certainly no Society pressure. No angry papa after him.

Still, he had done it. He had married her. He had stolen her away the instant he thought he might lose her.

She had married him, of course. What other recourse did she have? What were her options? Poverty? Ruin? Lawrence?

It made him ill, twisted his stomach into knots to think she had married him because he was the least *bad* option.

He didn't want to be her savior.

He wanted her to want him. *Him*. Not what he could do for her. Not what he brought to this marriage. Foolish, he supposed.

Marriage was only ever a negotiation. It didn't have anything to do with softer sentiments. Marriage was an exchange of goods. What one person could bring to the other. He had done this before, after all. He knew what it was all about.

He'd told himself he would never repeat that mistake.

His marriage to Mary Beth had been every bit of that. True, they had been childhood friends. There had been an attraction. At least on his part. But he knew she would have never married him if not for his title. She had been fond of him, but *in love* with his title.

Mary Beth had died cursing him. In pain. Agony. Her lifeblood ebbing away as the midwife attempted to revive both her and their stillborn son. All for naught.

He'd told himself he would never do it again. Never go through that.

He enjoyed his life now. Or rather, the way it had been.

But then he had changed it. He had changed everything. Now he found himself married to a female with appetites that matched his own. She didn't keep him at arm's length. She was insatiable, craving him as much as he craved her.

This could be different. Not like before.

The treacherous voice whispered through his mind.

He entered the house, his steps at an eager clip. Despite their earlier fight, he hastened upstairs, wanting to see her, *needing* to see her.

"Oh, there you are, Your Grace!"

He looked up to see one of Marian's sisters hurrying toward him. Charlotte, he thought her name. He winced. He really should learn the names of his sisters-in-law. Nora, he remembered. She had made quite the impression upon their first meeting, after all. Charlotte was the quieter of the two.

"Are you looking for me?"

"Actually, we've been looking for Marian. She's been gone for quite some time. We thought you might know where she is. It's nearing the dinner hour and we were a little concerned." Charlotte nodded to the younger girl beside her. "Nora rode to our house to see if she was still there, but there's no sign of—"

"She went to your house? Alone?"

Charlotte nodded.

Uneasiness curled through him.

Without a word, he turned and headed back out the way he had entered, the speed of his strides steadily increasing until he broke into a run.

MARIAN WOKE TO the gradual awareness that one side of her was pleasantly warm and the other side jarringly cold. She kept her eyes closed and held herself still, assessing, aware enough that something was not right. *What happened? Why was her head throbbing?*

A loud boom of thunder sounded overhead and she flinched. Rain pattered on the roof.

She shifted slightly and pain jolted through her at the motion.

Her mind backtracked, reaching for memory, struggling to recall what happened.

She'd gone to her house.

Lawrence had been there.

He struck her. *Lawrence.* He had done this to her.

She resisted surging upright. No sudden movements. She needed to think. She needed to be calm. She knew this. Somehow, instinctively, she knew this. If she panicked, all would be lost.

The rain continued to beat a steady rhythm on the roof. A fire crackled somewhere close. Hard ground was under her, but she didn't think she was still in her house.

She inhaled. It didn't smell like home. It didn't smell lived-in. It wasn't familiar. The air here was stale.

Ignoring the pounding in her skull, she eased open one eye, daring to take a peek around.

A great fireplace crackled in front of her, explaining why one side of her was so warm.

She was lying on a rough wood floor. No rug. Her nose twitched at the army of dust balls everywhere.

Another flinch as another boom of thunder reverberated on the air.

She opened both eyes. She knew this place.

She recognized it. It was the hunting cottage on Nate's property. She'd peered through the windows enough times to remember.

A neglected cottage in the middle of nowhere, forgotten by the world—that was why they had thought the place to be such a perfect location to meet for assignations. No one would ever see them coming or going.

Her stomach sank. *No one.* Because no one and nothing was out here. No one to hear her scream even if it wasn't storming.

It was strange to find herself in the place she had thought to be her sanctuary with the duke at one time. Their little love nest was now to be her prison. Her prison with Lawrence.

Perhaps even a coffin.

No. She would not die. She would survive this. Whatever was to come. Because she would be calm. She would not panic. She would think. *Think think think.*

The words wove as a mantra through her mind. She risked moving her head ever so slightly, ignoring the lancing pain in order to search for a weapon, something she could use to defend herself—

"Oh. You're awake. Excellent."

The heavy thud of footsteps resounded over the wood planks. "I must confess, you're a lot heavier than you look. It was quite a chore getting you here." His boots stopped in front of her line of vision. "But worth it having you all to myself."

She lifted herself up onto her elbows. Panting from the exertion and pain, she looked up at him. "You can't do this. I'm married now . . . Warrington will kill you."

"What makes you think Warrington will ever know what happened to you?"

He uttered the words so easily, so pleasantly. He was all the more terrifying for it. A chill shot down her spine.

She fought for composure. "He will know," she insisted. "If I go missing, he will know. He will figure out it was you. Everyone will know it was you."

He shook his head, his expression mild and oddly serene. "I've given this a great deal of thought. I don't think so. These are dangerous times. Highwaymen abound. You should have never gone out riding alone, Marian." He tsked and nodded confidently. "That is what people will think. That is what people will say."

Despair threatened to swallow her. Logical or not, he'd decided on his course.

There was no one to help her. No one would come. She was on her own.

She looked away from him, her gaze searching the empty room, tracking over everything feverishly. The place was vacant. There was nothing here. No furniture. No items of any kind. Nothing she could use—

Her gaze lighted upon the stack of firewood near the hearth. Except that.

She took a bracing breath. She had to reach the wood. Somehow. Before he knew what she was about. Before he could stop her. He was bigger, stronger. She needed the element of surprise.

She winced and made a show of touching her head. "My head hurts . . ."

"A headache is the least of your concerns."

Fabric rustled and she looked up. He worked loose his cravat. Pulling it free, he then removed his jacket. Both jacket and cravat in his hands, he glanced around, clearly looking for a place to put them. Apparently he was too fastidious to toss them on the floor.

He spotted a set of hooks nailed into the wall near the door and made his way toward them.

She took her chance then and dragged herself closer to the fire, to the woodpile.

"What are you doing there? Trying to run away? Ah, that's adorable. You think you can get away."

Sitting up, she turned to face him, her back propped against the woodpile. Her fingers scrambled behind her, trying to wrap around a log.

The fire popped and crackled beside her, so close she felt its singe on her skin. "Stay away from me."

He advanced on her, sneering. "Already talking like a duchess, giving commands like you're the bloody queen."

"I'm warning you . . ." Her fingers fumbled desperately behind her, her nails snagging and splintering against the rough bark.

He stopped before her and bent down, grabbing hold of her ankles. He yanked, pulling her toward him.

She slid across the floor with a squeak, but didn't let go of the log she had seized from behind her back. The entire stack tumbled. Logs went everywhere, several colliding into her.

Lawrence scowled. "What the—"

She swung. Using every bit of force she had, she brought the wood crashing against the side of his face.

He went down with a howl.

She hopped to her feet, ignoring the pain, fighting against the dizziness. Gripping the same log in both hands now, she lifted it above her head and brought it down on him. Several times she struck. His head, his shoulder, his chest. He brought his hands up over his face and she hit them several times.

He rolled, groaning. She lifted the log high above her head, ready to swing again, when she glimpsed his bleeding face. He looked a mess.

Deciding she had done enough damage, she tossed down the log and turned. Yanking open the door, she fled into the night, into the rain.

A single horse was tethered outside, suffering the downpour. She charged toward it. It backed up as far as it could with a nervous neigh.

"Whoa, easy there, easy now." She fumbled with the slick reins, trying to unknot them.

She cried out in giddy triumph as she freed them. A quick glance behind her revealed Lawrence staggering to the doorway of the cottage, blood streaming down his face.

Blast it. He was already to his feet.

She lifted a foot toward the stirrup, readying to mount.

Lightning split across the sky, striking somewhere close. The thunder to follow blasted over the night and rocked the earth like cannon fire.

The horse shrieked and reared, its hooves dancing on the air. She lost her grip on the reins.

Crying out, she dove for them, for the horse.

But it was too late. The beast was gone, galloping hard into the woods.

"No!" She sent a panicked glance over her shoulder.

Lawrence was out of the cottage, charging through the rain. Coming for her.

Swallowing back a scream, she turned and ran.

She plunged into the woods, running without direction, her only thought escape.

It was dark and the rain made it difficult to see where she was going, but she pushed hard, running blindly, weaving between trees, ignoring everything. The pain. The ground sucking at her boots. The incessant rain. The terror.

Fear egged her on.

She heard Lawrence crashing through the foliage behind her. She risked a glance and identified the dark shape of him. He was faster than she would have thought possible.

"Marian!" he roared.

She choked on a sob and pushed harder. She swung around a tree and dropped low, crawling as fast as she could and burying herself inside some bushes, hoping he would pass right by her.

Holding still, she waited. She heard him coming, getting closer.

"Marian!" he shouted her name in a singsong manner. "Come out, come out!"

She trembled, shaking violently, but it had nothing to do with the cold.

Moments slid past. Time stretched slowly.

Suddenly she heard him shout. Farther away.

Differently this time. She strained to hear over the rain. He sounded panicked.

"Help! Help me!"

She remained where she was, certain it was a trick.

"Help!"

She eased out of her hiding place, and moved stealthily through the woods, peering around her in every direction, braced for an ambush.

"Marian! Thank God! Help me!"

She stopped hard. His voice was close, but she couldn't see him anywhere.

"Marian!"

She looked down and there he was, chest deep in a bog.

"Help me. Get me out."

She hesitated. "Why would I do that?"

"I'll die."

"You were going to kill me!" He still would if he had the chance. She had no doubt of that.

"No. I won't do that. Get me out. I promise I won't hurt you. Please. Please! Don't leave me to die." His eyes gleamed desperately in a face speckled with mud.

She shook her head. Even after she had struck him he still came after her. She was stuck out here all alone with him.

She couldn't free him. Saving his life would not change his mind. He would not simply return her home unscathed. She couldn't risk it. She wasn't that great of a fool.

"Word of advice. Don't struggle. It pulls you down faster. I'll send help."

"There's no time!" he cried.

Turning, she fled.

Chapter 26

*I*t was almost morning, and they still had not found Marian.

Nate was sick. This must be where the expression *heartsick* originated. He'd never felt this kind of fear.

It came close to the night he had lost Mary Beth and their child.

He'd had the same kind of clenching in his gut then, too, when it became clear things were not going well with her and the babe.

It was the same chronic state of nausea. He hadn't been that afraid since then. Since he had allowed himself to care.

He hadn't cared since then. He hadn't cared about anyone.

Bloody hell. He cared about Marian. He more than cared.

He loved Marian. He had fallen *in* love with her. Of course he had.

He never would have married her otherwise. He never would have asked her to be his mistress otherwise. Only like a bloody cliché, it took the threat of losing her for him to realize that.

He gave himself a swift shake. He would not lose her. She was out there. He would find her.

He would find her and never let her go again.

He recalled the last time he had seen her—the crushed look on her face when he explained he would never give her a child. When he told her they could never have a child together. Never be parents. Never be a family. What a colossal ass he was.

He vowed he would never hurt or disappoint her like that again.

He just had to find her. Had to make it right. Had to have the chance to love her properly.

One of his men shouted, pointing up at the sky.

Nate looked up and spotted a stream of pale gray smoke against the blanket of darker night.

He dug in his heels and turned in that direction, cutting hard through the woods toward the smoke. It appeared to be originating from his hunting lodge. The very place he thought to make suitable for him and Marian.

Several of his men followed. For hours they had been combing the countryside, searching for any glimpse of Marian or Lawrence. Once they had verified Lawrence was missing, they concluded he had taken Marian. They had been searching ever since. It had not occurred to anyone to go to his hunting cottage.

He was so focused on reaching the cottage, he almost did not notice the shape emerging before him until it was too late.

He pulled back on his reins. His horse reared up with a shriek. The figure cried out as hooves crashed down on the ground.

He dismounted quickly, and then he could see quite clearly that it was Marian before him. Wet and bedraggled and the most beautiful thing he had ever seen.

He hauled her into his arms. She collapsed against him, breaking into sobs. She spoke quickly, practically incomprehensible. He pulled back to look at her, holding her face in his hands.

"Are you hurt? What happened? Did he harm you?" He looked her up and down as though he could verify.

She shook her head. "I'm fine. A blow to the head, but I will recover."

"Where is he?" Several of the men had gathered

around him by now, including Pearson. "Where is Lawrence?"

She motioned vaguely behind her. "I left him. He fell in a bog. I don't even know if he's alive."

He hoped he wasn't alive. The man had taken her. He meant to hurt her. Despite Nate's warnings, he'd dared to take Marian. If the man was still alive, Nate would kill him.

He gestured for two of his men to go and check on the bastard. He'd deal with Lawrence personally if he still lived, but for now he needed to attend to his wife.

He wrapped an arm around Marian, and turned her toward his mount. "Let's get you out of this rain and home. We'll have you in something warm and in bed in no time."

Nodding, she clasped his hand tightly in hers, as though she would never let him go. He hoped that would be the case . . . because he never intended to let her go, either.

MARIAN WOKE SEVERAL times through the night, frightened, crying out, her hands flailing, groping, clawing and struggling, certain she was being sucked down into a bog with Lawrence.

Then a hand would run soothingly over her hair, and warm arms would pull her close. "Shh, I'm here."

And he was. Every time, Nate was there, holding her, whispering words of comfort until she fell back to sleep.

When she woke in the morning, she actually felt rested. She rotated her neck on the pillow—wincing at the tenderness in her scalp—to find Nate sleeping beside her.

She watched him for a moment, so calm and serene in sleep. He was always achingly handsome, but in sleep he looked years younger. Vulnerable in a way he never was when awake. She lightly traced a finger over his brow.

Instantly, his dark eyes shot open.

"Sorry," she whispered. "I did not intend to wake you."

"How are you? Do you need anything?"

"My head is a little tender, but I'm fine. I'll live."

Something almost pained crossed his face at that utterance. "I'm so sorry."

"For what?"

"You're my wife. I should have protected you—"

"From a man like Lawrence? A madman? No. You could not have prevented it." She gave her head a small shake. "What happened to him?"

"Lawrence?"

She nodded.

"Dead."

"Oh. Did you . . ."

"I would have. But no. He drowned in the bog."

She expelled a breath, glad for that. Glad Lawrence was gone forever. Threat no more.

She was also glad it had not been from Nate's hand. She wouldn't have wished that awful memory on Nate. She didn't want him to have killed a man. Not for her. It shouldn't be something he had to carry for the rest of his days.

They stared at each other in silence for a long spell, both lying on their sides, only an inch between them. Even with an aching head, she was acutely aware of him—aware of the closeness of their bodies, the mingling of their breaths. "You came for me," she whispered.

"I will always come for you, Marian." He kissed her then, his tongue sliding inside her mouth, tasting her hungrily, as though she had been lost to him and he could not get enough of her taste.

She touched his face, her thumb brushing against his cheek, reveling in the scratchy sensation of his beard.

Suddenly, he pulled back. "I'm sorry. You're not well. I should not fall on you like some rutting beast."

"Shush." She pulled him back to her, clawing at him until he was over her—on top of her, his delicious weight pushing her deep into the bed.

She parted her thighs for him, and reached between them, freeing him from the breeches he still wore and finding his cock. She gave him several long pumps with her hand. "I need you. I need this. Inside me. Now."

She needed this. They both did. As an affirmation of life . . . an affirmation of what they had together.

He obliged, thrusting into her. They moved quickly against each other, their gazes never straying, never looking anywhere except into each other's eyes.

"I'm close," she gasped.

His face contorted in near pain, but he drove into her again and again. He reached between them and latched on to her swollen bud, squeezing and rolling it until she shattered.

She arched and cried out under him, her fingers digging into his arms.

He followed, pushing deep, burying his manhood inside her.

His gaze locked on hers as she felt his seed release inside her.

"Nate," she gasped.

His dark eyes held hers, even as he bent down and kissed her, slowly, achingly. Her heart felt close to exploding. She knew hope was a dangerous thing, but she felt it now. Hope emerged, bright and alive inside her, even as she told it to wait . . . to go away.

He pulled back slightly with a groan, trembling as he finished with his release.

Dropping to his side, he pulled her with him.

"Nate," she said in a rather strident voice. "What did you do?"

He propped himself on an elbow and looked down at her. "I'm giving everything to the woman I love."

She stilled.

Everything?

After a moment, she wet her lips and recovered her voice. "Wh-what?"

"I love you, Marian. I don't want to hold any part of myself from you. Whatever happens . . . I won't withhold my heart from you. If you want it . . . it's yours. If you want children, I'll do my best to give them to you. If you want me . . . you have me. I'm yours."

She couldn't speak, too overcome. Her chest constricted.

She could only stare.

"Say something, woman." He laughed brokenly, his dark eyes a little desperate. "I've just bared my soul to you. Please, say something. Tell—"

"I love you, too," she whispered, eagerly, hurriedly, as though all this might go away in the pop of a bubble. "I love you, and I'll take everything you have to give. Greedy soul that I am."

"No, not greedy." He stroked her face with his hand. "You're beautiful and more than I deserve."

She stared at him. "No. We both deserve this. We deserve each other."

Epilogue

One week later . . .

The entire village of Brambledon turned out
for Sunday church. It was standing room only.
Such high attendance was unprecedented. Even
old Mrs. Hurst, who had not stepped inside the
church since the death of her husband and son
in the war, was there in her too tight, ill-fitting
best dress.

Mrs. Ramsey, never one to attend Sunday services either, was also present with her maid in
tow. The self-proclaimed widow smiled to everyone and was even witnessed embracing the new
Duchess of Warrington before she settled into

her seat beside her maid and suffered the vicar's warnings of corruption and vice alongside all other attendees.

The vicar was later to have remarked that a spiritual awakening had overcome Brambledon. The deluded man must have failed to notice that all attention was directed to the Duke of Warrington and his newly acquired family in the front pew and not on him orating so fiercely from the pulpit.

Whispers abounded. Everyone was in agreement that the Langley sisters all sat pretty as spring flowers in their new, fashionable frocks.

Behind the duke's pew the Pembrokes sat, relegated to the second pew.

Young Mr. Pembroke stared in rapt fascination at the back of Charlotte Langley's neck, as if the trail of fair curls there was the most captivating sight on earth.

It was rumored that those two had renewed their courtship, and a betrothal would once again be announced between the quiet Miss Langley and young Pembroke. The fact that those rumors originated from Mrs. Pembroke was not a fact missed by anyone. That would be an interesting development to follow, indeed. Would the lass take him back after he had followed the urgings of his papa and ended their betrothal a year ago? Indiscreet wagers were already being made on the matter . . . in addition to the wagers being made on how soon before the Duchess of Warrington gave birth to the future Warrington heir.

Never had so exalted a peer sat in the tiny little church, and the denizens of Brambledon felt blessed. Clearly he was not a depraved duke.

His marriage to one of their own and his presence meant only one thing. He was *their* duke.

"To think," Mrs. Pratt whispered loudly from the middle of the church amid the vicar's long-winded homily, "he's married our very own Marian. Why, a fortnight past she couldn't even afford ribbons for her hair and now look at her. A grand duchess."

Look at her they did. Every single one of them. They looked at her and the handsome duke beside her. They noted their warm exchange of glances and how it seemed the duke had to be touching her at every possible moment. They looked their fill at the newly wedded couple and knew.

The Duke and Duchess of Warrington were besotted.

To Bed the Bride by Karen Ranney
Politics has introduced MP Logan McKnight to
many fascinating people, but Eleanor Craig of
Hearthmere outshines them all—even if she is
engaged to one of the worst men Logan knows. She
also seems lonely, so Logan brings her a friend, a
puppy. Thus should their acquaintance end, yet it's
only just begun.

My Fake Rake by Eva Leigh
Lady Grace Wyatt is content as a wallflower, focusing
on scientific pursuits rather than the complications of
society matches. But when a handsome, celebrated
naturalist returns from abroad, Grace wishes, for
once, to be noticed. Her solution: to "build" the perfect
man, who will court her publicly and help her catch
his eye.

The Men of Bitter Creek by Joan Johnston
From *New York Times* and *USA Today* bestselling
author Joan Johnston comes *The Man from Wolf Creek*
and *The Christmas Baby*, two classic stories of the
unforgettable Men of Bitter Creek, newly repackaged
and available for the holiday season.

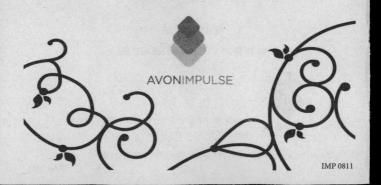